D1020135

QUESTORS

QUESTORS

JOAN LENNON

MARGARET K. McELDERRY BOOKS
New York London Toronto Sydney

Margaret K. McElderry Books

An imprint of Simon & Schuster Children's Publishing Division

1230 Avenue of the Americas, New York, New York 10020

First published in Great Britain in 2007 by Puffin Books

First U.S. edition, 2007

Book design by Debra Sfetsios

The text for this book is set in Weidemann Std.

Manufactured in the United States of America

2 4 6 8 10 9 7 5 3 1

Library of Congress Cataloging-in-Publication Data

Lennon, Joan.

Questors / Joan Lennon.—1st U.S. ed.

p. cm.

Summary: Three confused children are brought together then, with little training, sent off to save three worlds that were held in perfect balance until a cataclysmic disruption in the space-time continuum threatened their existence, which is just what their enemy desires.

ISBN-13: 978-1-4169-3658-9 (hardcover)

ISBN-10: 1-4169-3658-0 (hardcover)

[1. Space and time—Fiction. 2. Heroes—Fiction. 3. Brothers and sisters—Fiction. 4. Science fiction.] I. Title.

PZ7.L5393Que 2007

[Fic—dc22

2006028895

To Jamie, Davey, Thomas, and Callum—Lord Bullvador may say four's not a mythic number, but he's wrong.

I would like to thank Lindsey Fraser and Kathryn Ross, without whom Questors *would never have got much beyond a World and a half; and Yvonne Hooker, whose advice, even when I disagreed with it, was always backed up by thought, experience, and fabulous lunches.*

I'd also like to thank Margaret K. McElderry Books for taking on the American version of Questors.

QUESTORS

In the kitchen of The London House, a comfortable, round woman with a face made to smile was stacking a dishwasher.

Dishwashers with virtually infinite capacity are very, very expensive, but Mrs. Macmahonney had never considered good equipment a waste. *Her* machine was a great deal bigger on the inside than on the outside, which was just the way she liked it. So it wasn't the fact that she couldn't get everything in, that was forcing her face out of its smiley default expression.

It was the way the detergent was behaving.

There were no breezes or cross-drafts in her kitchen, yet, as she tried to pour the detergent from the package into the dispenser, it drifted and swirled, forming disturbing patterns in midair, and scattering messily onto the floor.

Mrs. Macmahonney frowned, went for a brush and pan, and bent to sweep the spillage up.

Her frown deepened.

The detergent had come out of the package clean, and her floor was, of course, immaculate, but what lay in the dustpan was inexplicably discolored and dirty-looking.

"It's getting worse," she muttered to herself in a troubled voice. She dumped the spoiled detergent into the garbage can. "I could be wrong, of course."

As if . . .

CHAPTER ONE

The girl in the back of the car looked
shell-shocked. The Courier, a friendly older man,
had given up trying to get her
to chat, and most of the drive through
the afternoon traffic had taken place
in silence.

It seemed Trentor children were all like that these days—tight,
and scared of putting a foot wrong. Maybe it was always that
way, though. Hard to remember.

Poor kid, he thought, checking her white face in his rearview
mirror. *Looks like she doesn't know what's hit her.*

He was right.

Madlen didn't see the London streets, the gray buildings, the
hurrying people with their careful clothes and their serious faces.
She just sat there, twisting a regulation school handkerchief
round and round in her hands, staring at nothing.

Should be in Physics, she thought, but it didn't seem real.
Nothing had seemed real, not since she'd been called in to Miss
Brack's office first thing this morning.

Only this morning!

In her mind she could hear Miss Brack's whiny, nasal voice going on and on. . . .

". . . Swithin Street School for Girls has been consistently producing successful Echelon candidates for a very long time indeed—and we are *not* an establishment that is used to having to deal with irregularities or . . . or . . . *surprises*!"

"I don't understand, miss."

"Madlen, you are to be removed from school."

There was a pause. Madlen remembered feeling . . . nothing. Numb.

"I have exams next week, miss," she'd said, as if that were the answer to it all.

"I know that!" Miss Brack had snapped. "But it doesn't change the fact that I have in my hand a letter which states that you are to leave, because your mother requires you. Right here." And she stabbed at the paper with her finger. "'Her mother wants her.'"

"I'm sorry, Miss Brack. There's been a mistake. I don't have a mother."

A part of Madlen's mind had noticed even at the time how calm she sounded, how controlled, and had approved.

Miss Brack, on the other hand, was becoming more aggrieved by the moment.

". . . most irregular and, and, *disappointing.* A car will be coming this afternoon to take you to The London House. The authority is not in question. See for yourself—here is the letter."

Madlen remembered holding out her hand and trying to focus on the words. Only one sentence was clear to her, and it leapt off the page and into her brain.

Her mother wants her.

She didn't remember leaving the office.

❖ ❖ ❖

Bryn found the young man who collected him good company, friendly, happy to make conversation, but completely uninformative. Every attempt to pump him was cheerfully sidestepped, no hard feelings on either side.

Once it was clear he wasn't going to find out anything about what in the Three Worlds was happening, Bryn settled back to enjoy the novelty of being out of the Castle, out of the mountains, out of the snow—and out from under the Steward's heavy fist. He rubbed his arm where the old man had caught up with him earlier, and grimaced a little. He'd been scared sick when Dane and his gang had cornered him and Nick in that dead-end corridor, but they'd scattered fast when the Steward appeared. Nick certainly hadn't waited around—he'd probably reached the other side of the Castle before Bryn had even finished saying, "I didn't do it, whatever it was!"

And now—all *this*! He shook his head, amazed. The things he'd seen—if only he could get *half* of it down on paper! Bryn kept his drawing things on him all the time—there was no place else safe enough to hide them at the Castle. His fingers itched to get at them now, but he wasn't stupid. The Courier man could too easily see him in the rearview mirror. He'd just have to remember it all and then, first chance he got to be by himself . . .

Cam shivered.

"Turn the heat up, please."

A clear, light voice, pitched to be heard, expecting compliance.

Nobody says no much to you, *do they, kiddo!* The Courier smiled to herself tolerantly, and bumped up the heat. *Still, no wonder you're cold, in those clothes.*

Dalrodian clothing followed a strict but subtle pattern. Everyone wore the same loose, long tunic and trousers. It was the most sensible way of dressing in the heat while keeping as much of the body as possible protected from the effects of the sun. It also allowed one Dalrodian to know at a glance exactly where in the social hierarchy any other Dalrodian might stand. They simply had to look at the material the other's clothes were made of. A finely graded progression distinguished a laborer's coarse cotton from the various grades of linen for administrators, and so on, up to the high-caste Holder's fine, flowing silk.

Cam wasn't thinking about any of that. *I'm not going to cry. I'm not going to hit anyone. Keep breathing. Back straight. Do what Ivory would do. Ivory. Ivory.*

A mantra helps sometimes.

As each of the cars pulled into Grenadier Square, they stretched, briefly, and then snapped back into shape, like cars in a cartoon. The Couriers checked their passengers' reactions. Temporal-spatial displacement can have unexpected side effects. But the three children looked only mildly confused. The odd feeling was just one more weird thing in a weird day, and over before they'd really noticed. The Couriers were relieved—they were saved having to explain how their charges had each started out in their own World and ended up . . . someplace else.

The three cars pulled up to the front steps of an elegant three-story house. It was, apparently, one of a row, but actually it was utterly and entirely one of a kind. As Madlen, Cam, and Bryn climbed out of their cars onto the sidewalk, however, they barely glanced at the house. They were too busy noticing the strangeness of each other. You could practically see their noses working and their hackles rising, like dogs meeting, or maybe young wolves.

This was a mistake.

Different clothes, different customs, different Worlds—it wasn't much, really, whereas the strangeness of the place they were about to enter was off the top of another scale altogether.

CHAPTER TWO

"Desirable Queen Anne House"

If The London House were ever to go on sale, it might be described in the real estate agent's literature like this:

> *11 Grenadier Square. Desirable terraced Queen Anne home in quiet street. High-ceilinged spacious reception rooms on ground floor with original fireplaces, cornicing, and central roses intact. First floor bedrooms and sitting rooms, ditto. Attic bedrooms with charming period roof beams and dormer windows. Large basement kitchen. At least 3½ bathrooms. Tastefully decorated throughout. Plumbing and wiring in excellent condition.*

The literature would probably *not* go on to say:

Known to be located on a cosmic cusp. Fine Queen Anne staircase equally useful for travel between floors and between points on the Space-Time Continuum. Rooms are liable to contain furniture (and, occasionally, inhabitants) from a variety of known historical periods. A floor plan is available on disk, but will require a computer of hitherto unimagined power to access. Particularly desirable as one of the few houses on the street without a historical plaque by the front door. This is due to temporal distortion—a feature reflected in the price. Known as "The London House" because, it is thought, in at least one alternate reality, there are no others. On-street parking only.

CHAPTER THREE

"This way."

That's all the Couriers had said. Then they'd left.

So now there were three people from three different Worlds—Trentor, Kir, Dalrodia—sitting by themselves in a room in a tall old London house, as the light outside began to fade, and the afternoon drew to a close.

Three people, sitting in an empty room, suddenly deciding it was silly not to talk.

"My mother sent for me," Madlen began. (She was, after all, the oldest.)

"Mine too!" said Bryn.

"She *says* she's my mother," muttered Cam. "Like I don't already *have* one!"

There was an awkward pause.

"Er, my name's Madlen," Madlen said. "Madlen Worthing."

"I'm Bryn," said Bryn.

"Cam Holder," said Cam. "Pleased to meet you."

The other two paused, aware of something odd about Cam but not knowing exactly what it was.

"You're from Dalrodia, aren't you?" said Madlen. That would

explain a lot. Everybody knew Dalrodians were *very* strange, and mostly crazy from all the sun.

"Yes," said Cam. Then, since there was a certain respect missing from their faces, "My mother's Ivory, the Lady Holder. I'm *Holder*." The others really didn't seem to know how to react. But of course the girl was obviously from Trentor, and the boy, with all that heavy clothing, must be Kirian. Not Worlds known for their great understanding of . . . anything much.

The three sat in silence for a while longer, Bryn chewing on a hangnail.

"It was news to me," he said suddenly, so loudly that the other two jumped. "A complete surprise. About my mother, I mean."

"That's . . . strange," said Madlen, frowning. "Mine was a surprise too. I was sure I didn't even have a mother—I mean, I thought she died years ago, when I was a baby, but she can't have—Well, obviously—"

"I've had a mother for *years*!" interrupted Cam. "And I don't care *what* this other woman says. I very nearly didn't come."

Bryn snorted. "Like you had a choice," he said scornfully.

Madlen's frown deepened. "That's very weird," she said. "Don't you think? I mean, all of us here, being sent for by mothers we never heard of and don't know at all?"

"*And* don't want to," muttered Cam.

"It's not very *likely,* though, is it?" persisted Madlen, but Bryn's mind wasn't on mysteries anymore.

"I'm hungry," he said.

"Me too," said Cam.

"So, let's go find some food," said Bryn.

Madlen looked horrified. "We can't do that!" she said. "We can't just go wandering off!"

The others stared at her. It made her nervous.

"At *my* school we learn to do as we're told," she said in a voice that sounded snooty even to her. "We're *supposed* to wait here."

"Says who?" said Bryn.

"Says . . . ," began Madlen, but then she realized nobody had *actually* told them to do *anything.* "Well, but, it was, um, implied . . ."

"This room is giving me the creeps," said Cam, jumping up. "I'm leaving."

Cam and Bryn headed for the door.

"But—," began Madlen. The sound of running footsteps out in the hall interrupted her. "Well, we'll just ask *them,*" she finished gratefully. She pushed past the others and opened the door.

"Excuse me?" she called into the hallway.

No one answered. There was no one there.

"You're too slow," grunted Bryn. He didn't like to admit that the House was beginning to make him jumpy too. Getting cross was more manly. "Come on."

The hallway was large and square, with a beautiful double staircase, and a number of massive oak doors, all shut. Madlen tidily closed *their* door behind them, which meant the three did not see a suite of furniture flick suddenly into view, lit fire in the fireplace and all. They did not hear the irritated grumble of the elderly gentleman sitting beside the fire.

"Well?!" he spluttered. *"Well?!"*

At which point, the gentleman, the fire, and the furniture as suddenly disappeared again.

"We just keep opening doors till we hit the kitchen," said Bryn, "or till we find somebody to tell us where it is—*if* that's all right with you." He made a face at Madlen.

She blushed. "All right, all right, don't get snotty," she muttered. "Just be *quiet.*"

It wasn't easy. The hall was like a big echo chamber, with its height and its marble floor and nothing to deaden sound.

Then they heard voices. It was nothing distinct, just a muffled murmuring, like a class of children before the teacher arrives, but it definitely came from the room opposite.

Cam walked over to the door and grabbed the handle.

"No! You can't just barge in! You should knock!" whispered Madlen urgently. She lunged at Cam, just as the door swung open, so that the two of them fell together into . . .

. . . another empty room.

Bryn peered in after them. "No food," he said. "No one to ask. Wrong again! Come on." He left.

Cam and Madlen stood in the doorway and looked at each other.

"I was sure—," began Cam slowly, when a man brushed past them. He was in a hurry; he was wearing peculiar clothes; and he had come from the empty room.

"Oh!" The man stopped in midstep and turned to look at them. "Oh. Oh dear. I do beg your pardon. I was late for my class, you see, so I took a shortcut. It's frowned on, of course, utterly frowned on. You're Present, aren't you—this is *really* not allowed. I would appreciate it so much if you didn't mention it? To anyone?"

"Don't worry. We won't tell!" Bryn had come up behind the man.

"Ohh! More of you! Oh my! Oh . . . thank you. I must say . . ." The man scurried across the hall and into another of the rooms.

The children turned to each other.

"Why didn't you ask him where the kitchen was?"

"Why didn't you?"

"He came from out of *nowhere*!"

As they walked away, the door to the empty room swung shut with a bang, and immediately faint sounds of an argument breaking out could be heard. The children froze.

"This is creepy!" muttered Cam. "I don't like this at all."

"Then why don't you just look in your crystal ball, or whatever you Dalrodians use, and figure out where the kitchen *is*!" sneered Bryn.

"At *my* school, *we* don't think it's clever to be rude," said Madlen smugly. "I guess it's different on Kir. You probably don't even *have* schools."

"Ooooo stop, you're hurting my feelings!" Bryn was going to each door in turn and dragging them open, until . . .

"Stairs!" he crowed. "Kitchen's bound to be down here."

He looked around at the other two.

"Hurry up!" he said.

Cam grabbed Madlen's arm and they ran.

They clattered down the stairs and into a large basement room that might have belonged to another house altogether. It was warm, and cozy, and full of comfortable and comforting things. This included a large table covered with food.

"Look who's here!"

A warm-looking, smiley woman came out of the larder with her arms full of even more good things to eat.

"So you found your way to my kitchen, did you? Good for you. Give me a hand unloading here."

They helped her set the things out on the table and then stood back, suddenly uncertain.

"Well, let me have a look at you," the woman said. "Well,

well. You wouldn't know you were a family, would you, not just by looking, but then I can see a bit of Kate in each and every one of you, and that's a fact. And you'll be Madlen, and you're Bryn, and you're wee Cam. And I'm Mrs. Macmahonney, so you must call me Mrs. Mac, for that's what everyone calls me round here. She's coming soon, your mother—she's been recalled, you know—but she doesn't know *you'll* be here, for you aren't expected for another ten years at least. It's this backwash, of course—very worrying! The letters went out in her name, obviously, but . . ."

Mrs. Macmahonney's warm cuddly voice faded away. Three numb-looking children stared at her. She stared back, a look of horror growing across her face.

"Nobody's told you, have they," she said at last. "You didn't know."

CHAPTER FOUR

<u>. . . and Relatively Stranger</u>

Before anyone could say another word, one side of the kitchen began to hum. And flash. And make urgent buzzing noises.

Mrs. Mac groaned. "I'm sorry, children," she said. "It'll have to wait. That's the dinner rush!"

If they'd noticed them at all, the children would probably have assumed the doors along the wall were just a lot of labeled cupboards. They'd have been wrong.

"They're a bit like dumbwaiters, if you know what those are," explained Mrs. Mac, as she began sliding doors open and pulling out order sheets. "This kitchen feeds the whole of The London House, and that means a lot of meals. And"—she grabbed sheets from behind the next two doors—"in spite of everything I can do to encourage *using* the randomization of the Space-Time Continuum, everybody *still* wants dinner at the same time!" She thrust order sheets at them. "Thanks! You'll find everything you need on the table. Don't try to do more than one at a time, though. It's easy to get in a muddle."

Mrs. Mac hurled herself at the next door, which had moved beyond polite beeping and had started to glow red in a demanding way.

Bryn read the label: PRELATES' LOUNGE.

They must really *be hungry,* he thought.

Then, for a while, they were too busy to think. The menus were as varied as their destinations. NORTHERN PROVINCES TRAINEE CLASS A had a huge order for fish and chips and mushy peas, but Mrs. Mac altered that one. "*Nothing* I cook is mushy," she said, and gave them salad instead. Some of the other training classes asked for things like shepherd's pie and lamb stew and great bowls of mashed potatoes and stir-fried veggies. "They're at that age," Mrs. Macmahonney said fondly. "Hollow legs, every one of them. I do love cooking for teenagers!" The COURIERS sent for sandwiches and thermoses of coffee and tea. "Packed lunches, night after night," she sighed, tucking in some extra fruit and cookies.

"What exactly *is* coddled mutton head?" asked Cam, holding up a sheet.

"Oh now, isn't that just what I was saying?" tutted Mrs. Macmahonney. "There's absolutely no need whatsoever for the Eighteenth-Century Training Class to be eating again just now. Just leave the Exotics to me, dearie. I'll know who's for what, and who shouldn't be, if you follow."

A silver tray with one boiled egg, three slices of toast, and a dish of curled slivers of butter had been prepared for the PERIODIC GENTLEMAN.

"Who's he?" Bryn managed to ask Mrs. Mac in passing.

"A damned nuisance," she replied. "Pardon my French."

By the time the flurry was over, the kitchen table was practically bare. The workers collapsed into chairs, panting a little.

"Thank you," said Mrs. Macmahonney. "That was splendid. It's been a while since I've had help." She snorted. "Funny how quickly people stop coming to see me at certain times of the day." She straightened up. "But you don't want to talk about that. You want to know why I said what I did when you came in. About your being a family."

The three nodded.

Mrs. Macmahonney heaved a deep sigh and sat up straighter. "I'm sure there are perfectly good reasons why no one has mentioned any of this before," she began, "though I'm sure I don't know what they are, and there are also *extremely* good reasons for why you were . . . What I mean is, the situation is very serious, and complicated, and *you* three, *well*! Though it certainly isn't my place to be explaining any of that—"

"Just give us the facts," said Madlen, in a strange voice that didn't sound like hers.

Mrs. Mac heaved a great sigh. "Right. Of course. The *facts* are, you are all related. You have the same mother, but different fathers. You were—"

"You're needed, Mrs. Mac. Upstairs." A girl had poked her head round the door, and then was gone.

Mrs. Macmahonney looked down at her hands for a moment, took a deep breath, and let it out again.

"Right," she said. "Don't go away. I'll be right back."

She heaved herself out of her chair, and headed off up the stairs.

In the silence that followed, the three children looked uncertainly at one another. Madlen seemed shell-shocked. Bryn had turned red, and Cam's eyes had become enormous.

"Well! A family! That's going to take some getting used to," Bryn began heartily. He turned to Madlen. "I never had a sister before." Then he turned to Cam. "Or a . . ." An uncertain look came over his face. "Or a . . . sibling of any sort."

Cam didn't seem to notice the boy's hesitation. "I've got

friends with sibs at home," the Dalrodian said. "It's okay, really, except they try to chew your stuff a lot when they're little."

"Sounds like puppies!" Bryn laughed, too loudly.

"A family," said Madlen in a flat voice. "A mother and a brother and . . ." She, too, hesitated as she looked at Cam. "You know—," she began, and stopped. They were no longer alone.

There, standing in the doorway, was a vision of black leather and gravity-defying curves. A gust of perfume washed across the room, and you could have sworn there was a bass beat coming from somewhere subliminal. *Boom—bapa—boom—bapa . . .* She took a few steps into the room, and spoke.

"Hi, kids. Mrs. Mac about? Oh, there you are," the vision said, turning as Mrs. Macmahonney trotted back into the kitchen and skidded to a halt. "I've been recalled—no reason, just 'Get your booty back to base.' And being the good little Agent I am, voila! Here I am. Any idea what the fuss is about?"

Mrs. Macmahonney seemed to have been struck speechless. All she could do was nod in a strangled sort of way at the children.

The vision looked from her, to them, bemused.

"New recruits?" she asked.

Meanwhile, the children were putting two and two together, and coming up with . . .

Mother? mouthed Bryn silently.

"Wow," murmured Cam.

All Madlen could do was stare.

Mrs. Macmahonney managed to find her voice. "Katharine," she said hoarsely, "I'd like to introduce Madlen, Bryn, and Cam. Your—"

"Oh, my giddy aunt, *it's the children*!" yelped the vision. "They're early—they *must* be early—they're ten *years* early— *why wasn't I told!*"

There was an eye-watering distortion in the light, and the leather sex bomb morphed into someone wearing what could only be described as a housedress. And a cardigan. The curves had gone south in a big way.

"Yurgggg," gargled Madlen.

The housedress-and-cardigan looked down. "I see your point," she said. "Too far by half."

There was another shimmy of light, and then . . .

"How's this?"

Their mother stood before them now wearing jeans and a soft shirt, with a body that had seen some use but was not yet dragging on the floor.

"Much better," said Madlen with relief.

"It's okay," agreed Bryn.

Only Cam seemed disappointed. "I liked it better the way you looked before."

Kate laughed. She reached out, as if to ruffle Cam's hair, but then pulled back. She was nervous, that much was clear.

Mrs. Macmahonney cleared her throat.

"Just *why* did they not know about you, Katharine? Or each other?" Her voice was very quiet, and even without knowing her, the children could tell this was a danger sign.

"Not my choice," said Kate, hands held up defensively. "It was a Council decision. They didn't want the children tampered with until they were ready to train, here, at The London House."

"Which was to have been . . . ?"

Kate was becoming more and more distressed. "Look," she said huskily. "None of this was my doing—I mean, the arrangements. It all happened years ago. I didn't know anything about *anything* in those days. I'd only just graduated. I must have been the most junior Agent around! All I knew was what they told me. They told me it was important. They said it was better if the children were left alone to grow up as normally as could be arranged, and then, when they were ready, they'd bring them here. When they were ready to *understand* what was being asked of them. And in the meantime, they said that . . . that it would be better if I had no contact with them whatsoever."

"And you agreed?" asked Madlen sharply.

The woman looked down. "I did," she said in a low voice. She looked up again suddenly and, almost as if she were pleading, said, "I was very young at the time."

"Older than us," said Madlen. She looked at her mother and her face was hard.

Kate drew a deep breath to speak.

"Katharine? You're supposed to report in."

A man stood in the doorway. He seemed embarrassed, and unwilling to intrude any more than he had to. Madlen couldn't help noticing he had beautiful hair.

Kate sighed. "Right. Thanks, Ben. You back for long?"

The Agent shrugged. "I guess. I've only just been recalled. This backwash is a killer! Good to have *you* home, though. Nice meal, Mrs. Mac!"

Mrs. Macmahonney lifted a hand in acknowledgment. As the Agent started to leave, he added awkwardly, "Nice to have you kids here too!" And left.

"How does *he* know about us," asked Cam, "when *we* don't know about us?"

Kate shook her head. "I can't explain any more now," she said. "I have to report in. And *you* need to sleep. It's been quite a day for you." She smiled at them, desperately trying to get them to smile back.

No one did.

Mrs. Macmahonney took over. "Right, Katie, my dear, off you go," she ordered. "I'll see to the children. Come back to me when you can, and then we'll talk."

Kate hesitated for a moment, as if hoping for something. Then, abruptly, she turned to go. Just as she reached the door, Bryn called out, "We'll see you tomorrow, then?"

She turned and gave him a grateful look. "You will," she said. "You definitely will!"

And then she was gone.

Madlen gave Bryn an angry glare, but he only shrugged.

"No more talking now," said Mrs. Macmahonney firmly. "It's some food and a hot drink and bed for the three of you. Come on."

She bustled them about, and they were all suddenly too tired and bewildered to resist. And sooner than they would have thought possible, she was herding them up a back staircase to the top of the House. A row of tiny attic rooms opened off a white corridor, each holding no more than a clean warm bed, a light, and a chair.

"Good night, now," Mrs. Macmahonney called. "If you need me, you know where I am."

As she started to undress, Madlen felt something small and hard in her blazer pocket. She put in her hand, pulled out a key—and instantly, in her mind, she was back at school.

Miss Gerard, one of the teachers, was speaking to her.

"Why are you still in uniform? Well, there's no time now. The car's here for you. You'd better get your blazer from your locker on the way out."

They'd walked together, down to the corridor near the front door, to locker thirty-seven. Madlen had unlocked it, taken out her blazer, put it on, and shut and relocked the door.

Not once had Miss Gerard looked directly at her.

It's as if I'm already gone, thought Madlen. *I already don't exist.*

And, in a tiny act of defiance, she had pocketed the key.

She stared down at it now.

She'd always hated school. She'd hated having to constantly pretend to be a good little Echelon candidate, keep her temper under control, keep her thoughts out of sight. But now . . .

. . . now all she wanted was to be back there, in her own bed. Back home.

Once started, the tears were unstoppable.

Bryn's preparations for bed involved taking off his shoes, and little else. He lay on the bed and thought for a time. It was strange, having a room to himself. He was used to the fosterings' dorm. He thought about his new mother. In his World, mothers were something boys did without for the most part—pleasant but distant figures who lived someplace else. Kate was news to him, but she fitted a familiar pattern. After a while he checked to make sure the door was shut, then pulled out a small sketchbook and a pencil, and began to draw.

"Bryn? Whatcha drawing?"

Cam had pushed his door open, silently, and stood there, looking at him.

"Not!" he snarled, stuffing the notebook fiercely into his shirt. "What do you think I am—*a girl*?"

Cam looked astonished and squeaked, "Why would I think you're a girl?" But Bryn was already backing down.

"Nothing," he muttered. "Sorry. You shouldn't sneak up on people, that's all." He stood up. "Look . . . truce. Okay?" He stuck out his hand, and, cautiously, Cam gave it a shake.

✸ ✸ ✸

Back in her room, Cam was lonely and cold. The skylight was propped open, but no one came to shut it. At home open windows let in the cool breezes, but it was different here. Ivory would have made everything all right, but Ivory was a World away. The Dalrodian didn't undress, just climbed into the bed and lay there, eyes wide in the dark, shivering.

Time passed. At last, high in The London House, three children slept.

CHAPTER FIVE

"Breakfast!"

"All *right*!" yodelled Bryn, and Cam called out to Madlen, "Are you up yet? It's breakfast. Madlen?"

"Coming," Madlen called back. "You go ahead—I'll be right there."

They clattered off down the stairs, and Madlen finished making her bed. A last look showed her a room as tidy as when she'd entered it. As she came out into the corridor, she couldn't resist peeking into the others' rooms.

Surprisingly, Bryn's was as pristine as her own. Cam's room, however, was a mess. Bedclothes trailed over the floor; the chair had been shoved behind the door; and the skylight was left propped open, in spite of a threateningly gray sky overhead. Madlen shut it.

There'd been girls like that at school. The ones who came from rich families, where there was always a nanny or a servant or somebody else to do the picking up. *Girls like that* . . . But Cam . . . ?

Madlen shook her head, and started thoughtfully down the stairs.

❁ ❁ ❁

When she entered the kitchen, the other two were already eating. And arguing.

"But why the fuss?" Bryn was saying, his mouth full. "On Kir, mothers stay with the girls and the boys go into a pack. That's just how it is. So I wouldn't have known Kate or Madlen *anyway*, not much. *You*, on the other hand . . ."

Madlen held her breath. If Bryn asked Cam the question, she wouldn't have to. They still hadn't noticed her standing there.

Then, "Look, kid," he said. "I'm not sure how to say this tactfully, but I've known you now for, what, *hours*, right, and I *still* can't tell . . ." He ground to a halt. His face was getting red.

"Can't tell what?" said Cam, concentrating on the food.

"I just can't tell . . . ," he started again, and then finished in a rush. "Look, are you my brother or my sister?"

Cam stopped eating and stared. "I'm neither."

Madlen made a choking noise. Bryn turned and saw her watching them. His face got even redder.

"No, you don't get the question," he said, turning back to Cam. "I know this must sound really, really stupid, but—I don't know what sex you are. You know, boy or girl, pink or blue, that sort of thing. To be honest, I really can't tell." He spread his hands. "Sorry!"

"No," said Cam. "I got the question, and the answer is—I'm neither. I'm an emergent." And as the other two stared, Cam said, "Give me a chance, will you? I'm only eleven!"

"What are you talking about?" chorused Madlen and Bryn in unison.

Cam looked from one uncomprehending face to the other. "You're Trentorian, right? And you're from Kir. Are you trying to tell me *neither* of your Worlds has emergents?"

"Yes," said Bryn, speaking very slowly. "That could very well be exactly what we're trying to tell you. *If* we had a clue what you were on about."

The Dalrodian leaned back and whistled. "Well, I never. You just assume, don't you, that everything's the same all over. My word . . ."

Bryn growled.

"Right! Right. . . . So, emergence—Well, it's like this. On my World we don't settle on a sex until we hit puberty." Cam paused at a sudden thought. "You do have puberty, don't you?"

"Yes, yes, we have puberty," said Madlen impatiently. "Of course we do. I mean, otherwise we'd all be children forever— but—are you trying to tell me you don't have a . . . a gender before *that*?"

Cam shook his—her—its head.

"What would be the point?" Cam said. "I mean, you have different sexes so you can make babies, right? And you can't make babies before you get to puberty, so why *have* a gender before that? It wouldn't make any sense."

Madlen and Bryn were openmouthed.

"But—but—," stuttered Bryn.

"But there's a lot more to being female than just . . . just . . . making babies!" squeaked Madlen.

"Yeah—and boys, er, male, too!" agreed Bryn.

Cam shrugged.

"Don't get all twisted," Cam said. "We just don't do it like that. With us, you're neither sex until you're ready to settle into the one you'll be as a grown-up. You're better able, by then, to know which one'll suit you."

"You mean you can *choose*?" Bryn's eyes had got huge. "You go up to somebody and say, 'I fancy being a man,' and they make you one?"

"No, no, no," said Cam scornfully. "You don't *tell* anybody. It just happens. You just gradually know and then it just happens. It's not a sudden choice—'I'll try this!' It's more of a growing certainty—'This is what I am.'"

There was a busy silence, as Madlen and Bryn tried to take on board what Cam was telling them.

"But what—," said Madlen.

"But how—," said Bryn at the same time.

They both stopped.

"You first," said Madlen.

Bryn looked uncomfortable and said, "No. That's okay. You first."

"This is hard to imagine . . . ," said Madlen slowly. "But listen, how do people know how to, well, treat you? With us, there are all these guidelines—unspoken stuff, you know?—about how you treat boys and how you treat girls, and how you're supposed to bring them up. Right from the moment you're born, practically. Stuff shifts as soon as everybody knows what sex you are. But with you—"

"Yeah, I can hear it now," interrupted Bryn. "The midwife's saying, 'One more push, dearie. . . . Congratulations, it's an *it*!'"

"Oh, shut up," said Madlen crossly. "At least I'm trying to understand. What was *your* question, anyway?"

Bryn looked suddenly reluctant. "No, it was nothing," he mumbled.

"Come on, Bryn," said Cam. "Go ahead and ask. I won't mind."

"Sure?" said Bryn. He was turning red again.

Cam nodded encouragingly.

"All right, then. What I wanted to know is, before you settle on a sex, you know, when you're still an emergency—"

"Emergent," said Cam firmly.

"Emergent, right. Well, so, how do you go to the toilet?"

There was a moment of total silence. Bryn nervously tried to fill it. "I mean, you can hardly wait till you're thirteen, or whatever . . . ," he burbled.

"Bryn," said Cam in a dead-flat voice. "In my World we do go to the toilet. We do not wait until we are thirteen. And we go to the toilet . . . IN PRIVATE."

Cam leaned across the table and grabbed Bryn by the shirt.

"IN PRIVATE, understand? None of your business, understand?" With each sentence Cam gave him a shove, and dragged him back again.

"Okay, okay, just wondering . . . ," babbled Bryn.

Cam shoved once more, and tipped Bryn onto his backside on the floor. "DON'T . . . WONDER." And then Cam grinned. "Trust you. Flipping trust you to ask something like that."

Madlen put out a hand to Bryn and pulled him onto his feet.

"Nice one, Mouth," she said. "Eat your breakfast."

"Getting to know each other, are you? That's lovely." Mrs. Macmahonney bustled into the room. It wasn't clear how much she'd heard, but she busied herself at the cooker and didn't look too closely at the three, as if to give them time to collect themselves. "Your mother isn't back yet—these all-night sessions aren't sensible for anybody, in my opinion—she's going to be good for nothing without some sleep."

"She's still not back?" asked Bryn. He sounded concerned.

"You're soft on her 'cause she wears tight leather," scoffed Cam.

Bryn looked aggrieved. "*Me?*" he spluttered. "It was *you* who said she looked better like that! The way you looked at her—I bet you grow into a male, I really do! Anyway, I think you two are too hard on her. It's not as if—"

"Kate!" Mrs. Macmahonney's greeting cut him short. "Come in and tell us all about it. Cam, get some coffee for your mother."

Cam started to protest—it was not used to being talked to like that—but then it saw how tired and pale Kate was. She leaned against the table, looking at them silently.

"Kate?" said Mrs. Mac again. "Is it bad?"

Kate shook her head. "It's worse than bad," she said wearily. "It's awful."

CHAPTER SIX

Council of the Worlds

There were always five of them.
Five Prelates in charge of the Three Worlds.
Over time the individual members had changed,
of course, but the number and the task
remained constant.

The current Council was made up of those who had reached that point of middle age that could be seen as old, but not dead old. They were:

Lord Metheglin—*tall, thin, nervy, a man given to finicky attention to detail and prone to migraine.*
Lady Vera—*large and bosomy, with a voice to match, and all the sensitivity and tact of a rhino with a sunburn.*
Lord Bullvador—*also built larger-than-life, a sentimental man, courtly and curt by turns.*
Lady Mary—*the motherly one, perpetually sorrowful that she was not a few inches taller and a few pounds lighter, trapped within the confines of being thoroughly, relentlessly nice.*

As a team, these four had developed a policy of downplaying the dangers of their work. The act of appearing to be ever so slightly bumbling was something that had evolved partly to suit their own eccentricities, and partly to reassure those in their care—if what looked like a bunch of old folk could keep the Worlds in balance, then the task mustn't be that big a deal. Not worth worrying about.

But then there was Lady Beatitude. The most recent recruit, she had been, at first, a striking exception to all that. Young, brilliant, and powerful, she did not spend long being overawed by the honor of her appointment. She proved restless at the pace of Council meetings, which exactly suited the other four; impatient at a style of working with enormous energies in flux that was second nature to her older, more experienced and, it must be said, more hidebound colleagues.

They tried to be kind, but it wasn't much fun for her, being the new kid on an old block.

All that, though, was before the accident. Lady Beatitude, still tall and elegant and slim, with flawless skin and pure white hair that floated about her, was now also, it seemed, several sandwiches short of a picnic basket.

"I've brought the hard copy you wanted, Vera," said Lord Metheglin as he bustled in. "On the Questors."

"Don't be pompous, Meth," said Lady Vera. "That's not 'hard copy.' That's *paper.*' Just put it on the table, will you? The others should be here any minute."

The Prelates took turns "setting up" for Council sessions. Lady Vera's idea of an environment within which to conduct business meetings was . . . businesslike. There was good electric lighting and a large table, behind which were five hard straight-backed chairs for the Prelates, and, facing the Council at a respectful distance, there had been placed four more chairs in a row. Her remaining colleagues, as they entered, sighed, wished they'd remembered to bring cushions, and sat down.

Vera wasted no time on preamble.

"As agreed," she began at once, "we've brought the Questors plan forward. The children have been collected and are now available for briefing. None of it is as we might have wished, but the situation has accelerated beyond anything we could have expected, and this and every other idea we've come up with has had to be pushed ahead to keep pace, and all I can say is, it's no blinking way to run the Worlds . . ."

Lord Bullvador leaned over and patted her on the hand. "Needs must, old girl. Needs must. And the Questors plan is still one of the good ones."

Lady Mary coughed genteelly. "As a brief reminder . . . ?" She paused and looked about at the others. A small hologram hovered before her. At Vera's nod of permission, she maximized it and moved it out into the center of the room. "As you may remember, I filed it under 'theperfectionoftheWorlds.doc.'" She smiled shyly, and the Prelates gazed.

"Fish!" cried Lady Beatitude in delight. "Beautiful fish!"

"Not this time, dear," said Lady Mary.

But it *was* beautiful. A horizontal triangle of light glowed and spun slowly in the air, and at each of its vertices they saw a figure: one silver, one bronze, and one gold. Each held an object. The figures were so luminous, it was impossible to see any detail to them or what they held, but there was also no doubt of their individual power and beauty. They were not the same, and yet they had an undeniable, indefinable family resemblance.

"Potential," murmured Lord Metheglin. "That's it, isn't it—that's what they've got. You could believe that anything is possible when you look at them."

Regretfully, Lady Mary made a gesture and the hologram faded. The room was a duller, more tired place without it.

There was a knock on the door, and Kate herded Madlen, Bryn, and Cam in.

The Prelates looked at them. Then they looked at one another.

"Are you sure these are the right . . . ?" whispered Lord Metheglin loudly behind his hand. The written descriptions of each of the Questors stared up at them from the table.

> *Questor One, from the Outer World, with the stature*
> *and strength of a warrior, a hunter's instincts,*
> *the epitome of courage and fortitude.*
> *Questor Two, from the Inner World, a visionary, richly imbued*
> *with the skills of the artist, and attuned to the intangible.*
> *Questor Three, from the Middle World, a strategist, versed in*
> *pure mathematics and, by extension, music, and able to*
> *reason out any material challenge.*

The Perfect Team, on paper.

While, staring back at them, round-eyed by the doorway, in the flesh . . .

Three children. Madlen was at least tidy, but the other two looked as if they'd slept in their clothes. The best you could say about Bryn was that he was too short to be a warrior; Cam was biting its nails in an anxious and very unvisionary way; and Madlen—well, she just looked inescapably *ordinary*.

"Whoops-a-daisy," said Lady Beatitude, though she was probably referring to something else.

It was an awkward moment, into which Kate charged. "You did require them *ten years early*," she snapped. "Just what were you expecting? Adults?"

The Council was taken aback. They were not used to being spoken to by Agents in quite that way.

"Well!" spluttered Lady Vera, but Bullvador waved a finger at her.

"It's the maternal instinct," he murmured. "She can't help it. Think of tigers."

Vera peered at him as if he were slightly crazed, but he just looked sentimental at her and shook his head.

"Yes. Well," Lady Vera said, turning back to the group by the door. "Come in. Sit down. There's a lot to discuss." She broke off and appealed to her colleagues. "This is not *at all* what I was expecting—just *where* do you suggest I start?" she said.

Lady Mary smiled at her reassuringly. "Just tell them *everything*, dear. That'll be best. They're *bound* to be exceptionally bright, even for children. But," she added in a whisper, "do try not to frighten them."

Lady Vera gave her an exasperated look, and began.

"Because of circumstances beyond our control, my colleagues and I find it is time to explain to you . . . er, *everything*. Even though you are somewhat younger than . . . It is earlier than . . . Let us begin at the beginning. You are, I'm sure, familiar with the Three Worlds Concept," she said, in a voice she felt sure was child-friendly.

Blank faces.

"You *do* know about Multiverse Synchronicity, generally, though," she continued.

Nothing.

"The Space-Time Continuum?" She was almost pleading now.

Madlen said, "Er," but got no further.

Lady Vera turned to Lord Metheglin. "Don't they teach them *anything* in those schools?" she hissed. "I hardly thought when I said I'd explain everything that that included *everything*!"

"It's our policy," Metheglin whispered back. "We instructed all the boards of education to actively discourage teaching about the other Worlds, or their special relationship within the Continuum. Even with government officials it's on a need-to-know-only basis. We *did* discuss this. Don't you remember?"

"Are you sure?" Lady Vera looked at him, incredulous. "And we thought that was a good idea?"

Lord Metheglin nodded emphatically.

"Divide and conkers," murmured Lady Beatitude.

There was the moment of bewildered silence that often followed Lady Beatitude's contributions. It was almost impossible to tell exactly when these were over, and no one wished to be rude. This time, however, there didn't appear to be any more to come.

Lady Vera shrugged. "Oh well, if we agreed it was a good idea, then it must be," she said. She patted down her hair, heaved up her bosom, and turned back to the children.

"So," she said. "I am to take it that you have little or no knowledge of any World, other than your own. Is that correct?"

Bryn stuck up his hand.

"Yes, young man?"

"I don't know any stuff officially, miss," he said, "but I did hear our Castellan talking with the Steward once, though of course he was pretty drunk at the time, and *he* said that everybody on Dalrodia was a spaced-out hippy, and everybody on the Middle World was a constipated number bumper, and none of them knew their elbows from their . . ." His voice trailed off as he realized that everyone in the room was staring at him.

"Come to think of it, *I* heard something about *your* World too," said Cam sweetly. "*I* heard that everybody on *your* World was *stunted*"—and the Dalrodian gave him a poke— "and *stupid*"—poke— "and covered with hair because it's so *cold*"—shove.

From the floor, Bryn looked up at Cam.

"I did say he was drunk," he said.

Cam made a disgusted noise and turned away.

Kate stepped in hurriedly. "There are bound to be, er, misconceptions, since the Worlds are kept so much in ignorance of one another."

"He's not very bright, our Castellan," said Bryn to Cam's back. "Even when he's sober."

"Perhaps we could continue with—," Lord Metheglin began, but Bryn was still trying.

"Absolutely right about the hair, though, if it's him you're thinking of. Hairier than a yeti's armpit, and only half as good at conversation."

There was a muffled giggle. "All right," said Cam, turning back again. "I accept your apology."

Bryn jumped up with a grin, and Lady Vera sighed noisily.

"*Might* we carry on, *if* all that has been cleared up to everyone's satisfaction?" she asked heavily.

"Certainly," said Cam calmly.

"Fine by me, miss," was Bryn's cheery reply.

Madlen fought the temptation to bury her head in her hands.

"Lord Metheglin," said Lady Vera in her most formal, and formidable, manner. "I don't feel we are getting anywhere quickly. May I suggest a rewind to the original conversation on the Questor plan, which, if memory serves me, includes a perfectly lucid explanation of *everything*."

Metheglin drew a hand across his face. "Thank goodness!" he said. "Sense at last!" And he pulled a remote from his robes and entered some numbers.

"What are they on about?" Cam whispered to Kate. "They keep video records or something?"

Kate shook her head. "*They* don't," she whispered. "The *room* does."

"*WHAT?*"

Kate just smiled. "You'll see . . ."

The three exchanged puzzled glances, and then squealed in unison as the room darkened, and began to spin.

CHAPTER SEVEN

Instant (sort of) Replay

The spinning stopped. They were still in the room—they could still see each other—but overlaying the Present was the room in a Past. It was dimly lit, and mysterious.

"Wow!" murmured Cam, but its voice felt woolly and muffled.

In the center of the room five ornately carved chairs had been arranged in a circle, in a pool of slightly lighter dusk. A chill wind sighed along the floor, then died away.

A black-robed figure, hooded and tall, prowled around the circle. He observed the layout of the furniture intently, went over to one of the chairs, and adjusted its position a little. There was another pause, and the sound of an irritated tapping foot.

"Something is . . . missing," the figure murmured. "It needs . . ."

He made a small gesture, and at once the air was flavored with an indeterminate damp smell, hard to pin down, that nevertheless whispered the word "GOTHIC."

"Ahhh," he purred. "Perfect." He placed one finger lightly to his temple. "I sense the others. They are coming . . ."

The robed man—it was Lord Metheglin—held his dramatic pose, smiling slightly, until—

"Blast and damnation!" Lady Vera's bosomy voice swore

somewhere in the dark. "Thirty shades of blood! I'll have to go back for my reading glasses. This murk is impossible."

A crash from the other side of the room heralded the arrival of somebody else.

"What idiot put a table here? Who turned out the lights?" It was Lord Bullvador. No one else could have produced quite that volume and bass-ness.

Lady Mary came in behind him, looking . . . different.

"Oh dear," murmured Lady Mary in the Present. "I knew I'd regret that hair color." She looked reproachfully at the others. "Someone *might* have said . . ."

"With your permission," said the Present Lord Metheglin hurriedly, "I'll fast forward."

It was weird how they could still see what was happening—Metheglin looking pained and the others gesticulating and flashing in and out and getting in more lights—weird and headache-inducing.

"About . . . *here,* I think," said Lord Metheglin, and the Flashback slowed to normal speed.

The five Prelates were at last assembled. Metheglin's Flashback self also held a remote. As he thumbed it, a hologram of the solar system appeared in the air before them. It was a lovely thing, detailed and exact, and one planet especially had the most dazzlingly rich colors. He pointed to it.

"The Three Worlds exist simultaneously in the same place, perfectly centered on a single, orbiting point. The balance of cosmic energy required to keep them that way has held steady for as long as records have existed. Minor adjustments, of course, have always been required and these fall to us. By dint of vigilance and hard work, The London House has kept the balance. Nothing short of a cataclysmic disruption in the

Space-Time Continuum could possibly alter it."

"Or so we thought," murmured Lady Mary.

Metheglin bowed solemnly in her direction.

"Or so we thought," he agreed.

The hologram began to change. The three overlapping Worlds were dividing out from one another, their colors beginning to bleed away as the Prelates watched. The members of the Council shifted uneasily, but no one spoke.

"Pause, perhaps, Meth?" rumbled Lord Bullvador in the Present. "To make sure we haven't lost anyone?"

Lord Metheglin thumbed, leaving the Flashback Council with unflattering, uncomfortable expressions frozen on their faces. The looks on the faces of the three children were not much better.

"Well . . . dears." Lady Mary decided to have a go. "I'm sure you understood all that, but just to recap . . . Simply put, there are Three Worlds—*your* three Worlds—that exist, at the same time, in the same place. That's what we call Synchronicity. To hold the Three Worlds in Synchronicity requires a great deal of power. But someone, or something, has gained access to that power potential and is draining it, a little at a time. Like a slow leak."

"I had a bicycle once that had a slow leak," said Lady Beatitude dreamily. "I never rode it. The servants could never find the pump."

There was a polite pause, while everyone waited to see if there was more, but Lady Bea just smiled in her vague way, and was silent.

"Yes, well," said Lady Mary with a cough. "As the power potential has lessened, the focus of the Worlds has begun to blur."

There was a pause, in which the churning of challenged brains could be heard.

"They are not as reliably simultaneous as they were," offered Lord Metheglin helpfully.

Around the room the desire to appear bright and engaged was now resulting in a variety of pained expressions.

Four members of the Council sighed as one. The fifth member appeared to be counting her fingers.

"Perhaps if we continue?"

"If you think it'll help."

"And now," said the Flashback Metheglin. "This is what we may reasonably expect in the Future, based on seventeen independent Forward Projection programs and three Prophetic Spells."

There was a profound silence in the room as the hologram changed for the last time. The Three Worlds continued to separate out from one another, the overlapping areas becoming thinner and thinner slivers of color in an increasing grayness. Then, they were completely apart. For a brief moment they moved on around the sun, perfectly parallel until, without a sound, they disintegrated, streaming out along the paths of their orbits in smaller and smaller pieces.

Then they were gone.

The Flashback Metheglin thumbed his remote, and the rest of the solar system faded away.

"The Three Worlds have enjoyed millennia of perfect con-centricity," he said. "Now they are threatened. An energy leak of unknown origin has weakened the necessary stasis. We have each tried to find the source, or sources, of the leak, without success. We have each explored all the obvious technical solu-tions to the imbalance, also without success. Time is running out. I suggest we now consider the *less* obvious options—"

"I see little point in bemusing our, er, young friends with

information other than that which directly concerns them," the Present Lady Vera interrupted, and again the room fast-forwarded. The Council engaged in a series of high-speed pantomimes suggesting all sorts of incomprehensible, intriguing ideas, returning to normal to the sound of Lord Bullvador's booming voice saying, ". . . excluding, of course, the use of butter."

The others nodded sagely.

"And then there is always the traditional option," said Lord Metheglin.

"Oh yes," said Lady Mary. "We mustn't forget that. A Quest. Of course. With a Hero? Or a Heroine?"

"The traditional option would require a Quest, and, of course, a Questor," agreed Lord Bullvador. "But I don't think we need be too exercised over gender." He stroked his chin. "The perfect candidate would simply have to be someone who represented in himself or herself the strengths of the Worlds." He shrugged. "Then I imagine it'll be a question of three significant magical objects to be retrieved, one from each World, probably, and brought together in a prepared place, so that their combined power may be used to seal the breach, and draw the Worlds back together again. That sort of thing, anyway."

"A Quest. A Questor. A Question," put in Lady Beatitude suddenly, and stopped.

"So," said Vera, "someone with the best qualities of all the Worlds?" She snorted. "That's quite a tall order. Who would you say we have—actually *available*, I mean—who fits the bill? *I* can't think of anybody!"

Apparently neither could anyone else.

The Council had at its disposal a substantial network of Agents, Couriers, and Trainees. Their abilities, weaknesses, and activities were known to every member of the Council capable of comprehending them, and there was no one person currently on the books who came at all near to meeting a Quest's requirements.

There was a long, dark pause. Then, "Well . . . perhaps we might consider a little DIY?" suggested Lady Mary brightly. "I mean, if we haven't *got* what we want, why don't we *make* what we want?"

The members of the Council stared at her in horror.

"Oh, I wasn't suggesting *us*. Not us *personally*," she burbled, embarrassed. "But, well, selective breeding has been very successful with, um, dogs. . . . Well, *some* dogs . . . not bassets, of course, but . . ." Her voice trailed off into silence, but it was a busy silence now. The Prelates looked at one another speculatively.

"How many generations—," began Lady Vera, but Lord Bullvador interrupted her.

"There's just no *time*," he said, shaking his head. "The kind of, er, controlled evolution we're talking about here, to manufacture the perfect Questor, would take more time than we have left, if the projections are even remotely accurate."

"All right, then," said Lord Metheglin slowly. "But what if we don't try to manufacture just one? What if we breed three—"

"*Three* perfect Questors?" blared Vera. "How would *that* help?"

Metheglin shook his head. "Not three who are completely perfect," he said, his voice growing in confidence. "Three Heroes or Heroines, with each one manifesting the strengths of one World *each*. Not the strengths of all three, in one. Are you following me here?"

"A *team* . . . !" breathed Mary. "We haven't done that since . . . oh, it must be since Jason and the Argonauts! That was quite a large group, as I remember. But you think three would be a viable size this time?"

"Three," said Metheglin firmly. "To match the number of Worlds. Representatives."

Lady Mary gave a little nod. She opened her handbag, brought out a small palmtop, and began poking at it with her discreetly pink lacquered nails.

"Don't you see—together they would make up the perfect *composite* Questor," continued Metheglin. "And they could be produced in a single generation! We have enough time for that. We'd have to choose the parents with great care, of course, to get the best possible genetic material."

"Three pairs of men and women, the cream of their Worlds, willing to be mated by request and then to give up the resulting child to the Council." Lord Bullvador shook his head anxiously. "It's asking a lot. Not everyone would be happy to be manipulated like that. Not everybody is as biddable as our Agents, you know."

"*Use* Agents, then," said Lady Vera brusquely. "Pick the best, and tell 'em to get cracking. It's their job to serve the Council, at least it was when I last checked."

"Yes, but this . . . It's a bit *personal*, don't you think?" protested Bullvador. "I mean, an Agent's usual orders don't include, er . . ."

"These are not usual times," said Lord Metheglin pompously, to which Lady Beatitude added, "Fish do it underwater," and shut her eyes. (Lady Beatitude in the Present promptly shut *her* eyes as well.)

"Still . . . ," said Bullvador. "Six Agents . . . And do we really want to spread this around quite so much? I mean, how in the Worlds are we going to keep something like that a *secret*?"

There was another, anxious pause. Questions of security loomed large in the Council's minds.

"Well," suggested Metheglin hesitantly, "could we manage it with, maybe, *one* Agent, who, er, engaged in three separate, um, encounters, with the best individuals the Worlds have to offer at the time?"

The Prelates looked at one another speculatively.

"You know, that might just work," said Lady Vera.

"It would certainly help with security," agreed Lord Bullvador reluctantly.

"How old would you say the Questors would need to be?" asked Mary. "I mean, how much time do we have?"

"Oh, we'd want them fully adult," said Vera. "If we go with Meth's suggestion, I'd think we'd need the eldest to be at least twenty-five, and the others a minimum number of years younger, in order to accommodate things such as, hmm, gestation, a brief courtship, and so on. We're all right for twenty-five years anyway, wouldn't you say?" She looked around at her colleagues.

"I'm sure we're safe for *that* long," said Metheglin. "All the Predictors are in agreement—there isn't such a rush."

"So, Vera, could you take—," began Lady Mary, but they didn't hear what else she was about to say.

This was because, in the Present, several things happened more or less at once. Lady Beatitude, who had been sitting perfectly upright with a look of rapt attention on her face (although with eyes still shut), suddenly began to snore. Madlen, out of sheer nerves, giggled loudly. And a man the three had never seen before walked through a Flashback chair and the figure of Lord Metheglin, causing both to flicker madly.

"I beg your pardon," the stranger said. "I had not realized the Council was engaged."

Present and Flashback froze for a moment, then the Present reasserted itself.

"Well, *really,* Cordell!" huffed Lord Metheglin, but Lady Mary shushed him.

"It's all right, you know. There's nothing more they really need to see," she said soothingly.

At which point, another man rushed in. It was the Agent they'd seen yesterday in the kitchen. He was out of breath.

"Apologies," he gasped. "This couldn't wait." He noticed Cordell, and paused in surprise. "Oh! There you are! Where've—" He shook himself and turned back to the Council members. "More tremors—projected in Tantalan, any moment now. They just showed up—on the scans—out of the blue."

"Vera?" said Lord Bullvador, pushing back his chair.

Lady Vera nodded, and looked at Kate. "Get them out of here," she ordered. "Finish the briefing."

"Right. Come on," said Kate, and Bryn and Madlen got up out of their chairs. Cam didn't move. It seemed stunned. Then it seemed even more shocked, as the chair it was sitting on disappeared and Cam landed on the floor.

"Tantalan's on Dalrodia!" it wailed.

Kate dragged Cam up and hustled them all out the door. Bryn looked back and saw the five members of the Council moving purposefully to different points in the chamber. The room was otherwise suddenly empty. It was unrecognizable, as were the Prelates themselves. They seemed taller, larger, more intense— even Lady Beatitude had completely changed. *Before, it was just five old sillies,* he thought, *and now . . .*

The door shut, and he caught Ben watching him.

"Disconcerting, isn't it," the Agent said, still panting a little. "They seem so . . . senile, don't they, in so many ways. And then you realize they're holding three entire Worlds together for breakfast, and juggling Space and Time for tea."

"But—but—," stuttered Bryn. "That Beatitude woman—you wouldn't think she even knew her own name!"

"Yeah . . . there was some kind of accident." Ben shook his head. "It must have been something unbelievably powerful. Before my time, of course, but some of the older Agents were there, and they say it was phenomenal, watching the rest of them rebuilding her afterward."

"What are we talking here—guts in the chandeliers, or what?" asked Bryn uneasily.

"No. No, her body was still there. It was more a kind of search for all the other bits of her. She was convalescent for ages. And it must have been exhausting being one down all that time for Council work—but they never gave up on her. And then, one day she was back on duty, pretty much as you see her now. Batty as a cave. When it comes to the work, though, she's there with the best of them."

Ben noticed Bryn's expression, and grinned. "Welcome to The London House, kid!"

"Come on, Bryn," Kate called.

"Off you go," said the Agent, and then, very softly, he added, "Lucky lad."

"Yeah . . . ," said Bryn. He ran to catch up with the others. When he glanced back, Ben was still watching, but this time it wasn't any of the children he was looking at.

Hmmm, thought Bryn, *I wonder if I could catch that look in a drawing?* Then he thought, *I wonder if Kate knows. . . .*

CHAPTER EIGHT

<u>What the Council Didn't See</u>

In another dimension, so as not to
interfere with the Prelates, the room
rewound itself to the Present. Much that was
wonderful and strange but, in fact, bog
ordinary to the workings of the Council flashed by.
As Metheglin had said, there was little that related
to the Questors. But one scene *was* of
interest. One scene that, had the room's
memory been allowed to play on, undisturbed,
only a little longer, might have surprised
everyone who saw it.

Or perhaps not everyone . . .

*The search for the special Agent was over. The flowery sofas
and chairs were gone, and only a faint odor of potpourri
remained of Lady Mary's turn at setting up. There was an
unsourced, ambient light (for reasons of cosmology, the room
never became completely dark). And into this default dimness
came a man.*

*Anyone in the organization would have recognized him at
once. He was called Alpine Cordell, and his job was to act as*

Private Secretary to the Prelates. He was as essential to them as the air they breathed, and as noticed. He was weedy, and colorless, and apparently humorless, and had a name that begged to be made fun of. And yet, somehow, nobody, not even the youngest Trainee, ever did make fun of him.

Now he stood in the silence, perfectly still, perfectly alone.

But not for long. A figure, hooded and robed, was suddenly standing directly behind him. Its arrival had made no sound. Perhaps it was only by a displacement of the air that the man had sensed its presence at all.

"Preceptor," said Cordell.

The figure glided round in front of him.

"Oh now," the Preceptor said. "And I made so sure you wouldn't know I was there."

Alpine Cordell did not respond. He rarely did. He had always found not responding to be an unbreachable defense in any but the most physical situations. For those, he had other aptitudes.

The figure made a tiny noise of distaste, and half-turned away. "Call it up," the Preceptor murmured.

Cordell held out a remote, and spoke a word.

Re-conjured, The Perfection of the Worlds began its stately dance in the air before them, the three figures at the three points of the triangle, lustrous and glowing.

"You are aware of what has been discussed?" the Preceptor asked, watching the triangle's slow spin. "The directions to which the Council is now committed?"

"Of course. I am the Council's Private Secretary, as you know."

The figure shrugged, as if it couldn't be bothered to acknowledge or deny the fact.

"It is dangerous," the Preceptor said. "I had hoped they

wouldn't consider the old ways. Until it was too late."

"Yes," said Cordell. "Keeping the leakage managed for our use only, and keeping the Prelates in the dark, have been hard enough. How can we hope to control a team of made-to-measure Questors?"

"We can't," said the Preceptor.

"But how can we eliminate them without being noticed? Denounced? Eliminated ourselves?"

"We can't," the figure said again.

Alpine Cordell had grown used to the way in which his special employer liked to conduct conversations. A sage of no inconsiderable power himself, Cordell was frighteningly intelligent, but he had never felt the need for public acclaim. He knew his worth, and did not care that others generally did not even notice he was there. It satisfied something in him to know that the people who ignored him were so often, in fact, his inferiors. The games he played with the Preceptor were more complex than that, for there he was dealing with someone who was not his inferior in any way. But Cordell understood quite clearly that he could never achieve as much on his own as he could in tandem with the Preceptor, and that was satisfactory too.

"We can't," repeated the Preceptor. "But then, we don't need to."

The figure was staring at the glowing images in the center of the room. It took a step toward them, and another, then slowly raised a hand.

"We need only touch a gene here . . . a chromosome there . . . gently . . . gently . . ."

The hand dropped through the lines of light connecting the points of the triangle. The lines bent and swirled around the hand, and then resumed their proper state, like candle flames ruffled by a breath. But they were not the same. The change in the lines of connection was subtle, almost undetectable, but it was there.

Cordell watched.

Three glowing figures. As each spun slowly past, the Preceptor reached out a finger and, delicately, stirred. As if in protest, the images blurred a little and their colors, primarily metallic before, silver and bronze and gold, bled together into browns and the odd smear of red. At last the Preceptor stepped back, cradling its hands, one in the other, while, for a long moment, it continued to watch the hologram. And as the Preceptor watched, Alpine Cordell watched the Preceptor.

"I wonder what, exactly, has been done?" the Secretary murmured after a while. "Which portions, exactly, have been altered?"

Within its hood the Preceptor smiled. It was a slow smile, and bore no relation to laughter or common joy. It was luxurious, and lazy, and evil.

"I have absolutely no idea," the Preceptor purred. "Isn't it delicious? All I know is that, now, whatever they are, our little heroettes—they're not perfect."

The Preceptor stretched, like a cat that has perpetrated a crime, and walked away.

"Tidy that, Cordell. In case the others fancy calling it up from the files from time to time, it should seem as nice and shiny as before. And then put it away." The Secretary had been dismissed, like any other servant, without a backward glance.

Alpine Cordell bared his teeth. It might have been a grin, or it might have been a grimace. His eyes gave nothing away.

Then he turned, and did as he'd been told.

CHAPTER NINE

In the Kitchen

"That's practically my home! Tantalan can't be more than half an hour away! What kind of tremors? How bad? *What can I do*?"

Cam's voice was shrill and panicky.

"It's all right," Mrs. Macmahonney was saying. They were back in the kitchen, clustered around the big table. "They'll have it under control in no time. I'm sure—"

"I'll go and find out," interrupted Kate, and was gone.

Cam just sat there, stiff and straight, not looking at anybody. Bryn leaned over to Madlen and whispered, "I wish I knew what was going on. I saw the Council crumblies as we were leaving, and you wouldn't believe . . . They'd gone all mythic, you know? I don't know about you, but I sure as snow don't know any of the stuff they were on about. Do you?"

Madlen shook her head. "We didn't do Mythic at school," she whispered back. "I don't even know what it is, really. They *must* have got the wrong kids."

And then, so suddenly that it made them all jump, Kate was back.

"It's okay," she said. "They stopped it before it happened."

Cam stared for a minute, and then sagged in relief. "Was anybody hurt?"

Kate shook her head. "No one will even know anything happened."

"Because nothing did," said Cam slowly. "It was going to happen, and the Council fixed it so it didn't."

"They sealed the leak," said Kate. "They're having to do that a lot lately, as more and more leaks appear. The backwash just compounds that, affecting weaknesses before they might otherwise begin to bleed, which then in turn affect other weaknesses. . . . Everything's accelerating. The time isn't so far off when the Council won't be able to catch it all. They won't be able to hold the balance."

Madlen leaned forward. "What *is* this backwash thing everybody keeps talking about?" she demanded.

Kate dropped into a chair.

"It's because of what's gone wrong—I mean, is going to go wrong—and the wrongness is backing up along the Continuum and messing with things that are happening now, here, at the cusp." She looked at them. "Look, nobody lower than a Prelate actually understands this stuff. We don't even know exactly when it *started*, though lots of us figure it began in the time when the Council was one player down. What we do know is the effect it's having on the Worlds."

"Earthquakes and stuff?" said Bryn.

Kate leaned back in her chair, looking thoroughly tired. "It's more than that," she said. "The nonphysical is becoming polarized as well."

"What do you mean?" asked Cam, whose color was starting to come back again.

"Things don't work anymore, because polarized Worlds aren't viable," Mrs. Mac said. "You'll all have noticed in your own Worlds how things have been falling apart. The systems just don't work so well anymore. Like, what used to be very formal, ritualized war games are degenerating more and more into the mess of the real thing in Bryn's World. And in yours, Madlen, there's all that tightening-up on things—and people—that aren't strictly scientific. And in Cam's World, well, fewer and fewer people are in control of the dreaming that's in control of everything else. . . ."

Her face was bleak. "Extreme stuff just doesn't work," she said. "Go too far out on a limb and, eventually, the limb breaks. But it's even worse than that. You've told me about the hologram—you saw how the Worlds *need* each other, not just to be rich and diverse and complex organisms, but to be . . . *at all.*"

There was a long pause.

"I really don't see what you think we can do about it," said Madlen suddenly.

"Yeah," said Bryn.

Cam nodded. "What exactly is supposed to be going on?"

Kate sighed. "What is *supposed* to be going on is," she said, "you three finish growing up, you get trained here at The London House, so that your native strengths can be honed, then, at the proper time, you are sent on a series of Quests to retrieve three Objects of Power, bring them back here, and reestablish the balance of the Worlds by placing the Objects in relation to each other, in a Magical Field specially prepared for that purpose."

She stopped for breath. The children waited for more, but that was it.

"You're joking, right?" asked Bryn.

Kate didn't answer.

"That *is* the traditional option," said Mrs. Mac carefully. "You're very special children, you know. It's a destiny thing—a great honor to be chosen—what you were, um, born for. . . ."

Cam turned on her abruptly. "Yeah, right, thanks a lot. It's not what *I* think I was born for."

"Shut up, Cam," said Madlen. The Dalrodian glared at her, but Madlen didn't notice. She was focused on the adults. "So tell us what's different now. If it's not going to work the way it's supposed to, what *is* going to happen? We just start training early, that's all, isn't it? And then in ten years we'll be all set to go do this Quest thing. There'll be lessons, and exams, stuff like that. It's just been a change in the timetable, that's all. Right?"

Mrs. Macmahonney shook her head. "I'm sorry," she said. "We haven't got ten years anymore. You've got to do it now." She lifted a hand. "But when I say 'now,' what I really mean is 'ten years in the Future.' We have the power to move you forward and back along the Continuum, using paths laid down by the backwash. Then you find the Objects of Power, bring them back here, to the Present, and the realignment can be achieved before any more damage is done."

"So . . . ," said Bryn slowly. "You want to send us off into the Future to collect these Object things. Why can't we just collect them in the Present?"

"Are you *sure* we can't wait till we're a bit older?" put in Cam.

"Or will we *be* older, when we get to the Future?" asked Madlen.

Mrs. Mac answered each question in turn.

"The Objects can't be collected in the Present, because they aren't *in* the Present. They *will* exist, but they don't yet, not as Objects of Power anyway. And we can't wait ten years for you to grow, or even one year, because there isn't time. The damage being done by the backwash has accelerated—you saw today—and we just don't *have* that long. And no, you'll be the age you are now, because otherwise you'd be unable to return. You'll have to trust me on that one—the Physics of intertemporal movement is the study of a lifetime."

"Or two," muttered Kate.

"This is just stupid," shrilled Madlen. "We're *not* grown up, and we're *not* trained, and we're not—what did you call it?—*honed.* So I don't see what earthly good our being here is doing, and I've got exams next week, and I'd like to get back to school today, if you don't mind, or yesterday would be better."

"I'm afraid that's not possible," came a new voice.

"Good heavens, what are you doing here?" squeaked Mrs. Macmahonney, and she turned bright pink.

CHAPTER TEN

<u>Previously, in the Council Chamber</u>

The Prelates clutched mugs of tea, catching their collective breath after dealing with the earthquake on Dalrodia. Lady Vera's lips were pressed into a straight, stubborn line, and Lord Bullvador was not looking at all happy.

"I don't like it," he rumbled. "I really don't think we can safely interfere. Shouldn't we have some faith—let them get on with it in their own way?"

"*Trust* them—have you *seen* them?" murmured Lord Metheglin.

"A delicate touch, here and there, that's all I'm suggesting," argued Lady Vera. "Nothing more."

"A hint," agreed Lord Metheglin.

"I really think that would be wise," added Lady Mary.

"Could it rhyme?" said Meth. "I haven't done a good cryptic couplet in ages!"

"Of course . . . that would be within the rules, I'm sure we'd all agree." Lady Mary smiled at him.

"And I'll help." Lady Beatitude beamed. "I know a lot of rhymes. Crimes. Times. Chimes. Limes—"

"Oh, Bull, stop scowling!" interrupted Vera. "We never *used* to send Questors out blind! We always provided guides and charts and things." Then she frowned. "Though, of course, they already knew what they were looking for, because it already existed. The fleece. The grail. The dead girlfriend. There was none of this waiting-to-see-what-evolves business before, that's true."

"Exactly," said Lord Bullvador. "This time, the Objects of Power do not yet exist. How can we tell these children what to find? We could be completely wrong."

There was a troubled pause.

"Could we check the database? See what the likely objects might be?" Metheglin was reluctant to give up.

"No harm in just having a look," agreed Lady Mary. Then, as each of the Prelates called up screens in the air before them, she groaned, "Oh no! I had no idea. It's . . . gargantuan!"

"Arrows, Cups, Rings, Stones, Jewels, Scrolls, Elixirs of Youth, Enchanted Fruits, Spells, Golden This, That and the Other, Dragon's Teeth, Tears of the Gods . . ." Lord Bullvador looked up at his colleagues a little smugly. "Ever so slightly surplus to requirements, wouldn't you say?"

"We'll just have to cull a little," said Lady Vera firmly. "There's no point putting it off."

With a collective sigh, the Council addressed their screens, and for a long time, the room was quiet.

Then, out of the blue, Lady Beatitude let out a whoop.

"YES!" she cried. "YES!"

The others jumped up, and clustered round to see what her monitor had to say.

It was a computer game, its title in lurid letters across the top of the screen—The Pinnacle of the Worlds.

"I won!" she exclaimed. "Now I can go on to Level Two!"

"Oh, *Bea.*"

The others started to go back to their seats, but Lord Metheglin stayed at Lady Beatitude's shoulder to watch for a moment. He reached over and pressed a few buttons on her keypad, and then, slowly, straightened up.

There was an extremely thoughtful look in his eye.

"You're not going to believe this," he said. "But it's all here—already—in this stupid computer game—exactly what we're looking for—"

"Oh, don't be dim!" snorted Bullvador, walking over to join him. "They build those things entirely out of clichés and stereotypes and . . ." His voice trailed off as he looked more closely.

"The Ribbon of Abstract Thought . . . the Crystal of Courage . . . the Fruit of Dreams . . ."

"What if they're not clichés and stereotypes, but icons . . . and archetypes!?" Lord Metheglin squeaked.

Bullvador growled, but the others were busy chattering about icons and iambic pentameter.

They didn't appear to notice when he stumped crossly away.

CHAPTER ELEVEN

Meanwhile, Back in the Kitchen

Lord Bullvador stood in the doorway, filling it completely, and looking awkward.

"Hello, Maggie," he rumbled. "We've . . . I've . . ." Uncharacteristically, he seemed at a loss for words. Then he shook himself, and tried again. "I've come to help," he said.

Mrs. Macmahonney was staring at him with her mouth open and her eyes like soup plates. When she realized everyone was now staring at *her,* however, she tried to act casual.

"Help, is it? Sit down, then!" she said, clearing her throat. "If you remember how!"

"It's been too long, Maggie." The Prelate smiled carefully. He opened his mouth slightly, almost as if tasting the air, then gave a great stretch. He grinned. "I'd forgotten how good this kitchen feels," he said. "The shielding . . . It's wonderful."

Mrs. Mac snorted. "You'll get antsy soon enough," she said. "You'll want to know what's going on outside. You never could just let things be."

Lord Bullvador bowed deeply. "Dear lady, how well you know me!" he said.

Mrs. Mac snorted again, and looked away.

Kate and the others exchanged glances, and wondered what

the story was. But whatever it was, it would have to wait. They turned expectantly to Lord Bullvador.

Prelates do not age the way ordinary humans do. Lord Bullvador gave the appearance of being vigorous, healthy, mature, with the incompleteness of youth left behind, and the frailties of age not yet on the horizon. In fact, he had been around for a very long time indeed, and he was an old man in the ways of the Worlds. He knew perfectly well the lure of what he was about to say, the almost irresistible attraction of being seen to be the Hero, of being needed, of being the one to save the World. It was a lure he had trailed before grown men and women, many of whom had excellent reasons for saying, "I won't. I can't. Not me. Choose somebody else."

They might start by saying that, but they always ended up by saying, "I will."

He didn't think that children could resist the temptation, any more than the adults had. But was it fair, to put three apparently pleasant adolescents to the test? Lord Bullvador was quite sure that it wasn't.

He sighed, and did it anyway.

By the time he had finished presenting the nature of the Quests and the role of the Questors, he was almost ready to sign up himself.

It was Kate who sat with them at lunchtime, and the great and mighty Lord Bullvador who scuttled about with Mrs. Mac, filling the midday meal order sheets. There was no sign of the Prelate about him now—he seemed much more like somebody's favorite uncle on a Christmas visit. And, if they hadn't known better, the children would have sworn that the two old people were flirting with each other. There was certainly much more giggling, and pretend tug-of-warring over dishes, and brushing up against each other, than seemed absolutely necessary.

It was very embarrassing.

Madlen noticed the frown on Cam's face and suddenly leaned over.

"What's your problem?" she growled, and then stopped. Even to herself she sounded spiteful. *But I'm not!* she cried silently. *I'm just scared.*

Cam's frown deepened, but it didn't seem to be in reaction to Madlen—more in puzzlement. And it wasn't about Lord Bullvador and Mrs. Mac's backstory either.

"What are all those people *doing*?" Cam said quietly. "All those stupid scraps of paper and people getting trained as Couriers and all that business with running about when you want to tell somebody something!"

Cam stared at Madlen, who stared back.

"I don't quite . . . ," she began.

"Why don't they use the phone?" exclaimed Cam. "Or e-mail? Or fax machines? Or flipping magic, for that matter. Runners went out with the Dark Ages."

"We still have Runners," Bryn butted in, loudly.

"My point," retorted Cam.

"None of those other things work here."

It was Kate.

"Not reliably, anyway," she went on. "Within a specific segment of The London House Continuum—a room, say, at a certain time—electrical equipment is fine, magic is fine. But try to send between rooms, or times, or combinations of both— forget it! You have no guarantee the message will arrive, or when it will arrive, or how it may have evolved on the way. And nothing like that works coming in or out of *here*." She waved a hand to indicate the kitchen. "Especially magic. Mrs. Mac won't have it. She says it gets into the food and plays merry hell with the vitamins."

"I might as well serve nothing but TV dinners and junk food." Mrs. Macmahonney bustled past, putting plates of food in front of them as she went.

Kate smiled at the children. "The kitchen is heavily shielded. It's like disappearing into a great black hole."

"Bit like what happens to my cooking," grumbled Mrs. Mac on the way back.

"You mean nobody can tell we're here?" asked Madlen.

"If the Couriers don't tell, and the Agents don't tell, and the postman doesn't let slip he saw you coming up the front steps— why, you might not even exist at all!"

"The *postman's* in on all this?"

"Don't worry, he's very discreet."

"I'm not hungry," said Cam, looking at its plate.

Kate looked sympathetic. "Me neither," she said. "But it makes sense to eat when you can. You learn that pretty soon as an Agent." She picked up a fork and dug in determinedly.

When you can . . . Cam didn't like the sound of that. It poked at the food a little, and gave up. It gazed aimlessly around the room, and then suddenly asked, "Is there really a London in every World?"

Kate smothered a laugh. "You know, I can still remember the time I asked that question. Lady Vera herself was teaching that class—I think the usual teacher had got caught up in some sort of warp delay—and she said 'Any questions?' and I said the first thing that came into my head. 'Is there really a London in every World?' And she looked me up and down and said, 'The universe has to have a center, and Londoners have always believed they are it. The strength of that belief transcends fact, time, and the Multiple-World Continuum.'"

The Dalrodian stared.

Kate coughed. "I guess you just had to be there," she said.

"Did anybody ever ask why there are only *three* Worlds?" said Bryn, his mouth full. "I've wondered about that. I mean, why not two, or six, or sixty?"

"Oh sure. That one came up. I remember some teacher or other saying, 'Three is not enough for you, young person?' but mostly they just maundered on about three being a special number, with a special tension, and we should consider the triangle, the triad, the trilogy, and don't forget Pythagoras." Kate shrugged. "It's my guess they don't actually know."

There was a burst of laughter from the workers, and a plate hit the floor.

"You all right there?" called Kate in a careful sort of voice. "Need any help?"

"No, no, we're fine!" Bullvador and Mrs. Mac chorused.

Kate hid a smile, and winked at the children.

"Look," said Madlen. "This is all very interesting, but let's stick to the important stuff, okay? Like, like . . . how are we supposed to know the Magic Objects? I mean, will there be a sign or something?"

"Oh yes, they'll all be labeled: 'Objects of Power—One per Household,'" said Bryn scornfully. "I can just see that."

Kate ignored him. "As far as I understand it, there will be a sense of . . . rightness," she said. "It's hard to explain, but apparently unmistakable. You will just *know*."

"Like, it'll sort of speak to us?" Madlen was struggling.

"Hellooo. Pick me uuuuuuuuupppppp . . . ," murmured Bryn.

"BRYNN!" Kate and Madlen turned on him simultaneously.

"Do you want me to knock him over again?" asked Cam sweetly, but then another voice intervened.

"Lord Bullvador?" A Courier was at the door, not one they'd seen before. "You asked to be told as soon as the Council was to reconvene."

Lord Bullvador was suddenly standing by the table. He no longer looked like somebody's favorite uncle. He looked grim, and powerful, and even . . . sinister.

He looked like a Prelate.

"Thank you, Simons. That's all for now."

The Courier nodded, and left.

There was a pause. Then, "It's time," said Lord Bullvador, squaring his big shoulders.

Everyone stared at him. His expression was unreadable, but in the sudden silence his words rang in the air.

It was time.

TRENTOR

CHAPTER TWELVE

It Begins

"How will they travel?" Mrs. Mac's voice was all business now.

"By Tube," replied Lord Bullvador.

"What's a tube?" Bryn whispered to Cam.

"I think it's a kind of wormhole," Cam whispered back. "Must be time travel of some sort."

Madlen turned on them fiercely. "Don't be so stupid. Not 'a tube'—*the Tube*! The Underground! You know—little smelly trains that take people around London in tunnels. About as cosmic as toast."

Kate put out a hand. "You're right, Madlen," she said. "But . . . you're also wrong—"

"There's no time to explain," interrupted Bullvador. "Maggie, the Grenadier Platform. Factor in a ten-year Future-lag. Where would you like us?"

Mrs. Macmahonney appeared to listen for something, and then said, "If you would all just go into the larder and come out again, that would do nicely."

Kate and Lord Bullvador headed for the larder door. The children looked at one another, and then shrugged. It was just another thing that didn't make sense. They did as they were told.

Going in was completely ordinary, but as they came out again . . .

"Urggh—what *is* that!"

"Did you feel that before—in the cars?"

"Dimensional shift—nothing to worry about," Mrs. Mac called reassuringly to them.

"I thought you said there was no magic here," Madlen muttered sullenly.

"There's more than one kitchen, Madlen," said Kate. "They're not *all* shielded."

Mrs. Macmahonney was standing now beside the heavy sideboard against the far wall. As soon as Kate and Lord Bullvador joined her, she turned round and opened a drawer. Then, with a perfectly serious expression on her face, she took out two forks, gave them a quick rub on her sleeve, put them back, and then removed a teaspoon. She looked at this for a second, dropped it into her pocket, and . . . with a reluctant grinding noise, the sideboard swung away from the wall.

They all jumped back. Madlen caught a glimpse of forgotten buttons and coins, glinting among the dust balls on the floor. *Does the law of treasure-trove apply to the underneaths of sideboards?* she wondered manically. *With the right equipment you could make a decent career out of extracting lost change from down the sides of sofas, from the uncharted realms below furniture generally. . . . I wish I could stop sweating.*

There was a door in the wall. Mrs. Mac put her hand to the handle. She looked at the three kindly.

"Ready?" she said. Cam shrugged, and Madlen and Bryn nodded. They all looked green.

"Jolly good," she said, and opened the door.

A blast of warm air came out to greet them. It was musty and metallic, just a breath away from the smell of toilets infrequently cleaned. It was a smell anyone who had ever been in London would know immediately. Bottled, you could export it to home-sick Londoners in Kafftanistan, and there among the alien smells of yak's butter and wet felt, they would inhale and recognize their roots.

The Tube.

Stairs, lit by low-wattage lamps behind wire mesh, led down. The three stepped forward and peered into the depths. At their backs was a kitchen full of human comfort. At their feet something altogether less cozy beckoned.

One by one they started down the stairs.

As soon as Mrs. Mac shut the door, the blurring sensation returned, then passed over.

"Shielding's back," she stated in a flat voice.

There was a moment's silence in the kitchen. Then Bullvador spoke.

"I should go. But . . . I need to talk to you first," he said. "There's something badly wrong, and I need your help."

Kate didn't want to talk anymore. She just wanted to go someplace quiet and worry about the children. Her children. The Council represented collectively more power, skill, experience, and knowledge than she could even *imagine,* let alone aspire to. Agents, Couriers, they were all only fingers and feet for the Prelates. There were plenty of them, and they worked to keep their particular bits of reality ticking over nicely. But the Council—*they* held the entire picture in their heads, maintaining (and in some senses creating) it, both forward and backward along the Continuum, while playing three-dimensional chess to keep the rest of their brains from getting bored.

Let them solve the problems of the Worlds. Let them just leave her alone.

"What is it, Bull?" asked Mrs. Macmahonney gently.

Lord Bullvador drew a deep breath into his huge chest, and let it go. Speaking quietly was clearly an effort for him, but it was an effort he was prepared to make.

"I have reason to believe," he said, "that the source of the energy leak, the point of origin, is not anywhere in the Worlds. There are subsidiary weakenings there, of course, and there's all the backwash damage—but that's not where it starts. . . . It starts *here*. In the House."

Kate's mouth dropped. He had her attention now.

"But—but," she spluttered. "But we've been looking *in the Worlds*! All of us! For years. *How* could it be here? We all *live* here, for crying out loud—*You* live here! How could you possibly not have noticed—"

"Kate!" interrupted Mrs. Mac. "Mind yourself!"

But Lord Bullvador only shook his head. "I've been asking myself the same questions. And the only answer I can come up with, is that we were meant not to notice, and the one who meant us not to notice is someone of exceptional power and ingenuity."

There was a heavy pause. Then, "What do the other Prelates say about this?" asked Mrs. Macmahonney.

"I haven't spoken to them about it."

Kate drew her breath in sharply. "You suspect somebody on the Council?" she exclaimed.

"I don't suspect anyone," he said slowly, with a strange tinge to his voice.

Kate's heart jerked. "And this has to do with the children, doesn't it?" she said. She was standing now, though she didn't remember doing it.

"I'm afraid they'll be tampered with, yes," answered the Prelate. "Failing in the Quests would mean unthinkable disaster—but any success they achieve will undoubtedly increase the danger they are already in. I am turning to you, to both of you, because I know that your loyalty to the children cannot help but be clear."

Mrs. Macmahonney stood up, slowly, massively.

"And you have no other reason to trust me?" she said, so quietly it was almost a whisper.

Lord Bullvador looked at her. "I trust you with my life, Maggie. But this is more important than that."

For a moment it seemed as if Mrs. Mac were about to walk out. She didn't, though. She sat down again, and Kate stopped holding her breath.

"What do you want us to do, Lord Bullvador?" Kate asked.

"I want you to watch, and listen, and protect the Questors from anything that might affect them. *Any* advice, *any* hints as to what they should be looking for, could so easily steer them away from the truth. And I want you to report exclusively to me."

"Just you? But what about the Council?"

Lord Bullvador gave them a strange look. "I'm not asking you to do anything I'm not willing to do myself."

He stood up, and looked from Mrs. Mac to Kate and back again.

"The Questors must be allowed to complete the Quests without interference. They are the key. Think about what I've said. The Quests must be completed.

"And I must go," he added. He started to walk away, just like that, as if there were no more to be said.

Mrs. Mac didn't agree.

Just as the Prelate reached the door, she called out quietly to him. "Don't be a stranger, Bull," she said.

He didn't turn around. "I don't want to draw danger to you any more than I have to," he said. "But I wish . . ." Then he was gone.

"I think I'll go check out the, um, in the larder," said Kate, carefully not looking in Mrs. Mac's direction.

"Would you look at the dirt behind that sideboard!" exclaimed Mrs. Mac huskily. "It's a crying shame . . ."

Somewhere in The London House

"Preceptor?"

"Not yet, you fool! It is a matter of monitoring progress only at this stage. And, Cordell . . ."

"Yes, Preceptor?"

"Don't approach me again. If I want you, I will let you know."

"Yes. Preceptor."

As the Courier entered the kitchen, the first thing he saw was Mrs. Macmahonney's bottom in the air, as she attacked the dust behind the sideboard with a brush and pan.

He was only a Junior Courier, and this was not something he had been prepared for, not in any of the training courses he had taken so far.

"Errrgle?" said the Courier.

"Acckkk!" said Mrs. Macmahonney, rearing up, dropping the dustpan and banging her head on the wall.

"Spring cleaning?" squeaked the Courier.

"Spring cleaning," said Mrs. Mac at the same time. She waved the brush about, casually. "I had it out, you see, and it seemed . . ." She waved the brush again.

"Er, can I push it back for you?" asked the Courier politely.

He had an ailing mother of whom he was fond, and he didn't like the idea of any lady struggling when there were big strong men about.

"You're a thoughtful boy," said Mrs. Mac, "but I'm just fine." She made a mystic sort of gesture with her hand (while unobtrusively shoving the cutlery drawer shut with her hip), and the heavy sideboard rumbled back into place. The effect was spoiled a little by the sound of the forgotten dustpan being crushed into tiny pieces, but the Courier was still junior enough to be impressed.

"Yes, *ma'am*! I've brought a communication for the Questors. From the Council Secretary. Mr. Cordell said it was imperative I get it to them before they leave. Ma'am."

"I'll give it to them," came a voice from behind him.

The Courier whirled, and there was Kate, leaning in the larder doorway. She smiled a slow smile, and held out her hand.

"I'm supposed to deliver it directly to . . . ," he began, but Kate shook her head gently. Her hair swayed mesmerizingly.

"Trust me," she said. "I'm an Agent."

The Courier's thoughts were full of things he wouldn't be telling his ailing mother about.

"If you're sure," he said weakly.

"I'm sure," said Kate, her voice deep and sultry. She took the message from his unresisting hand, and gently sent him on his way. Then she turned on Mrs. Mac.

"Mrs. Macmahonney! I am *shocked*!" Kate said, one eyebrow up. "Pretending to move the sideboard by magic like that. Fooling that poor boy."

Mrs. Macmahonney huffed. "I don't know what you mean. Anyway, it taught him a valuable lesson—he's not too young to learn things aren't always as they seem. Besides, *you're* one to talk!"

"I just asked him nicely," protested Kate.

There was a pause.

"Want to have a look?" she said, holding up the envelope.

Mrs. Mac nodded, and joined her at the table. Kate slit the envelope open with a knife and took out a single sheet.

After they read, they sat, for a long time, and thought.

CHAPTER THIRTEEN

The Tube

Deep below The London House, Madlen, Bryn, and Cam stood on the platform. Already it felt as if they had been waiting there for a dingy lifetime. The station was badly lit and bare. There were only the grimy tiled walls and a cement floor blotched with unidentified stains and dirt to look at.

Cam and Bryn wondered about the World they were entering. They'd heard rumors—how all the power was in the hands of the Echelon; how math was the measuring stick for everything; how if you didn't make it as a candidate, you didn't make it as *anything*. But, frankly, Trentor had never seemed attractive or interesting enough a World for them to want to find out more. And at the moment Madlen didn't look as if she felt much like filling in the gaps.

They'd just have to wait and see.

So they waited. And waited some more . . .

Nobody had said anything for a long time, when Bryn suddenly burst out, too loudly and much too cheerfully, "Well, no trains today!"

He made as if to head back up the stairs.

"Oh, don't be stupid!" snapped Madlen. "We have to wait!"

"We have to wait!" he mimicked. "Don't get your knickers in a twist." He made a rude face at her.

There was an unhappy silence for another long while, and then Bryn and Cam became aware of a strange sound in the air. It was a sinister, unearthly sort of buzz, apparently without source. They looked around in alarm. The sound went away, and then returned. It scuttled. It grated.

They peered about anxiously. Then they noticed something odd. Madlen wasn't reacting. She was showing no sign of worry, as if she weren't even *aware* of the sound. She was just standing there, staring gloomily at her feet, and rocking back and forth a little.

Unnoticed, they moved closer to her, and exchanged puzzled looks. Could the noise really be . . . ?

Bryn reached out and tapped her suddenly on the shoulder.

Madlen shrieked—and the strange sound stopped.

"What did you do that for?" she yelled. *"You scared me half to death!"*

"Yeah?" said Bryn. "Well, *you* scared *us*! What kind of awful noise do you think you were making? We thought it was a monster or something!"

Madlen looked horrified. "Oh no," she said, putting her hand over her mouth. "Was I humming?"

"Is *that* what you call it?" muttered Cam.

"Look . . . I . . . I'm sorry," said Madlen. "I only do that when I'm nervous. I . . . I'm . . ." Astonishingly, she seemed about to cry.

"Okay, okay, don't go squishy," Bryn said brusquely. "So you've got the voice from hell—just keep it to yourself, will you?"

Madlen didn't answer, but now her silence was making him uncomfortable.

"Look, I don't care. Do what you like. I don't know what you're getting so obsessed about. It can't be that important, whether you can do anything as arty-farty as sing. You don't do *that* at your precious school, I bet."

Madlen bristled. "We're not learning pretty little tunes, you moron. Harmonics is practically math—but why should I expect *you* to know anything, being educated in some stone outhouse someplace where they don't even know what the *Tube* is!" She turned her back.

"It is not music as we know it," Cam said in a spooky voice.

Bryn stared.

"No, really," Cam continued. "They study Frequencies, Patterns of Vibration, Auditory Energy, that sort of thing."

Madlen turned round, mouth open.

"I did an essay on it once." Cam shrugged. "It was a punishment assignment for goofing off in choir practice."

"Phew! That's tough!" Bryn whistled. "When I goof off in choir practice, I just get strapped."

"I'm Holder," said Cam. "They're hardly going to strap *me . . .*"

There was a little pause, in which Cam listened to its own words and, for the first time, realized how they might sound. Ivory would never have said something like that. She would have *thought* it without a blink, but she never would have *said* it. She'd have had everything smooth as milk, everyone acting as if they'd been friends all their lives.

Instead of family.

It'd be a lot better if it were Ivory here, and not me, Cam thought.

Anybody *but me.*

"So you can both sing?" said Madlen, trying to appear casual about it. "I guess it fits for you, Cam, but Bryn's supposed to be training as a soldier."

Bryn grinned, and broke into a rousing marching song with some extremely doubtful lyrics. "And that's just the official version," he said. "You should hear what we sing in the dorm at night. Or"—he gave them a sideways look and leered—"maybe you shouldn't. Got to protect my sibs' delicate ears."

Madlen snorted, and Cam stuck out its tongue.

"Go on!" Cam said. "I dare you!"

"You're on!" said Bryn, and drew a breath.

"Stop!" interrupted Madlen.

Bryn looked smug, and started to say, "Can't take it?" when the Trentorian shushed him again.

"Listen," she whispered. "I think . . . it's a train coming!"

"At last," grumbled Cam, but there was a quaver in its voice.

Bryn gulped.

The noise grew, an echoey rumbling. A tide of stale air came on before it, so that their hair lifted and grit got in their eyes. Cam and Bryn covered their ears. It was hard to believe the din could possibly get louder—and then it stopped.

The train had arrived.

CHAPTER FOURTEEN

The Train Now Standing at Platform Nine

And it wasn't empty.

Through the greasy windows they could see that gray figures filled each of the carriages, heads down, reading newspapers or books, or dozing, or staring at the floor.

The doors slid open with a *phush* of air. No one got out. The three children had no desire whatsoever to get on the train, but it was as if they had no choice, as if someone were physically pushing them forward.

They got on.

They stood by the doors, clustered awkwardly around a pole. The doors slid shut, and with a lurch the train began to move. It was very rattly, too noisy to talk. The carriage was even older and more decrepit than the ones Madlen remembered—not that she went out of school much. All the color seemed to have been leached out of this train, and the upholstery was well past repair.

It was strange how quickly the swaying and the stuffiness and the grayness began to feel like being in a trance. The London House had been weird, but there was always something happening there. This was different. Here it was as if nothing *could* happen, almost as if they were between times, all of them, all of them neither here nor there, just in between. . . .

Madlen stared at the map of the Underground over the door. It looked as if water had got to it somehow, because it was too blurred to read. It was *so* blurred, in fact, that she began to feel a little seasick just staring at it. It didn't make sense to think it was *moving,* but that was exactly what it seemed to be doing.

Less of a map and more of an amoeba. Madlen smiled thinly to herself. *You're cracking up,* she thought. *Quietly, tidily, definitely, you're losing the thread.* She looked away.

Beside the central doors there was a feeble-looking hatchet in a glass cabinet, with the notice IN CASE OF EMERGENCY, KINDLY BREAK THE GLASS. Madlen wondered idly if there *was* any kind way of breaking glass.

She let her eyes drift to the nearest window. There was an impression of slimy black walls beyond as the train trundled through the tunnel. There was the reflection of the three of them, standing in the lit carriage. *What an unlikely lot!* she thought. *What a bizarre family. The angle of the window must be really odd, though, because I can't see the other passengers reflected in it. Just Cam, Bryn, and me.*

She shifted a little, but there were still only the three of them. *Some kind of optical illusion?* She leaned forward, peering at the glass.

A trickle of sweat ran down her back.

They were clearly there, three unlikely companions, reflected in the window. But no matter where she looked, she couldn't see anybody else.

Cam noticed her uneasiness, and leaned over.

"What's up?" Cam said into her ear.

Without taking her eyes off the window, Madlen hissed back, "Something's wrong. Look. See the other passengers—they're not there." Her voice began to rise in pitch. "*We* have a reflection, but THEY'RE NOT THERE!"

For a long moment Cam looked at the window, and then suddenly turned and looked straight at the other passengers.

"*Don't do that!*" cried Madlen. She was horrified, and frightened, and she didn't know why. "*You mustn't look at them!*"

Cam turned back to her in surprise, but it was too late.

All over the carriage, newspapers were lowered. Books were closed. Slumped figures straightened. One after another, the other passengers stood up.

A small part of Madlen's brain noticed that their clothes were all shades of gray, and baggy and oversize, as if the wearers had all been ill for a long time and had wasted away inside them. Their skin and hair were dull. There was no color anywhere, nothing to distinguish one passenger from the next, hardly even woman from man. That small part of her mind was screaming, *Why? What's the matter with them?*

The rest of her brain was just screaming. Because that was the part that had noticed their eyes.

They didn't have any.

CHAPTER FIFTEEN

Where their eyes should have been, there was only a dead, black blankness.

"We've got trouble," came Bryn's voice above the train's rattling. Madlen looked over her shoulder at him, and felt sick. The passengers from that end of the carriage were starting to lurch toward them. Cam grabbed her arm—the ones from the other end were also on the move.

"What do we do? What do they want?" Cam yelled. *"What are they?"*

The passengers made no sound that could be heard above the clattering of the train. They didn't speak, or cry out, and there were no expressions on their faces that Madlen could read. They just came closer, and closer, and they had their hands held out toward the children like muffled claws.

"Stay back!" Bryn squealed. "I'm warning you!"

The sound of his voice was swallowed up, and the gray people kept on coming. They didn't attack—there was no hitting or kicking or scratching—instead they pawed at the three, patting, patting, little touches that didn't stop. It was horrible, like being suffocated in a dream. Cam brushed their hands away again and again, batting at them as if they were insistent cobwebs or a swarm of insects. Bryn seemed paralyzed now, unable to do anything. Madlen could tell from his face how helpless he was feeling. Nothing he'd learned at the Castle would have taught him about fighting this kind of battle. He had his back to the wall, and was beginning to disappear behind a slow inexorable wave of . . .

. . . *zombies.*

Madlen went cold, as the memory of a forbidden book flared in her mind. The girl who'd smuggled it into school was removed not long after, but not before everyone in Madlen's year had had a good long illegal look.

That was what they were. They were gray, blank-eyed zombies, and everybody knows what zombies want—

Something else tripped inside her head, a switch that opened out a whole section of herself she hadn't even known was there. This wasn't a logic thing. There weren't any rules and there weren't any right answers. It was just about family—

Nobody's going to suck the life out of my family!

That's what the Hero in the book had said. . . .

"Stop it! Stop it!" she screamed from out of this new place inside her, but it had no effect. Desperately she looked about, for something, anything.

Her eyes lit on the cabinet on the wall.

"Get back!" she hollered, wrenching it open and pulling the hatchet away from its fixtures. There was a strange buzz as her hand met the handle, like an electric shock. It was heavier than she'd expected too, and she almost lost her footing as the train leaned around a curve.

She staggered again, and instinctively flung out the arm with the hatchet to rebalance herself.

"Hey!" screamed Bryn, as the blade almost connected with his head. "Watch it!"

But the effect on the gray figure behind him was even more dramatic. It reared back and let out a thin wail. Its eyes began to flicker—one second, black and blank; the next, real eyes with pupils and irises and whites; then, blank again.

The train lurched back the other way, and Madlen stumbled forward. As the hatchet flailed about near the zombies, the flickering of their eyes increased. They fell back from Bryn. Madlen swirled and thrust the blade near Cam. The gray people flinched away, like animals near fire, and their eyes juddered and flicked.

The real eyes were blue and brown and green—real colors—and they seemed to be frantic, in those seconds when Madlen could see them, as if they were calling out to her without a voice.

"What does it mean?" she screamed. "I don't understand!"

"I can see a light ahead!" yelled Cam, who was now pressed against the window. "The tunnel curves—there's a station coming!" Cam's voice went up to an even shriller pitch. *Why aren't we slowing down?*"

Madlen didn't stop to think. With her free hand she lunged for the emergency cord overhead—and pulled.

Metal shrieked against metal; there was a horrible burning smell; the carriage strained and jerked from side to side as if it were trying to escape the rails. Bodies staggered about. Madlen slammed into the others, dropping the hatchet as she tried to find something to hold on to, something to save herself.

Then everything was still. They had stopped at the station.

Madlen could hear Bryn and Cam panting, and her own ragged breath, and the creaking of metal adjusting. She dragged herself to her feet. The gray people were all standing again, but the flickering of their eyes had died away. Only the black blankness remained. Cam and Bryn got up, and stood beside her, desperate to make their escape, but nothing happened.

"Why don't the doors open?" whispered Bryn through clenched teeth. "Why don't they open?"

Raggedly, the gray people began their advance on the children again. Madlen stumbled back, and her foot struck something on the floor. The hatchet. Instinctively, she reached down for it, and a long collective sigh issued from the gray people's mouths.

Madlen looked down at the hatchet in her hands, then around at the gray faces. The yearning, living eyes were there again, there and gone and there. It was clear a battle was raging inside them, and the hatchet she held was in some strange way a weapon in the war.

She came to a decision. She stuck out her jaw.

"Kindly break the glass . . . ," she muttered. "Madlen, do as you're told."

"What?" said Bryn.

"Duck!" yelled Cam.

"YAAAA!" Madlen screamed. She spun on her heel and swung the hatchet up, and over, and down.

The glass in the door exploded. She struck again and again. Her technique was terrible, but she made up for it with a ferocious energy she didn't know she had. She slammed and gouged with the blade until the doors were in tatters, and then—

"Look out!" yelled Cam and Bryn together.

Madlen just had time to turn before the tide hit her—gray people pushing and shoving and clawing to get out. Each of them had living eyes again, filled with expressions of frantic urgency. Still clutching the hatchet, Madlen managed to squeeze back against the window as the gray people scrabbled their way out of the carriage and onto the platform. It was hard to believe there had been so many in the carriage, for the stream of bodies seemed to go on and on. But then, suddenly, they were gone.

The three Questors staggered out of the train.

They were alone.

"Uh, nice one," said Bryn to Madlen, very carefully, since she was still holding the hatchet and looking wild-eyed. "Er, would you like me to carry that for a while?"

"I'm fine," croaked Madlen. "I'm fine."

"Of course you are," said Cam soothingly. It turned to Bryn and continued quietly, "Let's get out of here."

There was only one door. It was marked EXIT, and led to a flight of stairs. It was the route the gray people had taken, but given the choice between following them and getting back on the train, there was only one answer.

Up.

Nobody spoke as they climbed the stairs. It seemed to take forever. Then, suddenly, Madlen began to laugh.

Cam and Bryn exchanged worried glances.

"Swithin Street Station!" wheezed Madlen, pointing to a sign at the top of the stairs. "I can't believe it! All *that,* and we've ended up at Swithin Street Station! Of all the—"

She shook her head, panting.

"So?" said Bryn.

Madlen tried to get a grip.

"Swithin Street is where my school is," she managed. "I only left yesterday! Don't you see? We go through all this craziness and where do I end up? Back at school in time for tea!" She grinned weakly at the other two. "Come on, and I'll sign you in as visiting family members."

The three ran out into the daylight and Madlen looked about for the familiar bustling streets and buildings.

She looked, but they weren't there.

CHAPTER SIXTEEN

<u>. . . and Above</u>

Bryn and Cam looked around them.
This was *not* what they'd been expecting.

"But—but," stammered Madlen. "It was all right yesterday!"

Her knees gave way, and she sat down suddenly on the curb. She looked half-horrified—and half-apologetic.

"It's ten years into the Future, remember," said Bryn, carefully. "A lot can happen in that length of time."

Madlen didn't hear him. This wasn't the World she'd left. Even in the poor parts, the Servers' Sectors, there would never have been anything like this neglect, this ruination.

"What happened?" breathed Madlen. "And the people, all the people, where *are* they?"

"I don't know. But whatever it was, all this didn't happen this morning," said Bryn again. "Or last week, either. It's been going on for a good long while." He looked about, scratching his head. "It's like everybody just gave up or something, and it's all been falling apart ever since."

"I want to see my school," said Madlen suddenly. She pulled herself up. "Now."

She headed off shakily, and the other two trailed after her.

"It doesn't have to be *the* Future," said Cam, who was

worried about the color Madlen's face had turned. "It could just be *a* Future. Ten years into *a* Future. Nobody said anything about this stuff being fixed. I mean, that's what *we're* all about, isn't it, putting things right?"

Cam was talking to itself. Madlen was beyond listening, and Bryn . . . Bryn was deep in thoughts of his own.

There was danger here. It didn't take a lot of brain to see that bad things had happened, and there was no reason to believe they were over. And there was no way of getting around the fact that he was *the boy*. As far as you could tell . . . Though, now he'd decided Cam probably would be female. He'd heard it cry at least once, and those clothes weren't exactly butch. On the other hand, Cam definitely packed a punch when riled, and it didn't walk like a girl—but anyway that was all beside the point. No matter what Cam ended up being, Bryn was and always would be the oldest boy. It was his job to protect the women and children.

And he had to face up to the fact that, once again, he'd been a failure. He'd been utterly useless in the Tube. He'd frozen stiff when those *things* started touching him—even thinking about it now made him shudder.

He felt the old round begin again: fear shame anger shame fear . . . If he were big or strong or good at something manly, then he could break the round and be the way he was supposed to be—eager for danger, keen to meet the enemy, to be the Hero.

Two days ago he was still one of the ones being protected. He had a castle, an army, and a Castellan (with a smart Steward to tell him what to do) between him and any known danger.

Now *he* was the Castellan, in a way (minus the Steward), with no castle and no army and no way of knowing one danger from the next.

He was the man.

What a joke.

So why was nobody laughing? And why—Madlen's voice broke in on his thoughts.

"That's it," she said in a strangled voice. She pointed. "Over there."

At first glance the school building didn't look too bad. The big front doors had splintered, a few of the windows were cracked, and the sign announcing THE SWITHIN STREET SCHOOL FOR GIRLS hung at an angle—but there was nothing much a lick of paint and a few screws wouldn't fix.

It was only when they looked at the upstairs windows that they saw daylight where it shouldn't have been.

"The roof's come down," said Cam. "That whole top floor's gone."

"That's where the dorms are," whispered Madlen. "That's where I sleep. Slept. What if it came down in the middle of the night . . ."

"Keep talking," said Cam quietly. "And don't look at me. Just go on as you are."

"What?" said Bryn. "Oh." He turned back to Madlen. "No, there'd have been a warning. A big cave-in like that couldn't just happen out of the blue. Here, look at this." He went over to Madlen and put his head close to hers, pretending to show her something.

"I think something moved over there," he breathed, carefully not looking up. "I didn't see what it was. Maybe a dog, maybe—"

A sudden high-pitched squealing made them both jump, and bang the sides of their heads together hard. Clutching their ears, they were in time to see Cam drag an extraordinary-looking creature out from behind some rubble.

For a moment they couldn't tell what it was, because dirt and hair and the way it was struggling in Cam's grip obscured its shape.

Then, suddenly, it wasn't alone.

A tall, beautifully dressed man with a silky blond beard and silky blond hair was standing there in the street. He should have looked completely incongruous. He was wearing a really expensive suit, shirt and shoes, and a tie that probably cost more than everything Madlen and Bryn stood up in, and he didn't look the least bit out of place. Standing there in the middle of a demolition site, he looked . . . perfect. He *exuded* rightness. Under *any* circumstances, he had it right, and everyone else was wrong.

The thing squirmed out of Cam's grasp. It was a boy, though it would be hard to say how old.

"Get rid of them!" he shrieked. "They touched me! Make them go away!"

"No," said the man.

Why did the three suddenly shiver?

He turned his attention back to them, and spoke.

"My name is Erick," he said. "You may call me *Master* Erick, since you are children, and *I* am *not*."

He flicked a finger in the direction of the boy. "Fred. My servant."

The boy almost exploded in indignation. "Your s-servant?! That is such a lie. You are such a—"

The man yawned. "I'm bored," he said. "I'm taking them home. You'd like that, wouldn't you." This was addressed to the three, and it was not a question.

Bryn's mouth hung open. There were danger bells clanging in spades inside his head *Just* look *at him!* he thought. *The man's practically* pretty! And yet it seemed inconceivable that they would not go with him.

Cam was perfectly familiar with elegant authority figures, and it knew there was something wrong with Master Erick. Cam also knew it would do anything Erick told it to.

Madlen felt utterly dirty and insignificant in his presence. Even her shoelaces were undone. She bent to retie them, and as she did so, the hatchet fell out of the inside blazer pocket she'd stuffed it into. It clattered onto the ground.

"Ernurgggg!"

Erick's face had turned pale, and his eyes were big with horror. He grabbed Cam and swung it bodily between himself and Madlen.

Madlen and Bryn stared in amazement.

"Um, what's wrong?" asked Bryn.

The tall man seemed to be struggling to regain his poise.

"We . . . ," he said, and then coughed as if to hide the quaver in his voice. "We appear to have a dilemma. The . . . horrible little implement the young lady has suddenly produced, I wasn't expecting . . . It shouldn't be . . . I'm allergic."

There was a bemused pause.

"Allergic?" repeated Madlen, unable to believe she'd heard correctly. "To hatchets?" She picked the hatchet up and peered at it in amazement.

"THAT THING STAYS HERE!"

The last words were spoken in a voice of absolute authority, which had Madlen automatically beginning to put the hatchet down again, even while protesting, "But . . . I can't just leave it lying around. It's sharp!"

"I am beginning to wheeze," said Master Erick, "even at this distance. My allergy is severe."

Madlen hesitated for a moment, and then turned on her heel.

"I know where to put it!" she said, and before anyone could stop her, she ran up the steps of the school and through the ruined double doors.

She thought she could hear Cam calling to her to come back, it wasn't safe, but she shut out the sound and ran on.

See? If I'd handed over my key to Miss Gerard yesterday, I mean, all those years ago, the way a good girl would . . .

Her heart was beating hard as she hurried along the shattered corridor. There must have been a fire at some point, for the walls were sooty and scorched. The ceiling over her head bulged down under the weight of the fallen roof. It creaked menacingly. She tried to move weightlessly; she tried not to breathe.

And then she was there. The lockers stretched along a section of corridor that was amazingly undamaged, though the soot and the dirt everywhere would have made Mrs. Alastair, the caretaker, weep. Madlen set the hatchet down in front of locker thirty-seven and, wiping the sweat from her hands onto her blazer, scrounged in her pocket for the key. She had trouble getting it into the lock at first. She was starting to shake all over with the urgency of the message from her brain—*GET OUT, GET OUT!*

Then, just as the key engaged, she froze. Something impossible was happening, just there, just out of the corner of her eye. Something . . .

She let her hand drop and spun around to face whatever it was, except that when she did, it wasn't there anymore. Just the ruined building, the dirt, the decay. Nothing.

Slowly Madlen reached for the key in the lock. As soon as her fingers made contact, it—whatever it was—was back, just there, at the edge of her vision. There were faint noises, and colors, and even smells. Madlen held absolutely still, fighting the urge to turn and look. The powerful aroma of Mrs. Alastair's pol-ish flooded her senses, and she felt a ridiculously overwhelming nostalgia for the good old days—for yesterday. She was aware of clean uniformed girls rustling up and down the corridor behind her; whispers that rose and fell as teachers paced majestically by; the faint leftover odor of burned breakfast toast; and a feel-ing of being absolutely sure of what the day would hold. It was almost more than she could bear. It made tears prick her eyes.

The tears spilled over, and everything went blurry. Working almost blindly, Madlen turned the key and pulled open the door of locker thirty-seven. She felt about on the floor beside her, found the hatchet, and pushed it inside. She could still hear and smell the lost world going on behind her as she fumbled the door closed. For a long moment she stood, her hand on the key, the tears still running down her face. Then, slowly, she removed the key from the lock.

The sounds of girls and gossip, and the smells of polish and disinfectant, faded. In their place she smelled damp and decay, and heard only the random creaking of a ruined building. She scrubbed the tears out of her eyes, and drew a ragged breath.

Stumbling a little, Madlen made her way back to the night-mare World outside.

As Madlen emerged from the school, she found it had started to rain. The others were looking anxious and miserable, except for Master Erick, who only looked majestic.

Bryn ran up to her, but Cam just stood where it was, fists on hips.

"Are you all right?" asked Bryn.

"I thought the whole flipping roof was going to come in on you!" yelled Cam. "Don't you know how dangerous that was?"

Then the tear smudges on Madlen's face registered. "Yeah, so, are you okay?" Cam mumbled, embarrassed.

"*Shall* we?" interrupted Master Erick impatiently.

"Let's go," said Madlen. Her voice was a little hoarse, but she managed to keep it from wobbling. "I'll tell you about it later."

Master Erick strode off down the street. At some point the boy Fred had disappeared again. No one had seen him go. The three looked at one another, shrugged, and headed out.

They found they had trouble keeping up with the man's long legs. No matter how fast they walked, or even jogged, he always seemed to be just too far ahead for comfort. Surprisingly, though, he didn't seem to be having the same overawing effect on them when he wasn't right in their faces anymore.

"Why can't the wretched man slow down?" grumbled Madlen.

"*Because you are children and he is not!*" Cam mimicked, and Bryn made a rude gesture at Erick's back.

There was no way Erick could have known what they were doing or saying, and yet . . .

"Naughty, naughty," he called back. At the same moment the rain got heavier, and a nasty wind sprang up that chilled and bit, driving the wet into their faces no matter which way they turned.

They were zigzagging through the streets, skirting piles of rubble, and sometimes cutting through the ruins themselves. Madlen was too unhappy to pay close attention, and Cam was too cold and out of breath, but Bryn struggled to keep track of their route. He'd learned many of the skills of the hunter and tracker with his pack, though in a built-up area and without the sun, he was finding it hard to keep direction clear. Even so, he began to suspect that Master Erick was leading them in elaborate circles, as if he wanted them to be unable to retrace their steps. Then, he stopped suspecting. He knew. The stranger was trying to get them lost.

He stared at the man's back, frowning, and then he noticed something else.

Master Erick was dry.

Bryn and Cam and Madlen were drenched, and shivering, but the tall man's hair and clothes weren't even damp. How? Why?

Bryn said nothing. There was no point in worrying the others.

He was worried enough for all three.

CHAPTER SEVENTEEN

<u>Camping In</u>

"Aah!" said Master Erick. "Home at last!"

The children hesitated at the bottom of a flight of steps.

"But . . . ," said Bryn. "This is a *church*!"

It was the last thing either Cam or Bryn would have expected on Trentor, and it certainly seemed an unlikely home.

Madlen looked uncomfortable, and a bit defiant.

"We're not *barbarians,* you know!" she hissed at Bryn. "The people in the Service Sector have a perfect right to their own ethnic traditions, as long as they're discreet about it!"

And she stumped up the steps.

The other two raised their eyebrows, but followed on anyway. They bumped into Madlen just inside the big doors, and peered anxiously about.

The church was high, and echoey, and cold, and dim. It took a moment for their eyes to adjust, and then they saw that the nave was a mess of overturned and broken pews, ripped-up hymnbooks, and scattered debris. Partway along, a space had been cleared and there was an open fire on the flagstone floor. Fred was kneeling beside it, feeding it with bits of wood. He peered at them sideways from under his mess of hair, and then looked away. The three began to pick their way through the clutter toward the fire.

"Sausages," said Master Erick. "Potatoes. And marshmallows." He smacked his lips. "Fab!" He looked at them impatiently. "Oh, stop pissing about there! I certainly hope you're not going to be *boring*."

Fred sniggered.

"Sausages sound great," said Cam hurriedly.

"Yeah!" agreed Bryn.

"Thank you for having us," said Madlen politely.

The man glared at her in disgust.

"You sit there," said Master Erick to Bryn and Cam, turning his back on Madlen and pointing to a great heap of pew cushions, vestments, and altar cloths by the fire.

"You—sit over there," he grunted at Madlen, indicating a kneeler on the other side, farther back from the fire.

"And *this*," he said, sitting himself grandly in an ornately carved thronelike chair, "is where *I* shall sit." He struck an elegant pose. "I look better in a chair like this than some fat-assed priest. Don't you think?"

Fred let out a guffaw, and the others smiled nervously.

It was a bizarre picnic.

Fred served up food to Master Erick and Bryn and Cam; Madlen, after a moment's hesitation, helped herself. Erick was working his way steadily through a cache of beer by his chair. There was nothing for anybody else to drink, but that didn't seem to embarrass him. And in the end it just felt good to be stuffed and drowsy around a campfire, even if it *was* a campfire inside a church, surrounded by a dead city in an incomprehensible Future.

Master Erick belched, and then gave a huge yawn.

"Go away," he said, swinging his long legs over the arm of his throne. "I'm sleepy."

There was a startled pause.

"Go? Wh-where?" stammered Cam.

The man waved a careless hand. "Put them in the balcony, Fred," he said, closing his eyes.

With that, he fell asleep, and began to snore through his elegant nose.

The children looked at the boy. He didn't meet their eyes, but then, he never did.

"What now?" asked Cam, and Fred indicated the back of the church with a jerk of his head. A balcony of pews was there in the darkness, with a set of stairs up one side.

They carried bundles of cushions and cloth up the stairs, and constructed makeshift beds on the hard pews. Fred showed them how, but when they tried to thank him, he ran away. Back down the stairs he scuttled, as if they'd offered to hit him. No one commented.

The three lay down as the last light of the day disappeared from the stained glass windows. There was silence for a little, and then Bryn spoke.

"So what happened in the school? If you want to tell us," he added cautiously.

Madlen had been lying, stiff and staring in the dusk. It was a relief to tell the other two what had happened to her in that familiar, unfamiliar place.

"It was as if it were all still there, all still going on, as close as I am to you, and yet . . . I couldn't *get* to it," she finished at last. "And I was *desperate* to. Which is so weird. When I was there, before, I mean, properly at school—I hated it. I never fitted in and I was always scared they'd find out, you know?"

"Yeah," said Bryn, and "Yes," said Cam, both speaking fervently in the dark.

That's strange, thought Madlen. *I'd have said those two were just right for their Worlds. I wonder what they think they're doing wrong.*

But tiredness is a powerful force . . .

CHAPTER EIGHTEEN

*The carriage was old and decrepit . . .
All the color seemed to have been leached
out . . . Less of a map and more of an
amoeba . . . gray people—but where were
their reflections? . . . "They're not there! They're
not there!" . . . "Don't do that!" . . . too late.
They're coming, closer and closer, those ghastly
eyes, blank, black, she knew she had to do
something but she was frozen, she couldn't
move, and they were coming closer, they were
all around her, bending over her, and their faces
were all she could see—*

Madlen hit the floor, cracking her elbows and knees hard. Something was tangling her legs so she couldn't get up. She seemed to be in a kind of open box, like a coffin, and the sides rose up around her in the dim light. Her heart thudded against her chest, and she was trembling and sweaty. She lay, rigid, until at last her brain caught up with her adrenaline-crazed body.

This is the church, she told herself. *I've been asleep on a pew. I must have fallen off. The others are here too.* By craning her neck she could see them, farther along the pews, two quiet bundles, wrapped up. That must be what was pinning her legs—she must have got herself tangled up in her own make-shift sleeping bag when she had the dream.

It had been a dream.

Still shaking, Madlen freed herself, and struggled upright. It was cold. She wrapped herself in the bedding and sat for a long while, feeling stiff and miserable and on the verge of tears. It was only gradually that the pounding of blood in her ears quieted, and as it passed, she became aware of voices in the nave below.

Treading as lightly as she could, Madlen crept to the edge of the balcony. Slowly, silently, she leaned forward until she could just see over the railing.

It was a strange scene.

The fire burned irregularly in its crude hearth, the flames leaping up and throwing huge shadows against the blank windows, then dimming, then sparking and hissing as the varnish on the wood caught. The pile of satin vestments and shiny cloth flickered in the light. And there was Fred, squatting in the midst of it, like a toad in the princess's bed. Master Erick, awake again, paced back and forth, his tall figure foreshortened from this angle. She couldn't help noticing a small bald spot in the middle of all that silky hair.

" . . . What did you bring them here for, then?" the boy was saying. "*I* don't want them. I don't want *anybody!*"

"Why did *I* bring them here? I didn't *bring* them—I found them! Wandering about. Poking their noses in. Getting their hands on *you*. They're dangerous, that's what they are, and they don't belong." Master Erick's voice had a brittle edge to it. "I want them where I can keep an eye on them. Even you must have felt the energy coming off that wretched little axe. The girl still stinks of it! They *all* smell wrong. . . ."

Then his tone changed. "Anyway, you don't think *you're* adequate company, do you?" The man preened. "I was ready for a little proper appreciation, a little *adoration,* and I got it! You could see they thought I was fabulous. And I am. Look at everything I've done for you, you little brat." He made an expansive gesture at the ruination all around them, and laughed. "And to think I used to be just a bit of *you,* trapped inside that miserable boy's body—it hardly bears thinking of." He gave a theatrical shudder. "You did a good day's work for yourself when you split *me* off, I can tell you!"

Madlen was bewildered. *What is he on about?*

"You used to be all frustrated and helpless, didn't you, until you figured out how to use your little number games for yourself. Once *I* existed, all the gray people just knuckled under, didn't they? You had the power then, didn't you? Feeling cross? How about smashing something? Don't like somebody? Poof— they're gone. Everything and everybody, just the way you want them. A little god."

Master Erick turned suddenly on the boy. "Except you couldn't do it by yourself," he spat. "And that's what you made me for, isn't it? Because I'm everything you're not. I'm big, and important, and people listen to me, and they *believe* what I'm telling them. Isn't that right?"

He loomed over Fred, who was cringing now in his satin nest.

"Leave me alone," the boy whined. "Don't forget—I can get rid of you anytime I like. *You're* the one who's nothing! I get tired of you and—poof!—*you're* gone!"

Master Erick looked down at his elegant fingernails with studied insolence. "Are you sure?" he said.

His voice was suddenly so quiet Madlen had to strain to hear, and so sinister it made her shudder.

"Are you certain that is still the case?" He turned slowly back and fixed the boy with his eyes. "I've been separate for quite some time now, my dear, and I've developed a taste for it. Oh yes. I wonder if you have been noticing anything, anything in the nature of a change, hmmm? In our special relationship? Are you sure you want me to call your bluff, little friend?"

Madlen was holding her breath. The man was so threatening, so powerful . . . What would Fred do? How could a boy fight someone like that?

He didn't.

He crumpled, and began to snivel into the satin. Only muffled bits of what he was saying reached the balcony.

". . . It wasn't supposed to be like this . . . ," he moaned. "It was supposed to be better . . . You were supposed to take care of things . . ." Then Fred lifted his head and wailed out loud, *"It was supposed to be fun!"*

And Master Erick slapped him. It was so sudden, and so vicious, that Madlen gasped, then clamped her hand over her mouth. But he hadn't heard. He had hold of the boy by his shirt and was shouting, and hitting him with each word.

"It's . . . fun . . . for . . . me! . . . It's—"

"STOP IT! STOP IT!!" screamed Madlen. She couldn't watch anymore. *"Leave him alone!"*

There was a horrible moment of silence, with nothing but a sick, panting sound in it. Madlen realized the sound was coming from *her*. Her heart was racing, and she felt as if she were going to throw up.

"Aah," said Master Erick, tilting his head slightly to stare up at her. "It's you. Join us."

Madlen shook her head, dumb with fear.

He continued to look at her while, almost casually, he shifted his grip to Fred's throat and started to squeeze. The boy made a gurgling noise, and clutched at Erick's fist with both hands.

Madlen scrambled to her feet. "Okay, *okay,*" she said. "I'm coming! Let him go. Don't kill him!"

Master Erick laughed, and dropped Fred. "Of course not," he oozed. "What an idea! Why, the boy's like . . . a *brother* to me. And bring the other two with you. I'd like us all to be together, if only for a while. . . ."

Madlen turned and staggered back up the balcony steps to rouse the others. But it wasn't necessary. Her scream had already woken them, and they were sitting up in their pews, wide-eyed and disheveled. Without a word they followed her down the stairs, and into the nave of the church.

Master Erick was waiting for them.

CHAPTER NINETEEN

Madlen, Bryn, and Cam stood in a row.

"What are you going to do with them?" asked Fred. His voice was hoarse, and they could see red finger marks on his throat.

Master Erick stroked his beard and smiled. It wasn't a pleasant sight.

"What do we normally do when we come across something we don't like?" he mused. "Oh yes, I remember. We *eliminate* it. We tap into our clever little computer and we access their irritating little bubbles of life force and—hey presto!—*they don't exist.* Well, they're still around, aren't they, but they can't quite remember who they are anymore, or where they were going, or what it was they were going to do."

Madlen shut her eyes. *Zombies*, she quavered inside her head. *They make zombies.*

"But that's getting a bit boring."

Her eyes snapped open again.

"I don't think we'll bother with that this time." Erick was almost purring. "I'm going to think of something *new*. All I have to do is act out some of those things *you* used to imagine. Don't you remember? You used to look at the *lucky* ones—just like these specimens—the ones who didn't have to be *special* like you. And you used to imagine nasty things. . . . Oh yes, there's a lot I can do to our little friends, without *beginning* to strain my ingenuity. And all thanks to you . . ."

The three looked uneasily at Fred.

"That was different," he mumbled to the floor. "That was before . . ."

"Before *me*!" Erick laughed, and lunged at the same time. He caught Cam by the hair, wrenching the Dalrodian's head back cruelly. "I can see this lasting a good long time—entertainment on tap."

The horrified looks of the children seemed to interest him, the way a cat is interested in the terror of the mouse.

"But I don't want to hurry. The vestry would be a good place to store you just now, I think," he said. "The other two might like to lead the way."

He twisted his grip in its hair, and Cam gasped.

"Okay, okay, we're going," said Madlen quickly. "Where is it?"

The man indicated a door at the side of the nave, and Bryn and Madlen moved toward it.

"Quicker!"

Another gasp from Cam had them running, and Erick followed with his captive. He shoved Cam into the room behind them, and slammed the door. There was the sound of a key turning in the lock.

Bryn went to Cam, and Madlen hurried over to the door.

She pressed her ear against the wood and listened.

There was the echoing of footsteps. It sounded as if Master Erick were leaving. A voice called after him.

"Where're you going?"

Madlen could hear the note of panic.

Master Erick chuckled unpleasantly.

"Oh, don't worry, little Freddy," he called back. "Don't fret, little boy. I'll be coming home to run things for you. But first I think I deserve another drink—and *everyone* should get what they deserve, just exactly what they deserve, don't you agree?" He chuckled again, and then added, "Don't try to go anywhere, now, will you."

It seemed as if Master Erick had gone. Madlen pressed her ear harder against the wood, straining to hear more. For a long moment there was nothing, and then she drew back sharply.

A key scraped in the lock, and the door swung inward. Fred stood in the doorway, a grubby, pathetic, white-faced figure.

"Help me," he said.

CHAPTER TWENTY

<u>Fred + Erick = ?</u>

All at once he was shaking. Madlen made a move
to put her arm around him, but he curled back
his lip and snarled at her.

"You aren't allowed to touch me!" he screamed. "I'm special!
You'll give me germs! You'll make me sick!"

They looked at him, appalled.

"Who said we shouldn't touch you?" asked Bryn. "Your
parents?"

As soon as he'd spoken, it seemed like a dangerous sort of
question to ask, but Fred had suddenly gone calm again.

"My parents don't tell me what to do," he said, matter-of-
fact. "They're just gray—gray people who go off to work. I have
tutors, and analysts, though, and people who watch me, and
people who watch the tutors and analysts . . . but I got rid of
them."

Madlen felt a cold shiver down her back. "*How* did you get
rid of them?" she asked.

Fred looked at her. "That was one of the very first things I
did," he said. "People needed to pay attention—they needed to
stop pushing me around. If you look like a kid, nobody listens,
do they? So I divided off a bit of me so that the rest of me could

get some peace. That's Erick's job—to keep all those gray people off my back."

Cam was frowning. "Fred . . . Erick . . . Fred . . . ," it murmured, then almost shouted, "Oh, holy desert, are you trying to say you're *Frederick,* and then you split yourself, and you called the bits *Fred—*"

"And *Erick*!" Bryn groaned. "That is just so tacky! You could at least have gone for something like, I don't know, Terry and Dactyl. Or how about Cat-Ass and Trophy?"

"Cat-Ass and Trophy, oh yes, now *that's* tasteful!" tutted Madlen. "Frederick's a perfectly normal name."

"Normal has nothing to do with it," muttered Bryn, but he subsided when Madlen kicked him.

Fred's face darkened, and he started to say, "You're not *allowed* to make fun—" when Cam interrupted.

"Is that *possible*?" it asked. "To do . . . what you said?"

"Oh yes." Fred tried to sound casual, but didn't succeed. "With access to enough power. Nobody else had noticed it, but *I* did. Staring them all right in the face!"

"What was?" asked Madlen.

Fred looked at her with complete scorn. "The imbalance, of course. In the power potential. Like a weak place, I guess you'd say. Siphoning the energy through was easy—for me, anyway. I could show you the math, but you'd never understand."

"Where'd you learn to be so charming?" said Bryn, but Cam cut in again.

"What did your parents think . . . of you making Erick?"

And Fred crumpled into tears. They seemed to explode from his eyes, and his nose ran. It was a very sad, very unattractive sight.

"*They* wouldn't know," he gulped. "What do you expect? They were just Servers—they handed me over years ago. It's obvious, isn't it, even to stupid people like you? *They didn't love me.* "Then, still leaking, he half-whined, half-jeered, "You don't know anything. I don't know why I thought you could help me—you're just *ordinary.*"

He made it sound like something dirty. He turned and started to walk away in disgust, until he heard a low laugh. It was Cam.

"I *used* to be," it said. "Ordinary, I mean. And I used to know what was going on, and what was what. I'd give anything to make things back the way they were then. But they aren't anymore. And I guess they never will be again."

Fred was intrigued in spite of himself. "Why—what changed?"

Cam's voice was low. "I found out the truth," it said. "I found out my mother had me as part of somebody else's master plan, and then she gave me away."

Fred lifted a tear-streaked face. "She gave you away?" he whispered. "That means you're . . . you're just like me!"

Cam looked horrified at the idea, but managed to nod. "Want me to tell you about it?"

Fred nodded solemnly. And he listened to every word. He listened as he hadn't listened to a soul in years. Another voice, another face, another story—for the first time, something outside of himself was becoming really real.

"I'll show you my math now, if you like?"

Cam heaved a big sigh, and nodded. Fred trotted off into the darkness.

"Got yourself a bosom buddy now." Bryn giggled softly. "You're just so *lucky*!"

"Shut up, Bryn," growled Madlen. "Cam handled him beautifully. I didn't notice *you* being very useful."

Cam was too tired to even kick Bryn properly, so it just made a rude sign at him instead. He snickered, unrepentant. Then they heard the clunk of a switch being thrown.

At once the whole front of the church was illuminated by hard, bright spotlighting.

"The vicar had all *that*?" Madlen gasped.

"Don't be stupid," said Fred, returning. "The vicar had an old Xerox machine and a manual typewriter. I brought this lot over from the lab where they used to keep me." He snorted, and dragged a sleeve across his nose. "Totally blew the wiring, first time I booted it."

The equipment covered the altar, and spilled over onto chairs and the pulpit and the floor. It was matte black and chrome, lean and powerful-looking, and it didn't take much technological insight to guess that it would use an astonishingly huge amount of energy to run. At the moment, though, it was only humming gently, as if working on some problem so simple it could do it in its sleep. Fred moved between the monitors, checking and pressing buttons. Streams of equations began to trundle down the screens and disappear, like shoppers on an escalator.

"I keep it running most of the time," he said. "There's a lot of stuff I've never been too impressed by—quantum theory, basal physics—so I'm reconfiguring a lot. I could really do with a better rig. This does okay, but it's just not very fast. Later I—DON'T TOUCH THAT!"

Cam leapt back as if stung. It had been bending over one of the monitors with a particularly complex cascade of numbers and symbols, which flickered and changed color, and generally managed to look pretty and dangerous at the same time.

"That's the mother program," said Fred flatly. "It is *not* something you want to mess with."

Cam held up its hands. "Okay, okay, not a problem."

Fred nodded stiffly, and then looked away. The Dalrodian shrugged and wandered off to another display.

But Madlen didn't. A peculiar expression had come over her face, and she crept up to the monitor Cam had just left, as if approaching something miraculous. Bryn was watching her. There was an almost visible shimmer of connection between her and what to him were only scribbles on the screen. She was hardly breathing. He moved closer to her.

"Madlen?" He spoke quietly. "You okay?"

She took a deep breath and sighed it out. "So beautiful," she murmured.

Bryn scratched his head. "What . . . *that?*"

"Yes. It's just so . . . right," she said fervently. Then she grabbed his arm so hard it made him squeak. "That's it!" she whispered urgently. "Remember what Kate said? *It would feel right!* What if this is it . . . It must be—it's what we're looking for—the Quest Object! *This* is what we're supposed to bring back. . . ."

"That? A bunch of *numbers*? How can you know—," began Bryn, but Cam, who had caught the end of the conversation, cut in with "Never mind. Just write it down quick! So you don't forget it."

Madlen shook her head. "You can't really write it down, but it isn't something you could forget," she said.

"I told you, you won't understand that," Fred interrupted loudly. "I'm the only one who can." He was watching them now, swinging back and forth on a swivel chair.

Madlen was still staring at the screen.

"You really are a genius," she said quietly.

"What?" Fred abruptly stopped swinging. "How can *you* tell?"

"This is how you accessed the energy leak, isn't it?" Madlen asked, with wonder in her voice. She reached out a finger but didn't touch the screen. "It's a Nonrepeating Möbius Strip Equation—a Ribbon! I've only read about those—I never believed I'd ever see one." She turned to face Fred. "And you did it!"

Fred's face was turning redder by the minute, and his mouth was hanging open.

"You did it," Madlen continued, her voice suddenly husky, "and now you're going to have to terminate it."

Fred's head dropped, and he glared up at her from under the mat of hair like a malevolent goblin. "It's mine!" he growled. "Mine!"

"It's *not* yours," she said. "I think you know that, really. Stuff like this—energy like this—it doesn't just lie about for no reason."

No response.

"You must have thought, you must have wondered, 'If I'm taking it, who's losing it?' I don't believe you didn't wonder."

Still not a flicker.

Cam sighed, and stepped forward. "She's right," it said firmly. "And you know it. It's over, Fred. Time to turn off the computers, seal the leak, get rid of Master Erick, and then . . . Well, we'll see where we are."

Fred's face was sullen and bleak, but he nodded.

"And turning off the mother program is the way to do it, right?" Madlen persisted. "Stop the flow of energy, and the separation between you and, er, the rest of you won't be maintained anymore?"

Fred was looking shifty again.

"Is that right?"

"Yeah," he said. "Probably."

"What do you mean—*probably*?" shrilled Cam.

Fred scrubbed his nose on his sleeve and shrugged. "Turning off the power might not be enough," he said.

CHAPTER TWENTY-ONE

"What!"

"I'll probably need to use Harmonic Disruption." He wasn't really talking to them. "If cutting off the power isn't enough."

"What?"

But Fred had stopped answering.

"I hate it when people do that," muttered Madlen.

"This Harmonics thing," said Bryn quietly. "Is that like 'The Fat Lady Who Can Shatter Glass'?" He caught the expression on his siblings' faces and blushed. "I saw a circus once," he continued. "One of the acts was this great fat woman who could sing really loud and screechy, and she had this table of glasses on it, full of water, you know, and she made them explode. . . . It was funny. The people in the front row got all wet—"

"A few glasses?" sneered Fred. "And that passes for ability in your World, does it?" He'd been listening after all.

"Yeah!" Bryn bristled. "Yeah! I thought it was pretty cool, actually!"

"Anybody can do it," said Fred dismissively. "All you have to know is the Resonant Frequency Range of an object and then take a step beyond, so to speak, in any of the standard Harmonic Dimensions and—hey *presto*!"

"Oh yeah? That's all there is to it? Right. Shatter . . . *that*, then, if it's so easy!" Bryn pointed to a thick, extremely ugly coffee mug decorated with luridly purple thistles and the phrase "I ♥ Auchtermuchty" in repellent red, which the vicar had long ago set down and forgotten.

"Fine."

Fred swiveled to a keyboard and typed in: "*ceramic *hollow *displacement 300 mls *fired/glazed molecular discrepancy." Then a program sequence. And "process." Almost immediately the screen offered a pattern of frequency blips. Fred glanced at them casually and, without even turning around, cleared his throat and sang. One note, peculiarly between the tones the others were accustomed to.

The mug shuddered, and was gone. A small apologetic shower of china dust trickled down from the shelf for a moment, but that was all.

Fred swiveled back and gave Bryn a look.

Bryn wasn't keen to meet his eye. He scuffed at the flagstones with the toe of his shoe instead. "Yeah. Well. You still needed the computer," he said grudgingly. Cam snorted. Bryn glared, but added with a poor grace, "Oh, all right. ALL RIGHT! You did it. Jolly good, and all that. And you're planning to shatter Old Man Erick next?"

"More rearranging him at a molecular level, but yes, you could say that," said Fred snootily.

"And you're sure that won't shatter *you* at *your* oh-so-self-satisfied molecular level at the same time? Not that I'd mind, of course."

There was a pause. In spite of himself Fred had to admit it was a good question.

"I don't know, not for sure," he answered sullenly. "But on

the basis of the original program, and assuming a stability of parameters consistent with standardized Midlothian logarithms . . . Look, I'll try to put this simply. If we take as given that each of us exists as a collection of energies, acting in particular relation to one another to create bone, tissue, skin, mind, et cetera— then I'm almost certain *I've* got more of my collection here, in this body, than *he* has in his."

"So, like, he's thinner?" said Bryn.

Fred stared. Bryn stared back.

Madlen smothered a giggle, and interrupted. "So what note would you use on Master Erick, then?" she asked.

Fred shook his head. "It'd take more than just a note. A chord, at least. Probably with a succession of individual Related Frequency Selections leading into it. And a finely controlled Differential Dynamic."

Bryn groaned, and buried his head in his hands.

"You mean a song," said Cam calmly. "With loud and soft bits."

Bryn looked up.

Fred shrugged, and said, "You could call it that. If you wanted."

Bryn collapsed once more. "Oh no," came his muffled voice. "Mr. Wonder Erick wants to skewer us, slowly, painfully, and many times—and we're going to *sing* him to death. This is getting stupider by the minute."

"Can you do it?" said Cam. "There isn't much time left—and if you need the computers to work it out, well, it has to be done before we pull the plug."

"Obviously." Fred was just sitting there, staring into space.

"Well? Can you?" Cam insisted, its voice getting shrill. "Oh, sainted sand snakes, we don't have time for this!"

"We don't *not* have time for this," Fred flared. "I have to think. If I get any part of this wrong, and I translate that into Harmonics, and we use the Harmonics, SPLATTT!" He threw his arms in the air. "That's us, bloody gobbets on the walls."

"But—"

Fred began to scream, "Do you have *any* idea the kind of power we're talking about here?"

"*I* do," interrupted Madlen. "And Cam's right. We're running out of time."

With one decisive shove she swung Fred's chair round and pushed him at a monitor.

"Get on with it," she ordered.

Fred glared at her, but started calling up files.

"Bloody . . . bloody . . . gobbets . . . ," he muttered as he worked. Then he swung over to another monitor. "I'll need all of you," he continued, bent over the keyboard.

"Except me," said Madlen, taking an almost imperceptible step backward. "Of course. Three's the magic number, after all."

"No." Fred shook his head. "All of you. Four voices—four Harmonic Dimensions."

Cam leaned aside to Bryn and asked quietly, "The kid'll be a treble, but what about you? Can you sing tenor at a pinch?"

Bryn nodded. "You?"

"Alto. We call it Second. So, Fred's First; I'm Second; you're Third . . ."

"Bit of a problem, then."

Cam put its hand on Bryn's arm. "I've got an idea. Wait here."

It took Madlen by the hand and drew her away from the others.

"I can't sing; you know I can't sing," she was babbling.

"Sing," said Cam.

"I CAN'T!" yelled Madlen.

Cam reached out and deliberately pinched her. Hard.

"Ouch!" squawked Madlen. "What did you do that for?"

"Right," said Cam, ignoring her indignation. "That's where we start." And the Dalrodian made a sound as close to Madlen's squeal as it could manage.

"Now, walk down. With your voice. Come on, we'll do it together."

Madlen stared at Cam as if it were mad.

"Come on, I dare you!"

Cam made its version of Madlen's noise again and then began to drop down, a note at a time. After a moment Madlen joined in, lurching now higher, now lower, with her amazingly sour voice. Further and further down a nightmare version of a scale they went, lower and lower, until Cam had to stop.

"That's as far as I go," it called to Madlen. "You keep on!"

Madlen did, lower, lower, and then something strange began to happen. Madlen's voice took on a new color, a rich sort of amber sound. And finally, she hit a note, one perfect note, and she looked at Cam as if she couldn't believe her ears.

She sang it again. And again.

There was a grin on her face that must have hurt, and Bryn and Cam grinned back.

"Did you hear that?" she crowed. "Did you *hear that*?"

"You just never found your range before," said Cam. It turned to Fred. "Right, get going. Build it from there."

"One note!" scoffed Fred. "Not exactly what I'd call a range! And anyway, who ever heard of a *girl* singing as low as—"

Bryn turned toward the younger boy. "Shut up," he said.

Fred started to protest, took one look at Bryn's face, and shut up.

Madlen's smile faded. "Will it be enough?" she asked.

Bryn loomed at Fred. "It will be," he growled softly. "You'd better *make* it be."

"Can you do it?" asked Cam.

Fred shrugged. "Uh . . . I'm not sure," he muttered gracelessly.

Bryn made a sudden move toward him, and the younger boy jumped back. "It'll—it'll be fine," he babbled. "Yeah, great, fine! I can do it."

"Good boy," said Bryn, and he patted Fred, hard, on the head. "Just what we wanted to hear." He turned. "Cam, maybe you should stay with our little friend here while he gets this weird weapon built. Madlen and I'll go on lookout duty, keep an eye out for Mr. Master Erick. Be as fast as you can. It's not far off daybreak, and he won't stay away forever."

He bustled Madlen out of the vestry and down the side aisle. They stopped just outside the big front doors, where the shadows kept them hidden while they watched. Three rubble-filled roads that met with the church as their apex were visible for some distance now in the gray predawn light. Madlen shivered, and then suddenly clutched Bryn's arm.

"There!" she whispered. *"Something moved! He's back already. We must go tell the others!"*

But Bryn had seen movement too. "I don't think it's him," he said quietly, knowing how much further whispers will carry. "Look—there—and there!"

They could see now that the ruins around the church were full of gray furtive figures. Some stood still; others drifted from one area of rubble to another; all were strangely familiar.

"It's the zombies!" moaned Madlen. "They're coming to get us!"

"I don't think so," said Bryn. "Look. They aren't coming any closer. It's as if they aren't allowed to cross the road or something. . . ."

It was true. The gray people seemed to have washed up at the foot of some kind of barrier. The church drew them—the attention of every figure was focused on it—but they did not, or could not, approach.

Then, suddenly, they were all gone. They melted out of sight so quickly that Madlen started to step forward out of hiding because she couldn't believe her eyes. Bryn dragged her back into the shadows just in time.

"It's him," he murmured in her ear. "Master Erick is coming back. Tell the others."

Madlen nodded, and scurried back into the church.

"He's coming," she called quietly.

She could dimly see Cam and Fred, two figures huddled by a monitor at the far end of the building.

"I don't think I can do it," whimpered the boy.

"I don't think you have any choice," Cam answered.

With a sob Fred reached a single finger, pressed, and the screen went blank. Cam squeezed his shoulder, and this time he didn't shrink from the touch.

Madlen watched them, her mouth dry and her heart thudding, until Bryn ran back in.

"Well?" he said. "Has he pulled the plug yet?"

Madlen stared at him. "Yes," she whispered. "Didn't it work?"

Bryn sighed, and shook his head.

"He stumbled a little, but that was all. Master Erick is still on his way."

CHAPTER TWENTY-TWO

Battle Hymn

Back in the vestry the four children listened breathlessly to the sound of Master Erick's shoes on the flagstones. They heard him bang into something, and curse.

"He's drunk," whispered Fred. "That'll help."

Then they came out of hiding, one by one.

Master Erick was at the front of the church by the altar. The high stained glass windows were just beginning to lighten into pale color behind him. They could see his face was flushed, but nothing else had changed.

He was the adult, and they were the children. He was right, and they were wrong.

Then Fred stepped forward. "We've got something for you," he said.

Erick frowned. "I thought I locked them up," he said, as if to himself. He leaned back against the altar, but didn't notice that the monitors around him were dark and still.

Fred took another step. Now there was only a long arm's length between them. He was being careful not to look Erick in the eye, careful not to alert him in any way, but behind his back the others could see his fists were clenched.

"I've written you a song."

Master Erick yawned, covering his mouth with the back of a hand. "Is it long?" he said.

"Not very."

"All right, then." He yawned again. "If you must."

The Questors shuffled nervously. But Fred wasn't paying any attention to them. He simply began to sing.

It was a wordless melody, high and cold. Fred's voice was perfectly clear, pitched in the exact center of each note, without a trace of tremolo. He sang for a moment, and then paused.

Master Erick had abandoned his show of boredom. He said, "You sing beautifully, boy. But that's the strangest tune. It makes me feel—"

"There's more," interrupted Fred. "It's not over yet."

He began to sing again, a version of the original sequence, and as he sang he turned round to the others and gestured for them to join in. First Cam and then Bryn added their voices to his.

"They're not a patch on you!" Master Erick called out, but Fred didn't respond. With one hand he called for more and more volume from the two children, and with the other he drew Madlen in as well. She had only one note to give. She gave it now.

Master Erick was becoming agitated.

"It's too loud!" he called to Fred. "Turn it down, you stupid boy!"

And still Fred's eyes bored into theirs, asking for more. His own voice soared over the others as the music built up into something little short of a wall of sound. Madlen could see Erick, as if pinned against the altar, mouthing curses and cries but unable to escape.

Then, just when it seemed there could be no more, Fred

pivoted, faced Erick, and hurled the final chord at him as if it were a spear. The children held their notes, and held them, until the tall stained glass windows behind the altar began to quiver and rasp against their leading. Fred was looking Erick in the eyes now, and holding him there. Terror distorted the man's face, and they could see he was screaming.

But still it was not enough. Raw energy hurtled about the nave, burning and twisting in the air, and still Erick stood and the four children faced him, and then—

Bryn's voice broke. Under the strain of holding a single note at full volume for so long, he lost control, and the note screeched, an agonizing glissando, up into another range.

The effect was cataclysmic. Erick staggered and shrieked, covering his ears against the sound. The window exploded behind him, hurling colored sharp-edged light into the nave. Bryn, Cam, and Madlen all ducked down instinctively when the glass shattered, but Erick and Fred remained as they were, upright and exposed.

A huge splinter of glass leapt from the window, hitting the man full in the back with such force that the point of the shard emerged from his chest. Arms flung out to the sides, he was thrown forward with huge force, down the steps—and onto Fred.

The two bodies crashed to the floor, pierced by the same blade. There was a moment of horrible silence, broken only by the panting of the three children, and the occasional clatter of the last remaining pieces of window as they hit the flagstones. Then there was a sigh, and where there had been two bodies, there was only one. Frederick lay on the cold stone in a pool of blood, alone.

Madlen, Cam, and Bryn stared at one another. They were too shocked to go to him, too shocked even to move.

Then, out of the deafened silence came a rustling sound. Hesitant at first, it grew and grew. It was the gray people, coming into the church, silent except for the way their too-large clothes whispered against their wasted bodies. Two, a man and a woman, came right up to the boy on the floor and bent over him tenderly, hiding him from view.

"Is he dead?" asked Cam hoarsely.

The woman looked back at them and smiled. It was a rusty sort of smile, as if its owner were out of practice, but it was joyful nevertheless.

"He's alive," she whispered. "My son's alive!"

CHAPTER TWENTY-THREE

<u>Morning</u>

"Well, time to get the number thing back to base,"
said Bryn cheerfully. "A good piece of work,
I'd say, for the Questors Three. All
for one, and all that!"

It was full daylight as they came out onto the steps of the church.
There were more people on the streets now, though they still
seemed unsure of where they were, or what had happened.

"They're not so gray-looking," said Cam. "I think they're
coming back to life."

"Post-zombification," murmured Bryn. "Well-known as a
time of intensifying color."

"LOST, ARE WE?"

The three mighty Questors squealed in unison at the sudden
voice booming in their ears. Whirling round, they were faced
with an extremely tall, thin policeman wearing a faded uniform
several sizes too large for him. There was nothing faded about
his voice, however.

"GOT HOMES TO GO TO, YOU LOT? UNSETTLED TIMES,
THESE. I'D BE GETTING OFF THE STREETS, IF I WERE
YOU."

The three didn't know what to do. But the policeman showed

no sign of leaving them alone to figure anything out.

"WELL?" he boomed. "MOVE ALONG!"

Suddenly Madlen reached a decision. "Can you tell us the way to Swithin Street, please?" she said in her best boarding-school voice. "The Swithin Street School?"

"OH, YOU WANT TO GO THERE, DO YOU? WHAT YOU DO IS, GO STRAIGHT ALONG TALBOT STREET, SEE? RIGHT TO THE VERY END. THEN TAKE THE SECOND RIGHT, GO TWO BLOCKS ON, AND YOU'RE THERE. CAN'T MISS IT."

"But why—," Bryn began, but Madlen silenced him with a glare.

"Thank you very much," she said politely. "Good-bye."

"Er, good-bye," chorused the other two.

The policeman watched as the three children headed off along the shattered remains of Talbot Street.

"FUNNY," he mumbled to himself. "I THOUGHT THAT WAS A GIRLS' SCHOOL."

The policeman couldn't remember exactly what he should be doing, which was odd, but he was fairly sure that standing about looking official was part of it. So that was what he continued to do. He was still doing it when, a short while later, a man came up the steps toward him.

"CAN I HELP YOU, SIR?"

The man didn't answer. *He must have a cold,* thought the policeman, deducing this from the way the man was sniffing. *That can clog up your ears something chronic. He mustn't have heard me.*

He reached out a big hand and tapped the stranger on the shoulder.

"I SAID, CAN I—AAGGHHH!"

The man had snarled at him!

The policeman reared back, horrified.

"Forget it," said the stranger, and then he turned and walked away. He was still sniffing in that peculiar way. Almost like a dog. A tracker dog.

Right, the policeman said to himself, *we'll need a description of* that *one down in black and white.* He pulled out a frayed notebook and an ancient pencil, and began to write.

Suspicious character observed. Middle height, middle-aged, middle . . .

The policeman scratched his head with the pencil. He had seen the man only seconds ago. Why couldn't he remember what he looked like? Or sounded like, even? What had the man said to him?

Forget it.

That's strange, thought the policeman. *I have!*

As they made their way back to the school, the three could see signs that the city was beginning to come back to life. More and more people were appearing all the time, and some had started to pick through the rubble in a dazed sort of way. A few even threw speculative glances at them as they hurried by.

"They're starting to notice things again," said Madlen. "And I think we're going to be one of the things they notice first. We don't belong here. I want to be well away before they decide to ask us questions we don't know how to answer."

There was an edge to her voice that made Bryn and Cam nervous.

"Okay," began Bryn carefully, "you could be right about that. But—"

Madlen shook her head and just walked faster.

"Not now," she said. "Not till I'm sure."

They arrived at the front entrance of the Swithin Street School sweaty and out of breath. The street was empty. Madlen started up the steps two at a time, but the others held back.

Madlen stopped at the shattered double doors and turned. She beckoned urgently for them to follow. Against his better judgment, Bryn took the first step. Cam was still hesitating when a voice broke the silence.

"Hey! Who are you? You can't go in there!"

"RUN!" yelled Madlen. "NOW!"

Cam leapt as if stuck with a pin, and Bryn practically flew the rest of the way to the doors. The voice—a woman's—continued to call after them, but they didn't look back.

"Quick!" muttered Madlen. "Hide here." She pulled them into the porter's box just inside the main doors, and they crouched down out of sight.

"Children? Children! Come out of there. That building is clearly derelict! Where are your parents? Children?"

The woman came as far as the top of the steps, but made no attempt to follow them inside. After a while she stopped calling, and then they heard her footsteps as she stumbled away.

Bryn let his breath go, and turned to Madlen.

"Right," he said. "What's going on?"

Madlen gave the others a nervous smile, and licked her lips.

"It's tricky, you know?" she said. "And I could be wrong. But I don't think so. To be honest, I pretty much know so. It's just—it's a surprisingly easy thing to make a mistake about, for a while anyway. And I did. Make a mistake about it."

"What kind of 'it' are we talking here?" asked Cam, confused, but Bryn was sitting up straight with his eyebrows disappearing into his hair.

Madlen took a deep breath, and then let it out in jerks. "It's the hatchet. From the train. Not the numbers. I was wrong."

Cam's jaw dropped, and Bryn looked as if he were about to explode.

"The hatchet from the *train*?" he squeaked. "You mean, you're saying, *that's* the thing we've been supposed to be looking for? You mean, it wasn't the numbers at all, it was that stupid *axe*!" His voice was getting shriller and shriller. "You mean we could have got away *yesterday*? We could have just picked it up off the wall, caught the next train back to The London House, and *had tea*?!"

Madlen hung her head. "I was so sure when I saw the Ribbon," she said. "It felt so *right*. But now it doesn't. Now I think it's the hatchet. And it fits with . . . stuff. Don't you remember how Master Erick reacted?" She paused. None of them wanted to think about Master Erick just yet. She drew a ragged breath and stood up. "Anyway, that's why I have to go get it. You two wait here. I'll be back as soon as I can."

But Cam grabbed her leg, and pulled itself upright.

"Not a chance," it said. "We stick together. Come on, Bryn."

Bryn was still breathing hard with indignation, but he got up too. They could hear him muttering to himself as he followed them off down the corridor. "Could have gone home yesterday! I can't believe it! We went through all that and we *could* have not even *been* there . . ."

Cam gave Madlen a nudge and a grin, and Madlen smiled weakly back.

"This way," she said. "My locker's just along here."

The corridor was as she had seen it the day before—relatively undamaged, but filthy and cold. She took out her key.

"I'm going to unlock it now, and take out the hatchet," she

said breathlessly to the others. "Watch, and tell me what you see."

She'd told them all about it before, at the church, but even so they were not prepared for the colors, the smells, the sounds, that were suddenly all around them, just out of focus. Just out of reach. Bryn and Cam were mesmerized by the strange double vision. But as soon as Madlen took the key out again, it was gone, and everything faded back into desolation and gray.

"Bring it back!" cried Cam. "I want to look some more!"

But Madlen shook her head. "I don't want to just look at it," she said. "Just hear it, or smell it. I want to get through, get out of here. I want to get back!" She took a deep breath. "All this—it's so horrible, and we have to get back to them, to The London House—and this is where we do it. I don't know how I know, but I just do. This is the way back, *but I don't know how*!" She ended on a wail.

"Okay, okay, let's just think," said Bryn, trying to be calming. "The key lets us *see*, but only when it's in the lock. When you take the key out of the lock, the stuff goes away. And that means . . ."

He ground to a halt.

"Don't look at me!" said Cam. "I haven't got a clue."

"So, *what*?" Madlen was beginning to sound desperate. "What am I supposed to do? How are we supposed to get OUT?"

There was a frantic pause, and then—

"Go crazy," said Bryn. "And then smash it."

"What?"

"With the hatchet. Like in the train, remember? You went berserk, and smashed at the door, and that's how we all got out. It worked last time."

Madlen looked appalled.

"But I can't just *go berserk*," she wailed. "Not in cold blood, for no reason, just out of the blue like that."

She slumped down against the lockers. The other two joined her.

There was a discouraged silence.

After a while Cam asked, "Madlen?"

"Hmm?"

"What were you thinking about? In the train, I mean. Just before you flipped into crazy mode? Do you remember?"

Madlen chewed her lip for a moment. "I was thinking," she said slowly, "about you two. About how I didn't want the zombies to, you know, suck the life out of you."

Bryn made a choking noise. "Zombies *do* that?" he gargled.

"Yeah," said Cam. "Didn't you know?"

He shook his head.

"What did you think they were trying to do to us, then?" exclaimed Madlen, amazed.

Bryn was quite pale now. "I don't know," he said. "I just thought they were a bit, you know, over-friendly. . . . *Sucking—* that's gross!!"

There was another silence, in which Madlen peered gloomily at the hatchet in her hands, and Bryn looked as if he were going to be sick. After a while Cam leaned back its head and looked up. It stared fixedly, and its whole body went stiff.

"Madlen?"

No answer.

Cam coughed, a very quiet I'm-not-really-making-any-noise-at-all kind of cough, and then, a little louder, said again, "Madlen?"

"What?"

Cam swallowed audibly. "Don't look now," it said, "but I think the roof's about to cave in—"

"WHAT!"

Madlen screamed, leapt to her feet, swirled round, and slammed the hatchet into the locker door, narrowly missing Cam's head.

There was a nauseating shiver in the place where they stood and—

CHAPTER TWENTY-FOUR

<u>Ten Years Ago, Day Before Yesterday</u>

"Miss Worthing? Miss Brack wants to see you, right away . . ."

The Server's voice trailed off and her eyes went wide at the sight of Bryn and Cam, not to mention the state of Madlen's uniform.

"But . . . *they're* not allowed in here!" she gasped. "No visitors beyond the front lobby." She leaned toward Madlen and whispered daringly, "Who *are* they?"

"They're family." Madlen answered as best she could, given that her voice was only just under her control. "And you can go now. I've got the message about Miss Brack."

The Server nodded and hurried away. Madlen brought the hatchet out from behind her back where she had been hiding it. She took off her blazer and wrapped the axe up into a bundle.

"The front lobby's at the end of that corridor, then turn left," she said, shoving the bundle into Bryn's arms. "Through the swing doors. I'll meet you there, once I've seen Miss Brack."

Smoothing down her skirt and trying to tidy her hair at the same time, Madlen scuttled off.

Cam and Bryn went along the corridor she'd indicated, through the swing doors, and into the lobby. Everything was polished, tidy, aggressively clean—as different from the dereliction they had just left as it could possibly be. They sat on a bench against the wall, and listened to the indistinct buzz of life that was a genteel girls' school in action.

After a moment Bryn looked over at Cam.

"Was it really?" he asked quietly. "Was the roof really just about to cave in?"

Cam looked smug. "Nope."

"And who's a clever little pip-squeak?" asked Bryn.

"Me," said Cam.

They grinned at each other, and were still. They were both too tired to talk, to think, even to worry.

It was peaceful.

Then they looked up, and Madlen was standing there in front of them.

"There's a car being sent for me," she said, and they noticed how strange her voice sounded. "Apparently my mother wants to see me."

Cam frowned, puzzled. "What, *again*?" it said.

Madlen slumped down on the bench beside them and stared at the floor. "Not again," she said. "This is the first time. Apparently. A parent ly. Very funny. Boom, boom."

Cam and Bryn exchanged looks.

"Don't you get it?" whispered Madlen suddenly. "Don't you see? It's the day before yesterday morning—no, it's *ten years ago* day before yesterday morning, and we haven't even met yet and we're going to have to do it all over again, and all those people are . . . are *zombies* again, except the hatchet won't be there this time because it's here because I took it away. . . ."

She ran out of breath, and just sat there, shaking.

"Do you understand this?" Bryn said aside to Cam.

Cam shook its head. "I think we need to get her back to Mrs. Mac and Kate," it said quietly. "Back to The London House."

Bryn nodded. "Do we go now," he asked, "or do we wait for this car?"

Cam looked at Madlen anxiously. "Better wait for the car," it said. "I don't think she's up to a trek across the city just yet."

"Yeah," said Bryn. "They won't be expecting us, though, will they? Whoever's driving the car, I mean. Could be tricky, that." He leaned his chin on his hands, his elbows on his knees.

The front door swung open and a man with a cap looked in.

"Madlen Worthing?" he asked.

"Um," said Cam.

"You Madlen Worthing?" said the man.

"No, this is Madlen." Bryn pointed.

"But we're supposed to come with her," added Cam hurriedly.

The man shrugged. "Fine by me," he said. "Let's go."

CHAPTER TWENTY-FIVE

<u>Back, and Between</u>

When they tumbled down the stairs and into the kitchen, there was no one there.

Then Mrs. Mac came out of the larder, her arms full of food.

"Look who's here!" she smiled. "So you found your way to my kitchen, did you? Good for you. Give me a hand unloading here—"

Her smile died away at the look of horror on their faces. She frowned, and her lips moved as if she were silently going over a conversation in her mind.

"We've done that bit already, haven't we," she murmured to herself.

She shook her head vigorously, and banged at it with the heel of her hand.

"Mrs. Mac?" quavered Madlen.

Mrs. Macmahonney gave an enormous sneeze, and then said, a little tentatively, "What? Back already?"

Before she could say anything else, Madlen burst into tears and threw herself into the big woman's arms.

"There, there," Mrs. Mac crooned at the sobbing girl. "It's all right. I've caught up now. And here you are, successful I'm sure, and the job done so quickly you're back almost before you left. I'm a stupid old woman and I'll be mixing my quantum flux with my pedestrian crossing before you know it." She continued to pat Madlen's back in a comforting way, and said to the others, "Get the kettle on, and then we'll all be feeling better."

They did as they were told. It wasn't long before Madlen had cried herself out and then, all together at the big kitchen table, the three of them told Mrs. Macmahonney about Fred and Master Erick and the computers and the leak and the zombies and the key. It took quite a while because they kept interrupting one another, and arguing, and setting one another right. And, surprisingly, laughing. None of it had seemed funny at the time, but telling it over now—well, it was different.

Mrs. Macmahonney listened and exclaimed, and smiled secretly to herself at the changes she could see in the three.

Then, when they were finally finished talking, she just sat, thoughtfully fingering the hatchet that Madlen had handed over to her to see.

"Isn't that clever," she murmured. "Isn't that surprising. Not at all what you might expect. Not at all."

"Is she talking about that blasted hatchet, or us?" whispered Bryn to Madlen.

Madlen shook her head and lifted a shoulder. She seemed almost back to normal now, but there was still a question she needed to ask.

"Mrs. Mac?" she said softly.

"Yes, dear?" said Mrs. Macmahonney absently.

Madlen gulped. "Will we have to do it all over again?"

Mrs. Mac shook herself. "Hmm? Do what all over again?" she asked.

"All of it—the stuff we just did," said Madlen. Then everything came out in a rush. "The whole *thing*. I mean, if it was, what, two days ago we were at the school, no, I was at the school, and Kate sent for me, and then just now, all of us were at the school and Kate sent for me and it was two days ago, except that it wasn't, because the others were there, and they couldn't be—well, does that mean we have to go in the train and meet Fred and the gray people and—"

"No." Mrs. Mac's quiet voice cut across the rising panic. "It doesn't work that way. The leak is sealed; the hatchet is in your hand—well, in *my* hand; Frederick is back with his parents. That Future can go on from then, and, I hope, heal itself. You've bought them another chance, and you've bought yourself a little time. Which"—and she sniffed slightly—"I suggest you use *immediately* to get a touch more fragrant. And then a good long rest. I need to do some thinking, and your mother . . . Well, as I say, there's thinking to be done. Meantime—"

Mrs. Macmahonney picked up the hatchet and walked over to the far side of the kitchen. She seemed to blur slightly on the way, but that could just have been their tiredness seeing things. There was a microwave on the counter, which she opened, and then, weirdly, she shoved the hatchet in, set the timer for sixty-four seconds, shut the door, and pressed the button marked HIGH.

"What!"

"You can't do—"

"It'll fuse—"

She ignored them.

PING!

Mrs. Macmahonney opened the door, and brought out the hatchet. She juggled it and blew on her fingers. "Hot!" she exclaimed. But it was more than just hot.

It was tiny.

"You . . . *sh-shrank it*?" spluttered Cam. "In a microwave?"

Mrs. Mac nodded cheerfully. She was busy threading the miniature hatchet onto some string. "This'll make it easier to carry about, Madlen." She caught sight of their expressions. "Well, you can't just leave something like that lying around! It's sharp." She finished tying a knot in the string to her satisfaction, and then held the makeshift necklace out.

"Come on! In fact, all of you come on," she said. "No, not that side—Come along the other side of the table. To me. That's right!"

They didn't argue. One more strange thing—who would notice, the way life had been lately . . .

There was a pressure, a resistance in the air, just before they reached her. They stopped, hesitated.

"Come on!" repeated Mrs. Mac. "It won't hurt!"

Cam shrugged. "Okay." It grabbed Madlen and Bryn by their sleeves, and the three leaned forward.

There was a moment when nothing happened, and then, with a pop, they were through.

"Wow," said Bryn. "That was . . . What the . . . ? Where . . . ?"

The kitchen *looked* the same, but it *felt* completely different.

"We're still right here, in The London House," said Mrs. Mac calmly. "But this is one of the bits *between*. I thought you could do with a touch of peace and quiet. Can you feel it, how different it is? There's no responsibility here; this is a place where no decisions are made." She smiled at them.

She was right. There *was* something very soothing. The bits of The London House they'd been in up to now had been full of uncertainties and surprises. On some level that they had only partly sensed, the House had *pulsed,* as the energies of Time and Space rippled about, flexing their cosmic muscles. But here it was neutral. It was restful. You knew you couldn't stay here forever, because people aren't designed for nothing but rest, but it felt as if you could stay here *long enough.*

There was a collective sigh of relief.

"That's it," agreed Mrs. Mac. "And now it's baths and bed and a good night's sleep, to set you up for tomorrow—or when-ever—when the brave Questors will sally forth to manage the unmanageable, do the unthinkable, and achieve the unachiev-able."

"Sally who?" said Bryn, but they all ignored him.

"And, Madlen," said Mrs. Mac as she held out the impossibly microwaved necklace, "this is for you."

The late afternoon sunlight came in through the frosted window. Mrs. Mac had fed them, and patted them, found bathrooms and bath towels for them all, and left them in peace.

Cam lay back in the bath. It hadn't felt this good since it'd left home. This was a simple happiness that had to do with hot water and the undeniable end of a day. A kind of mindless body-peace.

Then the sound came. A faint sound, that stopped from time to time, and that seemed to be coming from somewhere else, not far away, inside the House.

Cam sat up, to listen better. The sound came again, low and throaty, *vibrating,* and for a long moment the Dalrodian had no idea what it could be.

And then it realized. It lay back in the water and smiled seraphically up at the steamy ceiling.

Madlen was singing in her bath, her one perfect note.

KIR

CHAPTER TWENTY-SIX

Night Maneuvers

In the darkened kitchen there was silence, touched only lightly by the occasional low hum of an appliance motor switching on, and then off again. Time loosened its belt, slumped in a chair, and nodded off. Moments stretched out. The peace was almost too good to be true.

When the figure slid into the kitchen from the stairs, it too was silent. Its presence was more a shifting, a displacing of the air, a shading of dark against dark, than anything with a real body. It glided round the room, pausing, moving on. By the sideboard it came to a halt and there was the faintest suggestion of a sound, almost as if the figure were sniffing. Was it disappointed? It moved on.

The circuit of the room completed, the figure turned back, placed something on the big table, and was gone.

The stillness settled again, and stayed for a long, long time, until . . .

There were rumors that Mrs. Mac never slept. Certainly no one who came looking for a midnight snack or some late-night tea and sympathy was ever disappointed. So it was not unusual for her to be padding about at all hours.

She was padding now.

"Eh?" she muttered sharply, and turned on the lights.

"What's this, then?" She picked up the thing from the table. It was a message, on official Council letterhead, and after she'd read it, Mrs. Mac stood for a long time, tapping it thoughtfully against her teeth. Then, "Hmm," she said. She took a step back and opened her hand.

The paper hit the floor, and was nudged firmly under the table.

As she walked away, Mrs. Mac turned out the lights.

In a corridor somewhere in The London House, someone whispered urgently.

"Well? Did you find them? The monitors have been going crazy—if anything, the backwash has become more erratic than before. So? Are they back? They were seen entering the building—but was it the first time or a second? If they've died, that would explain the readings, but if they've succeeded . . . Well?"

Alpine Cordell's pause was as subtly rude as he felt he could get away with. He was not impressed by panic.

"I was not able to locate them on Trentor," he answered. "When I returned and was able to search the kitchen"—he shrugged one shoulder slightly—"Mrs. Macmahonney had been diligent. She had cleaned thoroughly."

His listener stirred irritably and then stilled, as if deliberately choosing to be calm.

"It's not important. You will have proceeded on the assumption of, at the least, their continued existence. You have delivered the instructions in the manner I ordered." It was not a question. "The timing and location should provide a

reasonable possibility of success. The rest will be . . . clarified."

The speaker turned and walked away, but Cordell overheard its last remark, noting the renewed self-satisfaction in the voice as it repeated to itself, "There is no need to be impatient. After all, Time is on my side."

CHAPTER TWENTY-SEVEN

Life in the Freezer

When they came down the next morning,
there was no sign of Mrs. Mac, or
Kate, or anyone.

Madlen frowned anxiously. "What do you think we should do?"

"Have breakfast!" said Bryn cheerfully. He was already pulling the makings out of the fridge. "One egg or two?"

A while later they were all digging in, though Madlen still had worry lines between her eyebrows. She kept fiddling absent-mindedly with the miniature hatchet necklace. Cam watched her, and then turned to Bryn.

"Didn't Mrs. Mac say this was the worry-free bit of the House? No decisions, no responsibility? Stuff like that?"

Bryn kept chewing. "We're not in that bit anymore," he said with his mouth full. "I got up in the night for a pee, and you could tell then it'd shifted back." He reached for more toast. "By the way," he continued, "you snore. Looks like you're going to grow up to be a man after all, 'cause snoring is one of the really *manly* arts."

"Girls snore too," said Madlen.

They looked at her.

She spread her hands. "I lived in a girls' school for a million years, remember? I was in the dorm for most of it. So, take my word for it—girls snore too."

Bryn shrugged. "Okay. Live and learn." He pushed back his chair and stood up. "I hate drying, so I'll wash."

"No way!" exclaimed Madlen indignantly. "I hate drying more than you do!"

Bryn made a rude gesture at her, but Cam interrupted.

"Drying what?" it said.

The other two exchanged glances.

"Right! Cam dries!" they chorused.

The breakfast things cleaned and put away, Bryn reached for a broom.

"Here's another little delight for you to learn!" He pitched it at Cam, grinning.

"Oh, ha-ha," said the Dalrodian, catching the broom deftly. "I'm not stupid, you know. Just because we don't use *water* to clean dishes where I come from."

"No, you use servants!"

"Oh, very funny." Cam started to sweep. "You can pull out the chairs. Your brain must be getting tired with all this wit— Hey! What's this?"

The broom had brushed against something lying on the floor under the table.

"It's a piece of paper . . ."

The three gathered round, and read the message.

WALK IN FREEZER IMMEDIATELY.

"Oh cripes!" muttered Madlen.

They turned, and looked at the door of the big walk-in freezer on the other side of the room.

The door just stood there, blandly chrome, giving nothing away.

"It could at least pulse with an eerie glow," murmured Bryn. The others nodded.

"They could have made the message clearer," complained Madlen. "Do they mean *walk in* as in, walk into it? Or walk-in, as in, you know, big? And just when is 'immediately'? I mean, we didn't exactly rush breakfast." She was getting more and more agitated. "And which World are we supposed to go to next, anyway? I mean, is it Kir or Dalrodia? Mrs. Mac said we didn't have to go back to Trentor—"

"Chill out, Madlen," interrupted Bryn.

"That'd be what the freezer is for, I expect," murmured Cam.

Bryn groaned. "That was terrible. Just for that, you get to check it out first."

"Oh yeah, and I'm really dressed to go messing around in some big fridge!"

Bryn made a rude noise, and walked up to the door. He grabbed the handle, and looking back at them over his shoulder, he jeered, "Oh, oh, I'm so frightened—the big bad bag of frozen peas is going to get me!"

He heaved on the handle; the door swung open; he started to say something more—

And he was gone. The freezer had sucked him in. With a brief metallic boom the door slammed shut.

Cam and Madlen stared at each other in horror. The kitchen was quiet, except for the carefree hum of appliances. There was still a faint scent of toast and eggs in the air.

But there was no Bryn.

"Do we . . . ?" Cam looked longingly toward the door to the stairs, but Madlen shook her head.

"I don't think we can take the time to find anybody," she said in a tight, strange-sounding voice. "It said *immediately*. I think we have to go after him *now*."

"Yeah," said Cam. "He's not much good on his own, is he?"

Madlen gave Cam a forced little smile. "We'll go together," she said.

Cam nodded. They took hands and stepped up to the freezer door.

"NOW!" squeaked Madlen, and together they took hold of the handle and pulled—

A tremendous freezing suction dragged them forward, ripping the door from their hands and slamming it behind them. Cam caught a glimpse of metal shelving, with ice-covered packets of food on them, and then, strangely, stone—stone walls and stone shelves and then . . . That was it. They weren't moving anymore. They were there.

But where was *that*?

CHAPTER TWENTY-EIGHT

Out of the Icebox and Into the . . .

"There's a door over here," said Madlen. "Latched." She grunted. "Feels like it's jammed against something. Here, give me a hand . . ."

Cam came over and together they leaned into the door.

"It's stuck!"

"Push harder!"

"I *am*—"

Grudgingly, the door ground open, just enough for them to squeeze through. The light outside was dazzling, and the air was so cold it hurt to breathe.

"It's a fair guess this *isn't* Dalrodia," said Madlen.

"MADLEN!" squealed Cam in delight. "It *must* be Kir—there's snow! Look, it's real sn—"

There was an unexpected tackle from behind, and Cam found itself face-first in a drift of cold white wetness.

"Keep down, you idiot, and shut up. I'm going to take a look . . ."

It was Bryn's voice, but before Cam could splutter clear of the drift, he was gone. Cam rolled sideways and bumped into Madlen. She was huddled down on the snow and her eyes were very big.

"Well, we found him."

"Y-yeah." Cam's teeth were beginning to chatter. "G-good for us."

They were lying beside some sort of farm outbuilding, in the corner of an enclosure or pen. The bit of sky they could see suggested it was afternoon on a short northern winter day, with more snow expected. And there was a sound.

"What *is* that?" whispered Cam.

It was irregular, and coming from some distance away, a noise sometimes like a football crowd whose team is being trounced and sometimes like . . .

"Slaughtering pigs?" wondered Madlen.

"When have y-you ever been around a p-pig slaughtering?" said Cam, looking dubious.

"Well, I don't know, it's a farm, isn't it—," Madlen began, when suddenly Bryn was back.

"Come on," he ordered, panting clouds of white. "I'm pretty sure it's safe." Then, when they didn't move immediately, he grabbed their hands. "I really think it would be a good idea to get to shelter, don't you?" he insisted.

"No argument," groaned Madlen. "I just need . . . to get . . . started . . ."

"Come ON!" And glancing nervously about, Bryn dragged them out of the enclosure.

As soon as they came round the corner, the wind hit them. It was icy and heartless, and it immediately leached away what little warmth they had left in them. They were in a farmyard, with low outbuildings on two sides, and a farmhouse on a third. The ground was a churned-up mess of mud and snow, as if herds of animals had stampeded through it.

They stumbled across the broken surface to the house, and

Bryn pushed open the door. Even with the cold, Madlen hung back at first.

"You didn't even knock!" she protested.

"There's nobody home—I checked."

"But—how did you get in? Wasn't it locked?"

Bryn shrugged. "Country people don't lock their doors. We don't have a lot of crime on Kir. Now get IN!"

"G-go on," stuttered Cam, and pushed her indoors.

It was cold inside the farmhouse too, but escaping from the icy wind made it feel almost cozy. The place had that still, waiting feeling of a home whose people are away. Bryn headed for the stairs.

"Warm clothes, first thing," he said.

"What are you *doing*?" Madlen stood by the door. "You can't just tromp into somebody's house and *take* stuff!"

"*Borrow* stuff, not take. Borrowing's okay."

Cam looked at Madlen. "We do need warmer things. We'd ask if there was anyone *to* ask, but we have to get kitted up somehow."

Madlen shook her head, sighed, and followed the others to the door at the top of the stairs.

They found Bryn in a big loft bedroom. He'd dragged open a cedar chest and was pulling out warm woolens and furs.

"Okay, any skirts . . . any dresses . . . ," he muttered to himself as more bits of clothing flew out onto the floor.

"Sorry, Madlen," he said, when the chest was empty. "No women's clothes here at all. I'll try over there."

"What?" Madlen's head was just emerging from the depths of a fur-trimmed tunic.

"Women's clothes," repeated Bryn. "There aren't any. I'll go look—"

"Don't bother." Madlen flopped onto the bed and started to pull on some lined trousers. "These are big enough. I can stuff my skirt in at the top. It'll make another layer to keep me warm."

She stood up to do just that—and Bryn looked away in embarrassment. Which brought him face-to-face with Cam. He looked at it inquiringly.

Cam made a face at him. "You must be joking! I'm not wearing a skirt in this weather. At home, all right, but here . . ."

Bryn couldn't help taking note of that. *Aha!* he thought. *Wears skirts.* Must *be going to be a girl.*

"So you wear skirts at home, then?" he asked carefully.

"Of course. *Everybody* wears skirts—for formal events, like weddings and funerals, stuff like that. Not for everyday." Cam continued to speak and dress at the same time. "My uncle always looked fabulous in his." It grinned at Bryn, looking as if it enjoyed messing with his head.

. . . or maybe not, thought Bryn as his brain changed gear one more time. *Get into something warm, stupid,* he chided himself. *First priority, right?*

It was not long before the three shivering Questors were transformed into three Kirian bundles of wool and fur. Cam tottered across the floor with its arms and legs stuck out.

"Does my bum look big in this?"

"In those clothes I can't even tell where your bum is," replied Madlen, stuffing her hair up into a fur hat. She went over to rummage in another chest by the dormer window. "Hey, look! I've found boots!"

"Excellent!" said Bryn. "Pitch me those. They look about my size."

Madlen didn't answer.

"Madlen? Pitch me those boots, will you? . . . What is it?"

She was staring out the dormer. She pointed but didn't speak. Cam and Bryn looked at each other, and went over to see what could be affecting her like that.

"Over there," she said huskily.

Cam gasped. Bryn swore quietly.

It wasn't the view of mountains, or the sweep of the valley leading up from the farm, or the distant Castle presiding over it all that they were reacting to.

It was war.

The battle had evidently engulfed the farmstead not too long before, and then swept on. Its passage was marked by broken fences, snow and soil trampled together, and horrible, scattered humps of . . . they strained to see . . . dropped equipment? Lost clothing? Or the fallen bodies of men? The battlefront itself was several hundred yards away and still lurching up the valley. They could see it so clearly in the high, cold air, and yet there was a surreal quality to it all—the ragged groups of men that struggled together, slashing, grappling, bleeding, were entirely noiseless, their screams and grunts and the thud of weapons on flesh silenced by distance and the doubled glass. It was a horrible mime, choreographed by a sick mind. Then, as they watched, the bulk of the battle moved farther up, over a ridge, and disappeared.

For a moment nobody spoke. Then Bryn turned away from the window and began to drag on the boots. Madlen stared at him.

"Bryn! Do you realize—if we'd done what the paper said, if we'd come here *immediately*, we'd have walked straight into *that*? Straight into the middle of a battlefield, with no weapons and no equipment and no warning and no clue." Her voice quivered and stopped.

Cam gave her an encouraging shove. "Lucky for us we didn't, then, wasn't it!"

"The message was meant to get us killed," Madlen insisted.

Bryn looked up, red-faced from bending over. "We're going. Get ready."

"Going? Where?"

He stood up and stamped, settling his feet in the boots. "To the Castle. We're not going to find out anything here."

Cam gaped. "You want us to go out *there*? With *that* lot!"

"The fighting's moving away. And it can't be far off time for it to be over for the day anyway."

"Oh yeah? Nine to five, is it?" Cam scoffed.

Bryn nodded, and Cam looked confused.

"Go downstairs." He didn't want to talk—that much was clear from his voice. The others exchanged uncertain looks, and went.

As they headed for the door, Bryn stopped to tip some discarded clothes back into the chest. He followed the others. At the top step he turned to close the door.

When he turned back, everything had changed.

CHAPTER TWENTY-NINE

War on Kir

"War's over, soldier."

Bryn felt his blood jerk in his veins. The man in the room below was a complete stranger, but the cocked crossbow he held so casually in his hands needed no introduction. He must have been sitting, silently, out of sight, waiting for them to come down. It wasn't as if they'd been particularly quiet. Suddenly Bryn could hear his pack-master's voice. *Real war is real. It isn't a game. There's no "den" and no "time-out." Take it seriously and you may die. Don't take it seriously, and you* will *die. It's as simple as that.*

How could he have been so stupid? Of course there would be stragglers. Or maybe this one had dropped behind deliberately, in the hope of picking off strays from the other Side, or one or two of the walking wounded. He groaned out loud. The stranger's eyes flicked up at him for the briefest second, and then returned to their original focus.

Madlen.

With a lurch in perspective, Bryn realized what the stranger was seeing. Madlen, frozen on the stairs, would seem as tall as a man. She was dressed as a man, her girl's hair hidden under that hat. He and Cam were small. They looked like children.

But to someone who didn't know her, Madlen looked liked an adult male.

In the ghastly slow motion of nightmare he saw the tip of the crossbow rise, and the stranger's eyes narrow as he took aim at Madlen's heart.

Move! Shout! Stop him! Bryn's brain screamed at him. *I'm trying! I'm trying!* he screamed back.

With a supreme effort Bryn managed to stumble down a step and croak, "Nnnno—" just as the outside door slammed open. The stranger swung round, automatically releasing the crossbow bolt, which lodged itself solidly in the door frame about an inch from the head of another soldier.

"Cripes, Sarge!" the man shrieked. "What'd I do?"

The crossbowman swore with a creativity that made everyone blink. He continued to curse for some time, but eventually wound down enough to ask, "Well? What do you want?"

The soldier, still cowering by the open door, drew himself up nervously and saluted.

"Came to tell you the time, sir," he barked, parade-style, at attention and staring straight ahead. "Like you told me to tell you, sir. Almost Bells, sir."

A clanging sound drifting in from outside interrupted him.

"Er," the soldier's voice wavered a bit. "Not exactly almost, anymore. Sir."

For a long moment the ringing continued, and even grew louder. The noise would carry many miles on the cold clear air. The crossbowman stared at the floor.

Finally the clanging died away. Without a flicker of a smile the crossbowman looked up at Madlen on the stairs.

"Saved by the Bell," he said, and walked across the room and out the door. The unfortunate subordinate scurried away at his heels, closing the door carefully behind them.

There was a moment of shocked silence.

"Bryn?" quavered Cam, but Bryn shook his head. He looked as if he were about to be sick.

"We've got to go now," he said in a strange voice. "Up to the Castle. Before it gets dark."

The others didn't argue.

There was no one in the farmyard, but on the road beyond, travellers were beginning to appear. The three crossed the churned-up yard—Cam and Madlen peering about nervously, Bryn head down—and joined the flow of people.

They headed off up the valley. The traffic thickened as two lines of soldiers, moving in opposite directions, began to filter onto the road's easier surface from the fields around. Each line ignored the other completely. Transport trucks now rumbled by between them, turning the snow into a muddy sludge. Everyone seemed to know what they were doing, and everyone was doing it with the utmost dreariness.

Cam and Madlen waited for Bryn to start filling them in, but he just kept walking, head down, shoulders slumped.

Finally Madlen couldn't stand it anymore.

"Bryn," she said, and then louder, *"Bryn!"*

He looked at her, eyes dull.

"You've *got* to talk to us—we haven't a clue here!"

He nodded, and kept walking. "I know. I'm sorry. I'll . . . try."

Cam leapt in with questions. "So, what was that stuff with the bell? Why did the man stop trying to kill us? I mean, he just let us go! Why? It doesn't make any sense."

"And him trying to kill us in the first place *does* make sense?" shrilled Madlen.

Bryn checked that no one was in earshot. "Look, he didn't know it was you. I mean, he didn't know you were a girl. He thought you were a *man*."

Madlen started to look huffy. "Thanks a lot!" she muttered.

"No, it's not like that! He wasn't *expecting* a girl, and there you were, in men's clothes and that big hat and no hair showing. Anyway, that's not really the point." He stopped and pulled off his own hat, running his hand roughly through his hair. "The point is, we landed in a DBZ and since he didn't recognize you as one of his Side, it was fair to assume you were on the *other* Side, and then, of course, he left it too late, didn't he, and it was Bells, so that was that. . . ."

Bryn ground to a halt. The others blinked, and tried to look intelligent.

"DBZ?" ventured Cam.

"Designated Battle Zone," said Bryn.

"Bells?" asked Madlen.

"They ring this big bell so that everybody knows it's the end of the BD and it's time to stop fighting."

"And a BD is, um . . . ?"

"Battle Day. If he'd killed you *after* Bells, there'd have been a huge fine. His Side would lose points big-time."

Cam turned to Madlen.

"Not to mention the inconvenience to you," it added, but Madlen didn't respond. She was staring at a man, lying against a stone wall a little farther along the road.

He was dead.

Neither Cam nor Madlen had ever seen a corpse before. The man was on the ground, leaning against the wall, his legs sprawled out untidily before him. He had his hands clutched tightly over his stomach, his head thrown back, his face twisted in pain and at the same time utterly empty.

Whoever said that death was like sleep hadn't had this in mind.

Bryn had walked on. He was acting as if the man weren't there. He was acting as if *they* weren't there. They had to bustle to catch up with him.

"Bryn—didn't you see? Back there—there's a body back there! Shouldn't we—"

But Bryn interrupted her. "They'll collect it."

"But . . ."

"I said they'll collect it!"

"HEY!"

The three jumped and swung round to see that one of the transport trucks had stopped. A young man with a clipboard and his arm in a sling leaned out from the back and was calling to them.

"There's room. Get in!"

Madlen and Cam turned uncertainly to Bryn, but he was just standing there, stone still, with a strange expression on his face.

The young man called again, beginning to sound impatient.

"I *said*, there's room. But if you *want* to walk to the Castle . . ."

"Well I don't want to walk if I don't have to." Madlen headed for the truck.

Cam hesitated, then shrugged and gave Bryn a shove in the right direction.

As soon as they were in the back, the young man pulled down the canvas flap and yelled to the driver. The truck started up at once. Then he slumped down in a spare space and apparently fell asleep.

In the dimness they could see the truck was full of weary

soldiers, huddled in on themselves and paying no attention to the late arrivals.

Under cover of the noise from the engine, Cam spoke to Bryn. "What is it? What's wrong *now*?"

Bryn shook his head. "He didn't know me," he said. "He looked right at me, and he didn't *know* me."

"Who? The guy with the clipboard?"

Bryn nodded miserably.

"Well? Why should he know you? Who is he?"

Bryn's voice wobbled slightly.

"He's Nick—my best friend."

"Really?" Cam's voice rose involuntarily, and Bryn immediately put a hand on its sleeve in warning.

"Not a good place to talk," he muttered. "Keep your head down until I can figure this out."

Cam looked at him. He seemed older and more worn. He seemed like the soldiers around them. It turned to Madlen, but she had her eyes shut, as if she were pretending to be someplace else. Cam slumped back on the hard bench, gnawing its lip, and waited for the trip to end.

A long time later Bryn suddenly straightened up.

"Listen," he said.

The muddy lurching and slurping of the truck had changed.

"Cobbles. We must be getting to the Castle."

The soldiers shifted, trying to unstiffen after the long ride, and Nick with the clipboard woke up. The truck stopped. "We're here," he said, flipping back the heavy canvas flap. "Fun's over for today."

Grumbling, everyone piled out into the courtyard of the Castle. The sky was fully dark now, and the snow that had started to fall was lit in swirls and flurries by harsh electric spotlights from the walls. The place was packed with people, milling about in the cold. Nobody seemed to be paying them any special attention, but Cam and Madlen felt conspicuous—everything was so strange. Everyone must have been able to tell they didn't belong. And they didn't know what Bryn was thinking. He was giving no clues.

"Wait here a second," he said, and pushed off through the crowd.

There was a sullen air to the place. Maybe it was just the end of a long, cold day. Maybe people just wanted it to be done, and were thinking about food and dry socks, and that was why they seemed not to want to meet one another's eyes. Maybe. But it didn't feel like that. And there was something else. . . .

"Have you noticed," whispered Cam, "how everybody's sort of . . . *green*?"

"What?" said Madlen. "Who?"

Cam shrugged. "Well, maybe not green, but greenish. Sort of yellowy-whitey-greenish. Like they're all ever so slightly motion-sick?"

"You're crazy," Madlen said automatically, but then, as she looked more closely at the crowding Kirians, she added, "Or maybe you're not."

At that moment they saw Bryn shouldering his way back to them. He looked tired, and tense, and troubled, but the color of his skin was undeniably different. He looked basically healthy; the others looked as if they had been ill for a long, long time.

"Stick close," he grunted, and they didn't argue.

Once inside the building they joined a general shuffle toward the faint whiff of cooking. It was enough to start the Questors salivating. So when Bryn abruptly pulled them out of the crowd and into a dingy, dim side corridor, the other two were not best pleased.

"Bryn!"

"I'm *hungry*!"

But Bryn only tapped his nose knowingly.

"Trust your clever brother, little ones," he said. "This is a shortcut. Unless you want to spend the next hour waiting in line? Hmmm? I thought not."

He had just turned back, an irritatingly smug expression on his face, when a figure loomed suddenly in front of them, blocking their path. It grabbed Bryn by the coat, picked him up effortlessly, and slammed him into the wall.

CHAPTER THIRTY

<u>Welcome Home</u>

The man's white hair and wrinkled face didn't
seem to bear any relation to his strength.
He shook Bryn a few times for good measure, like
a dog worrying a rat, and then dropped him in a
heap on the stone floor.

"Right, boy," he growled. "Just what do you think you're play-ing at?"

Bryn gargled nervously. "Um, I'm not . . . Um, you . . ."

The Steward kicked him. "Don't lie. Do you think I don't know every boy who's ever passed through my hands? I'm the Steward. I know *everything*."

There was the sound of someone approaching down the hall. The old man frowned. "Can't talk here," he grunted. "Come with me."

He set off quickly in the other direction, not bothering to check that they were coming with him.

They came.

He led the way up a flight of stairs, along corridors, down other stairs, around corners, until . . .

"In here," he said, pushing open a door.

The room was warm and welcoming, with a good fire and

plain but pleasant furnishings. And there was someone there before them, unfolding himself from one of the chairs.

"Bryn? Is it really you?" It was Nick, the soldier with the sling. He was frowning at first, uncertain—and then his big open face broke into an enormous smirk. "It *is*! It's *you*! You little rat dropping—you haven't grown a bit!"

"*You* have," said Bryn, grinning wildly. "I bet they could use you to dust ceilings with your head!"

"Go find them some food, Nick, and yourself. You can do the reunion later." The Steward turned to the three. "You lot stay here. I have a few things to see to. When I get back, we'll talk."

He left.

Nick sidled up to Bryn and whispered loudly, "Listen . . . Bryn . . . I was just wondering . . . Does all this have anything to do with that . . . that *thing* you used to do?" And he made a scribbling gesture with his hand.

Bryn swallowed, and shook his head. "No, of course not. I grew out of that ages ago."

Nick shut one eye and tapped the side of his nose wisely. "Good idea," he murmured. "I was sure you would."

He nodded in a friendly way to Madlen and Cam and followed the Steward out of the room, presumably in the direction of the kitchens.

There was a moment's pause in which Bryn stared with hot eyes at the wall. Then, so suddenly the other two jumped, he exploded in a suppressed sort of way.

"I hope you're satisfied," he snarled from between clenched teeth. "Now you know. This is me. In my World. Makes sense of a lot of things, I don't doubt."

"What are you on about?" said Madlen, frowning.

"What am I on about? I'm on about *me*!"

"What's wrong with you?" said Cam.

Bryn snorted. "What's *wrong* with me! Just look at me!"

He swung round to face them and spread his arms out with pathetic melodrama. "Can you honestly say you see standing before you the makings of a six-foot-tall fighting machine that can draw an eight hundred-pound crossbow with his teeth and bounce rocks off his chest?"

Cam started to open its mouth, but Bryn answered his own question.

"No, of course you can't. If I make it to the Third Reserve Battalion in Charge of Cowering in the Cellars, it'll be a miracle. They probably wouldn't want me, though. I'd probably screw up their Cowardice Average."

Cam and Madlen had never seen Bryn in such a state.

"But you're still grow—," began Madlen.

"We like you the way you a—," protested Cam at the same time.

They both stopped and grinned awkwardly.

Bryn collapsed into a chair, groaned, and buried his face in his hands.

"Never mind," he said, sounding muffled. "I've finished." He took a deep breath. "Sorry."

Cautiously, Madlen went over to him and gave his shoulder a pat. Nothing happened, so she patted again.

"It's what Nick said about your drawing, isn't it," said Cam suddenly.

Bryn nodded, still not looking up.

"Is it really so bad?" Madlen asked carefully. "I know they don't like arty stuff back on Trentor, but what's the story here? There are pictures, paintings, and stuff in the Castle—I *saw* them!"

"Oh, art's okay," answered Bryn bitterly. "No, it's better than just okay. It's very valued. But it's a girl thing. Boys wouldn't even *consider* it."

He heaved a great sigh. "I could get away with it, maybe," he said sadly, "if I were huge. If I were huge and courageous and could do all the warrior stuff, people might be prepared to let it pass as, like, a quirk. But . . . this is me we're talking about. You've seen how I am—at the farmhouse, and with the zombies, and, and, all the time—I'm scared. I've been scared my whole life." He swallowed hard. "I'm a coward. There's no getting around it."

"Rubbish—"

"Oh, for crying out loud—"

The door opened, and the Steward came in. He looked at the three of them for a moment, and they instinctively felt guilty, as if he'd caught them out in something. Then he grunted, and poked the fire.

"Nick not back yet?" he said.

They shook their heads dumbly.

"Good lad, Nick," he went on. "Heart bigger than his head, of course. He won't have really cottoned on to the reason you're still such a runt . . . Bruce?"

"Bryn."

"Of course. Bryn. Should have remembered the name. Certainly remembered the face! But as I was saying," the old man continued, "time travel, distortion of the Continuum—not strong on that sort of thing, our Nick."

"Know a lot about time travel yourself, do you?" Madlen muttered, not very quietly. She was learning fast how much she disliked the Steward.

"Enough to know a fostering who should be ten years older

than *him* when I see one. You have to get up pretty early in the morning to fool *me*, boy." The old man turned to her, a smug expression all over his face.

"Oh yeah?" sneered Madlen. "That just shows what *you* know. I'm not—"

"From round here," interrupted Bryn, coming quickly into gear. "My . . . friend is not from around here."

"Tell me something I don't know," the Steward snorted. "Those two aren't from round here, and *you're* not from round *now*. And what does that mean? I'll tell you what that means. It means you're different. And to most people, that means you're spies." He leaned closer to the three. "And you do not want to know what we *do* to spies."

"But—but we're not spies," stammered Cam.

"Aren't you? Maybe not. But if you're not, then what are you?"

The Steward looked at them. Cam and Madlen looked at Bryn.

It was his World. It was his call.

For a moment he just sat there looking unhappy. Then he nodded to himself. "Right," he said hoarsely. "Madlen, you might as well take your hat off before your head cooks. This could take some time. . . ."

The fire had died down, and the food was all eaten. Madlen and Cam had finally succumbed to warmth and weariness, and had nodded off in their chairs. Nick, who had returned to listen openmouthed, was staring into the embers. Bryn had answered the old man's questions as best he could and was now just sitting, glazed and talked out.

"No, there's no two ways about it," said the Steward at last, after a long silence. "You'll have to go to the City of Ice."

"What?!" Bryn straightened up, shocked awake.

"Look, lad," said the old man gruffly, ticking off his points on gnarly fingers. "You can't stay here or they'll get you as spies. You can't go to any other Castle for exactly the same reason. The farms are empty this time of year, or if they're not, that's even worse, because deserters aren't very welcoming, if you follow my drift. But all of that's neither here nor there, because you can't go back to London without your mythic Object—and there's nothing like that round here. Most mythic object *I* know's my ass, and you can't have that 'cause I need it for—"

"But—you're talking about the *dragons'* City!" interrupted Bryn hastily. "You're expecting me to deal with *dragons*?"

Cam jerked upright. "I must be falling asleep," it squeaked. "I thought you said 'dragons.'"

The old man nodded. "No question. If there's anything of the sort you're after anywhere on Kir, they'll be having it."

Cam poked Madlen. "Did you hear that? We're going to see dragons!"

Madlen yawned hugely. "Don't be stupid," she mumbled. "There's no such thing."

Nick, Bryn, and the Steward stared at her.

"*Definitely* not from round here," the old man said.

Madlen looked at Bryn. "Enough crazy stuff, okay?" she appealed to him.

He nodded wearily. "Sorry, Madlen. There really are dragons on Kir," he said. "We just don't overlap much. Well, at all, really. They don't find people interesting."

The Steward agreed. "Keep themselves to themselves. Bryn'll know all about the Separation Treaty, but I wouldn't be surprised if they missed out teaching *you* anything about it—you not being from round here, sort of thing." He snorted, and rubbed his chin. "It isn't as if we could live where they do, anyway. They're right up north—too barren and cold. Very few of us have even seen one."

"But you're sure they do exist." Madlen was obviously reluctant to give up hope on this.

"Oh yes. They exist all right."

She sighed. "Okay, okay. So, how do we find these dragons?"

"We'll need to go to the glacier at the Lake of Perpetual Ice. That's the best place."

"And?"

The Steward shrugged. "Don't ask me. You're on your own. Oh, except for . . ." He got up and rummaged in a cupboard, then thrust something into Bryn's hand. It was a small black device, with a dial and pointer on the front and a couple of switches. "You can take that if you like. Got invented by mistake. They were trying to find a new device for detecting radiation when miners went into a new bit of mountain, but they ended up with this. It was only by chance they discovered what it really detects. Good story, that—I must tell you it some time. Anyway, it appears dragons give off some kind of radiation, and the box here picks it up. Basically, it's a dragon detector. It won't *do* anything about them, but at least you'll know when you're getting close."

Bryn hefted it thoughtfully. "Thanks," he said, and flicked one of the switches.

Immediately the pointer began to jerk. As he moved the device randomly about the room the jerking increased, until the pointer was practically invisible. Bryn frowned.

"You sure this thing works?" he said.

He tried the other switch, still pointing it at different things—and people. Now the box was humming. The hum increased dramatically when he aimed it at the Steward and Nick, for example, but subsided completely when he pointed it at Madlen or Cam.

Or himself.

He looked at the Steward inquiringly.

The old man grunted, took back the device, gave it a swift bang with his hand. It stopped altogether.

"*Supposed* to work—could be there's interference somewhere in the Castle, though."

But Madlen wasn't interested in dragon-centric technology. She had gone back to something the Steward had said earlier.

"Excuse me, but did I hear you right?" she said, frowning. "Did you say where dragons live is too barren and cold for people?"

The Steward nodded.

"And that's where we're going?"

He nodded again.

"And you don't see a flaw in this plan?"

"The sooner we get you out of here, the safer," said the Steward, standing up briskly.

"But how—," began Bryn.

"Caterpillar truck. Nick and I'll drive you up. Shouldn't take more than a day and a half, maybe two. But we have to leave *now*. Not even time to get that boy a hair cut." And he winked at Madlen. It was a wicked wink, and it left her completely unsure of what in the Worlds it meant.

Next morning, back at The London House, Mrs. Mac's blender began to whir just at the height of the breakfast rush. It was several moments before she even noticed it. When she did . . .

"Oh NO!" she shrieked, dropping an entire tray of egg, sausage, bacon, and tomato. "Not now!"

Sidestepping the mess on the floor, she lunged for the Puree/Divert button, but just as the tip of her finger reached it, the whirring stopped.

The Council's guiding messages for the Questors had been sent.

"Damn," she whispered.

"Damn!" said the Secretarial Assistant.

At the Dalrodian palace there was yet another power cut. The Assistant had just caught a glimpse of something marked "Urgent," before the system crashed. He was new at his job, and very earnest, and when the computers came back online, he searched diligently for whatever the message might have been. But no luck. It was well and truly lost.

Still, he comforted himself, *if it's important, they're sure to call again.*

And on Kir . . .

"Damn. . . . *Steward*!" bellowed the Castellan. "Stew-ard! Where are you, man?"

No answer. The Castellan stumped angrily back to the table, daring the Incoming Message button to still be flashing when he got there.

It was.

Blast the man! Where was he hiding? He knew the Castellan hadn't a clue how to get the computer to spit anything out. That's what Stewards were for. What they *weren't* for was not being there.

The button continued to flash. "Incoming Message. Urgent. The London House. Incoming Message. Urgent . . ." scrolled across the screen.

Even more than computers, the Castellan hated Urgent Messages from The London House.

"Argghhh!" he yelled, slamming a thick fist down on the desk so hard the monitor leapt. Then he stormed out of the room in search of the Steward, or breakfast, or a drink, whichever came to hand first.

Unheeded, the message button flashed on in the empty room.

CHAPTER THIRTY-ONE

Disjointed Conversations

The truck had four sets of paired wheels joined by caterpillar tracks that spread the weight, keeping them moving instead of sinking in. Their route seemed to be determined by finding the thinnest coverings of snow, along windswept ridges or flat plateaus that discouraged drifts. Roads didn't come into it much, particularly as the group got ever farther north.

The trip through the mountains, through some of the most spectacularly wild and beautiful scenery the Worlds had to offer, was pretty much a blank for the Questors. The truck was a slightly more comfortable version of the transport vehicle they'd arrived in, but still completely windowless and noisy. At least it was warm, with a small oil-burning stove at one end, and there were mattresses and bedding that could be spread on the floor, so they weren't having to sit up all the time. There was also a screened-off corner with a trapdoor-type toilet. But for the tag end of that night, and all the next day, and the next night as well, there was nothing but the black, swaying walls of the truck and one another to look at.

Nick and the Steward shared the driving, the one off-duty nipping back into the body of the truck to sleep and eat.

All that enforced togetherness should have produced many long meaningful conversations, but the level of noise made it seem too much of an effort to talk a lot of the time. It was hard to share anything very personal when they would have had to shout it. Some exchanges of information did occur, but there was always something piecemeal about them.

Over a series of disjointed conversations, Madlen and Cam learned more about the Battle Calendar, the system by which Kir's appetite for waging war was satisfied and controlled. The Steward seemed to enjoy educating them. He explained how fighting was allowed on certain days, in certain seasons, and between specific groups only. Night fighting was banned, because darkness made it too difficult to identify acceptable adversaries. Forms of combat that caused damage to property or livestock or crops were also not allowed.

"Properly managed, fighting can go on indefinitely. Most wars grind to a halt because of neglected or destroyed resources, but we've solved all that."

He beamed at them. Madlen and Cam could only stare.

"But . . . what about when one side *loses?*"

"Yeah. Isn't a war over when it's won?"

The Steward held up his hand.

"Of course! Of course you're right—in *feral* wars. But we've learned our lessons from agricultural domestication. For example, we've learned from the principles of crop rotation to move our battlefields about. We've learned to husband our resources, not squander them. And with the Point System, neither success nor failure need mark the end of a conflict."

Below a certain point, he went on, a Side wasn't viable and

dropped out of combat until it was able to remedy the situation either through recruitment from outside or as its fosterings came of age.

Cam found it all weirdly fascinating. Madlen found herself falling asleep a lot.

Bryn kept very quiet, but they could tell he was listening to every word.

Later:

"Bryn," said Cam.

"What?"

"I don't understand. If you have the technology for stuff like this"—and it indicated the truck—"how come that guy back at the farm came at us with a crossbow? And all the other weapons we saw—they're all so old-fashioned. I mean, why didn't he just, I don't know, bomb the place?"

Bryn looked shocked. "Don't you think that would be a bit barbaric?" he asked sarcastically. "Killing somebody without even seeing them?"

Cam shrugged. "Don't see the difference. They'd still be dead."

"*You don't see the difference?*" Bryn's voice cracked. He couldn't quite believe what he was hearing. "*Honor's* the difference! Isn't it obvious? I don't care how far into the Future we are—*that* hasn't changed!"

"Okay, okay, I was just asking." Cam made a placating gesture, but then realized Bryn wasn't looking in its direction anymore. He was staring at the Steward.

"Don't look at me like that, boy," the old man said gruffly. "Building bombs—it's only talk at this stage, and you can be sure I'll knock heads together if I catch wind of it in *my* Castle.

But my Castle's just the one, and you can't trust the Caithners. Never could. Or that lot over Tay way . . ."

The old man's voice trailed off.

Bryn refused to talk to anyone for a long time after that.

Another exchange:

Nick: Bryn, why does your friend Madlen have such long hair?

Bryn: Because he's not my friend. She's my sister.

Nick: (pause) Oh. Well, that explains it.

Some time later:

The Steward had just come into the back after a long stint in the cab. He was ready to sleep. Cam wasn't.

For Cam, the subject of dragons was the stuff of dreams. It couldn't get enough stories, which was basically all the Steward had to offer.

"So, dragons," Cam said. "Quite private, then, are they?"

"That's so," said the Steward, pulling his hat down over his eyes.

"So they won't necessarily be all that keen to help us? Or even see us?"

"Very true."

There was a pause. The old man was not taking any hints.

"What do they eat?" demanded Cam.

The Steward looked up from under his hat.

"They eat children," he said. "That's what I was told when I was young. Particularly children who ask too many questions."

With that, he turned his back on them pointedly and settled down. Cam stuck out its tongue, less than satisfied.

"He's kidding you," said Bryn. "If they only ate humans

they'd have starved to death long ago—the Separation Treaty's as old as the hills. And as to helping us—we'll just have to convince them. It's their World too, and anyway, they're supposed to be quite smart. They'll have noticed something's wrong."

Later still:

"Whatcha doing?" said Madlen.

Bryn froze, and then shoved the book into his coat, not quite quickly enough.

"Drawing a map," he said abruptly.

"Oh," said Madlen. "Right."

She made no comment on what she had seen. *Not* a map. In that brief glimpse she'd seen a sketch of a dead soldier, lying awkwardly in the snow at the side of the road.

At The London House, someone else was drawing too. It was Kate. She was tracing a pattern of spilled tea with her finger on the table. She was deep in thought.

"Well?" said Mrs. Mac, as she dropped into a chair opposite with a tired *hwumph.*

Kate looked at her, but didn't smile.

"I'm to report to the Basement." She stared down at her tea picture for a moment and then ran a disgusted finger through it. "I'm one of the best field operatives they've got, and they've assigned me to Research!"

Mrs. Mac clicked her tongue. "Somebody doesn't want you loose; that much's clear," she said. "How did Bullvador look— did he seem behind the idea?"

Kate shook her head. "Didn't see him. Didn't see any of them. Cordell brought the message to me here."

"Cordell?" Mrs. Mac looked surprised. "But that's a Runner's job! I don't remember ever seeing *him* doing running . . ." Her voice died away, and came back in a murmur. "Or do I mean, I don't remember ever *seeing* him doing running."

She was staring at the table now too, but not at Kate's tea spill. At a place further along, she remembered a night when a message had been left . . .

Kate was hard to convince.

"He's always seemed such a *nothing*," she protested. "Bit slimy, yes. But an evil mastermind?! Get a grip!"

"You agree he's a really good secretary?" Mrs. Mac asked innocently.

"Oh, that. Absolutely."

Mrs. Mac looked at her fingernails. "Only *stupid* people underestimate the sheer raw power of a really good secretary," she murmured smugly.

Kate stuck out her tongue. "Yeah, yeah, fine. So tack a tracking device on him, why don't you, and we'll monitor the progress of Mr. Alpine Deviousness. Oh no. Can't do that. If he is who you think he is, he's far too clever not to notice a tracking device, right after you stick one on him," said Kate.

"*Right* after . . . right *after* . . . ," Mrs. Mac murmured oddly. Then a positively sly expression slid across her face. "You're correct, of course," she said. "He'd be far too clever. But would he be clever enough to notice a tracking device *before* I stick one on him? Eh?"

Kate could only stare. Mrs. Macmahonney went to a cupboard and brought out a bottle of Extra Finest Malagasy Vanilla Essence. She caught sight of Kate's expression.

"Now don't look like that!" Mrs. Mac said. "I *have* to use this one; only the *best* vanilla is retroactive."

"Er," said Kate.

"I'll be right back," promised Mrs. Mac.

Mrs. Macmahonney seemed to be lost. She was wandering about in the upper corridors with none of her usual purposefulness, almost as if she'd forgotten what she was up there *for*.

Alpine Cordell allowed himself a slight irritation at the sight of her. He really had no interest in adding extraneous crones to his list of responsibilities just now. He gave a dry, inquiring cough.

Mrs. Macmahonney jumped. "Oh! Oh, it's you, Mr. Cordell," she said. And then, she just looked at him, blinking.

He sighed.

"Can I be of assistance?"

"Well, now, I'm not sure," said Mrs. Mac. "I have to tell you, I'm finding this backwash really very . . ."

She staggered suddenly, as if she were about to faint. Cordell tried to back away, but he wasn't quick enough. Mrs. Mac's hand shot out and grabbed his. Her touch was surprisingly hot.

Then, just as suddenly, she was steady again.

"I need a cup of tea," she announced abruptly, and walked away.

Alpine Cordell watched her go . . . and then put her out of his mind.

The Preceptor wanted him.

Back in the kitchen, Mrs. Mac took a number of storage jars down from a shelf. She removed their lids, shuffled them, put them back on in a different order, and returned the jars to the shelf. Then, eyes closed, she paused.

In the darkened kitchen there was silence, touched only

lightly by the occasional low hum of an appliance motor switching on, and then off again.

The figure that glided into the room was as shadowy as it had been on the night in question, and as silent. Sight and hearing were still of no use in identifying it, but there was another sense that suddenly came into play.

As the figure reached out its hand to place the paper on the table, a faint scent of vanilla drifted in the air.

In another time, Mrs. Mac, eyes still closed, murmured a single word.

"Gotcha."

Alpine Cordell and the Preceptor had found each other.

"Go. Now," the Preceptor said.

"To the Castle?"

"Fool. To the City, of course. Get there before they arrive. Make sure the Path of the Crystal continues to be strong. A little xenophobia goes a long way, but it needs careful nurturing. . . . I want the possibility of a hasty action, with unfortunate consequences, maximized. Chance is a fine thing."

CHAPTER THIRTY-TWO

<u>The Nature of Nowhere</u>

On Kir at dawn on the second day, the truck had stopped. They'd jumped out, unloaded the gear, loaded the sled, and stood around briefly, feeling awkward.

The Steward had said, "Right. It's over that ridge there. Be careful. Good luck."

Nick had said, "Oh. Um. Well . . ." and then punched Bryn in the arm. He'd half-waved at the other two, and scrambled into the cab.

Then they'd driven away, spraying snow and sliding sideways a little, leaving the three alone in . . .

. . . the middle of nowhere.

This was what the words had always meant.

Cam started to walk, and the others followed automatically.

Then, only a few steps from the churned-up snow and the lingering stink of machine, Bryn stopped, the sled rope slack in his hand. All at once, out of the blue, he found himself feeling . . . preternaturally alive. It was as if he could hear the crunch of every individual snow crystal under his boots; feel every little piece of freezing air as it came into his warm lungs and then out again in a cloud of steam; see the exact palette of colors that went into the dawn sky, the blacks and blues, the weird greens, the clear white of the sun as it rose out of a band of red and eclipsed the stars. Every detail, every texture. He'd seen how homesick Cam had been at first for the desert, but now he was feeling it too. Though how *could* you feel homesick when you were at home?

It was like sheer energy flooding straight in through his eyes.

Madlen came up beside him. He gave her an enormous grin, waving a mittened hand enthusiastically at, well, everything, and she smiled back.

"Okay, I admit it: Wow!" she said, and that was enough.

"Come on, you two," Cam called back. "I'm freezing!"

Bryn grabbed the sled rope and tromped off after Cam.

"So what do we do now?" asked Madlen, hugging her coat closer to herself against the cold air.

They'd come up over the ridge at the foot of the valley, with the glacier looming at the far end. Bryn had explained to them what a glacier was, how at some point the ice had retreated, and the valley had been left behind by its passage. But that wasn't how it looked. It looked as if the great ragged wall of ice were about to attack, topple over onto the frozen lake that was its prey.

"Well?" Madlen said.

Bryn didn't answer. Instead, he pulled the dragon detector out of his pocket.

"Oh, great," scoffed Cam. "Kir technology. That we already know doesn't work."

Bryn ignored Cam, and flicked the switch.

The whine the vibrating detector produced sounded thin and feeble in the hugeness of the landscape. Bryn held the box out in front of him and turned slowly through three hundred and sixty degrees.

"Down there," he said after a moment, indicating the lake far below them. Then he pocketed the detector once more.

Cam and Madlen exchanged looks.

"Dragons you can't see, a basically vertical slope and no road or path or handy lift. Of course. Where else would it be but *down there*?" asked Cam.

"Will you push me or shall I push you?" said Madlen. "When we reach the bottom we can easily continue the Quest as giant snowballs with broken legs."

"You first, sib."

"No, no, I insist, *children* first."

"Very funny," said Bryn. "Here, help me unload the sled." He began throwing things energetically onto the snow. "We can use the snowball idea for the packs. Take out anything breakable . . ."

It was Cam who thought of tying the packs up in the tent, making the bundle as round as possible. Then with a whoop they hurled it down the slope and watched with delight as it snowballed lakeward, spinning at last well out onto the frozen surface.

"Now us!" Bryn grinned manically at the others. "All aboard!"

"O-kay," said Madlen uncertainly, but Cam was well into the spirit of things now.

"Can I sit up front? Can I?" it shrilled.

Bryn arranged them on the sled, Cam in front, Madlen in the middle, and himself and the remaining pack at the back.

"Keep everything tucked in or you'll slow us down. Maybe even tip us over," he warned as they settled on the very rim of the slope.

"Ready. Steady. GO!"

They pushed off with their hands, leaning forward eagerly, ready for the mad rush of the wind, the grip of gravity—but nothing happened. The heavily laden sledge just stuck there, wedged into the snow at a ridiculous angle.

"Push!" grunted Bryn, and they all three heaved and strained.

With a groan of snow, the sled suddenly shot free, hurtled with stomach-lurching speed down the sharp slope, trailing Questor screams as it went, and thundered out onto the ice.

They zoomed past the bundle of packs, Bryn making a vain grab at them and nearly succeeding in capsizing them all. Madlen dragged him back on board the now wildly spinning sled.

At last they ran out of momentum. Giggling and gasping, the three Questors rolled off onto the ice and lay on their backs, letting the sky spin round high overhead.

"That . . . was . . . fabulous!" panted Cam, and Madlen turned onto her front and pounded her fists on the ice, squealing, *"Fabulous!"*

"Look how far out we've come!"

"And how far *down*! See how high the sides of the valley are!"

"Bryn—I'm convinced—Kir is a terrific World."

"Even the ice is pretty—look at the patterns in it."

"What patterns?" said Bryn, suddenly alert.

"These ones, like little lacey cracks . . . CRACKS?"

Madlen leapt up and tried to back away. The cracks followed her, audible now, as sinister as whip snaps. Instinctively, Cam grabbed hold of Madlen and clung to her.

"NO!" screamed Bryn. "Spread out! Spread OUT!"

Too late—the ice broke. Madlen and Cam disappeared,

shrieking. Bryn lunged for them, trying to catch their hands as they dropped out of sight.

"Wait!" he yelled like an idiot, and tripped.

Momentum slid him inexorably forward, and he vanished, headfirst, into the dark.

CHAPTER THIRTY-THREE

Strange Fish

It was hard to breathe.
So this is drowning, thought Bryn. *I thought
it would be . . . wetter!*

"Ooowwww," someone groaned. "Get off me, you lummox!"

Once he'd disentangled himself from Cam's fur coat, Bryn found that his breathing eased considerably.

"Right," he said. "We're not drowning. We're not in water. We're in some kind of cave-in, within the ice and over the lake. Okay. Is anybody hurt?"

"YES!" chorused Madlen and Cam.

Bryn sighed. "No, really," he said. "I mean, any broken bones, internal bleeding, concussion, stuff like that?"

"Well, if you put it like that . . . no," admitted Cam grudgingly.

"How about all-over third-degree bruising?" asked Madlen, but Bryn only grunted at her.

"People okay. Check. Now, equipment . . . We've still got one pack. That's lucky. So that means we still have"—and he rummaged through the bag—"emergency rations, water, med kit, one sleeping bag, my gear, and the detector. I wonder if it's broken."

He flicked one of the switches, and the device immediately began to vibrate wildly. The significance of this hit him just as he switched it off again . . . and part of the wall began to move.

"Gggg . . . nnnnngggg," he began to gurgle.

"What kind of fish are *you*?!" If walls have gender, this one sounded female.

The wall came closer, gradually acquiring shape. As it—she—passed under the hole in the roof, Bryn saw an angular, long-snouted face; enormous eyes; a neck covered with skin like a gigantic toad's; muscular shoulders; clawed feet that gouged tracks in the diamond-hard ice floor.

There are some fears that make you run like the wind, and others that make you instinctively curl in on yourself, close your eyes, cover up your ears. And then there is the kind of fear that makes movement of *any* sort impossible. Bryn found himself frozen with fright of this order: unable to hide, unable even to look away as the dragon came on, closer and closer, until—

—she stopped.

"Must be the light," she muttered, and at once something peculiar happened to those huge eyes. They blinked, and between one instant and the next, the color and strength of light in the surroundings changed. The dragon's eyes turned orange, and the ice walls glowed with an orange shade as well. Another blink, and eyes and ambient light switched to a rosy color.

She's lighting the ice—with her eyes! thought Bryn numbly.

Blink, glaring white, blink, a feathery gray.

The dragon shook her head and, with a final blink, lit the space in a quite pleasant soft cream.

"It's not the light," she announced. "You really *are* incredibly ugly."

It was an indication of just how terrified they were that not one of them, not even for an instant, felt offended.

"Er, sorry," said Madlen.

The dragon waved a claw. "Probably not your fault. I have to say, though, I've been fishing out this way loads of times and never come across anything quite like . . . what *are* you?"

"I'm not from round—"

"We're on a Qu—"

"He's a—"

The dragon clicked her claws together like a finger-snap, and said, "Got it! You're humans, aren't you! I've heard about you—didn't we do you in Beginner Zoology?—but how did you end up in here?"

Bryn looked up at the hole in the roof, and back at the dragon.

"Er, sorry," he said.

"What?" said the dragon. "Oh, that. Not a problem."

She reared suddenly up onto her haunches, causing the three to scrabble back nervously. And then she began to breathe, steadily, at the gap in the roof. Her head swayed back and forth, and side to side, and her breath came out in trails of translucent cloud, like twin vapor trails. The hole in the ceiling started to blur.

She's weaving! thought Bryn. *She's weaving with air! Warm wet air, it must be, from inside her, and then, see, it freezes when it's outside. . . . Amazing!*

Within moments the dragon had finished her repair. She gave her snout a vigorous rub with one foot, and looked at them.

Without being conscious of it, Bryn had been forgetting to be afraid, but suddenly, now, a new fear clutched at him.

"But . . . how do we get out?" he said.

"Do you want to get out?" she said, sounding surprised. "You just got here!"

"And here is . . . ?" ventured Cam.

The dragon stared at it. "You really *are* lost, aren't you! This is the lake. I thought everybody knew *that.*"

"We know *that*! Only we call it the Lake of Perpetual Ice," said Bryn stiffly.

The dragon snickered. "Sorry, but that's a pretty dumb name, you have to admit! I mean, it's like calling it Lake *Lake*, isn't it, really."

There was a bemused pause. Then Cam said, "Uh, we don't follow you."

The dragon shifted about, starting to look as self-conscious as anything that size could. "Well . . . lakes *are* made of ice. What else could they be made of?"

"Water!" exclaimed Madlen. At last they were getting to things she knew. "Lakes are made of water. Fresh water."

The dragon shook her head. "No, lakes are made of ice. It's the ocean *underneath* that's made of water. *Salt* water. You know, where the fish live?" No response. "You could hardly expect fish to live in ice, now, could you?"

There was another long pause, as the three humans tried to take on what she had just said.

"An ocean?" Bryn pointed at the ice floor. "Down there?"

But the dragon had lost interest. "Look, I need to go now. I took longer fishing than usual. It just gets harder and harder these years to fill your stomach, doesn't it?"

"Wh-where are you going?" squeaked Cam.

"The City. Where else?"

"The City of Ice?"

The dragon snorted. "You're doing it again. What else would you make a city out of? You really don't know much, do you?"

Bryn was about to answer but Madlen interrupted.

"Can we come too?"

For a moment the dragon didn't answer. She seemed to be thinking. The Questors braced themselves uneasily for questions they weren't sure about answering. But then, "No," she said at last. "I can't think of any rule why not. Let's go!"

She headed off down the tunnel, and after a moment the Questors scrambled after her.

"My name's Dagrod," she said. "What's yours?"

"Bryn," said Bryn. "And that's Madlen, and that's Cam."

"Weird na—Um, pleased to meet you."

CHAPTER THIRTY-FOUR

Journey Under the Ice

At first the strangeness of travelling through
the ice along dragon-size tunnels with an invisible
ocean beneath their feet was enough to
keep the Questors openmouthed and silent.
It was also more than a little unnerving, the way
they were moving in a kind of bubble of light that
centered around Dagrod—the ice was dark and
frightening only a few yards
before and behind her.

"It's amazing, how you do that," said Cam at last. "Beautiful."

"Do what?" said Dagrod.

"Make the light."

The dragon shrugged. "I guess so. Can't you do it?"

Cam shook its head. "No. Not at all. Dragons are very . . .
talented."

Dagrod preened a little. "That's nice. What else can I do that
you can't, would you say?"

"Oh, *tons* of things, I'd say." Cam cooed. *Flattery!* said the
Ivory voice in its head, and Cam was happy to comply. It
had known from knee-high this was a technique that rarely
failed.

Madlen thought it was disgusting. "Dagrod," she interrupted, "why is it your breath doesn't show now?"

It was a mistake.

"I *beg* your pardon!" The dragon squawked to a halt. She sounded totally offended.

"She means the way it was before," Cam put in quickly. "You know, when you mended the roof? It's not doing that anymore."

The dragon snorted. "Well, of *course* not," she jeered. "What do you think—I only have one pair of nostrils or something? Sheesh!"

Then, suddenly, she brought her head right round to peer at them. Bryn fought the urge to put his hands up in front of his face.

"Oh." The dragon's voice was much quieter now. "I didn't realize. I'm . . . very sorry. I had no idea humans were defor . . . made like that." She reared up. In a solemn voice she said, "I, Dagrod Nanrodstochter, do sincerely apologize, and assure you that no offense has been intended."

She grinned anxiously. The teeth this revealed were white, pointy, and large, and provoked an immediate response from the humans.

"Apology accepted!"

"That's all right!"

"We don't mind!"

Their eager chorus seemed to reassure the dragon, and she relaxed back into her usual slump. This brought her snout down to standing-human-eye-level again, and they were able to see that she did indeed have more than one pair of nostrils. She had *three* pairs, in fact.

"That's actually very interesting," said Madlen, who didn't

know when to leave well enough alone. "You're breathing with the front pair just now, aren't you?"

Dagrod nodded.

"So does that mean you have three pairs of lungs as well?"

"Oh, don't be daft. Three sets of lungs!" snorted Bryn.

"Well, what about cows?" Madlen turned to argue. "They have three stomachs, or is it four? And so do wallabies. We did that—"

"I know, *in school*," mimicked Bryn. "I never heard of half the stuff you did *in school*."

"Well, *that's* obvious," Madlen sniffed.

Cam ignored their squabbling. "So," it said, "you use one set for breathing, one set for making the vapor stuff, and one set for—what—breathing fire?"

Its words provoked another unexpected reaction from the dragon. Dagrod looked shocked and shamefaced at the same time, as if she had been caught doing something rude.

"I bet you're a totally amazing sight," Cam continued nervously. "When you're flaming, I mean. I could just see you—"

Dagrod backed away. "*When?*" she exclaimed. "*When did you see me? I was so sure* nobody *could see me. . . .*"

"What's the matter?" The Questors were bewildered. "What's wrong?"

"I don't know what you're talking about! Females don't flare. I mean, we're not supposed to flare. I mean, it's not allowed." Then something seemed to snap inside her. She stopped looking embarrassed, and started looking fed-up. "*Females don't flare,*" she mimicked. "*Females don't have adventures. Females don't speak in the Assembly. Females don't go to the Forbidden Places.*" She sighed. "About the only thing that's left is laying eggs, and we can't even do *that* properly anymore. Oh, come on. There's no point in talking about it."

Greatly daring, Cam gave her a sympathetic pat on the leg.

"Life sucks sometimes," Cam said.

"Tell me about it," the dragon replied with another sigh.

As the tunnel curved deeper into the heart of the glacier, the Questors learned more. Dagrod told them about unimaginably huge under-ice seas, where dragons swam in the darkness like glowing submarines, and hunted for days on a single breath. She told them about the 328 Rules of Behavior, and the boredom of Female School, and the rivalry between Lord Na and Lord Aggano over her third cousin Ro. . . . Dagrod loved to talk, and even Madlen found herself enthralled.

Still, it was a long journey for the merely two-legged, and the humans at last began to flag. Bryn handed out emergency rations from the remaining backpack, after explaining to the dragon that their species needed to eat more often than once a year. Dagrod seemed to find this very strange, and when Cam began to shiver visibly with cold, that was even stranger. Madlen did her best to explain other Worlds, hot climates, and the concept of clothes.

"If rest and warmth are what you need, would it be of assistance to sit up against me?" Dagrod offered, frowning anxiously. "You would be most welcome. Dragons are self-regulating, of course. One of the advantages of internal fires! If . . . you'd like to?"

Gratefully, Bryn dug out the sleeping bag to put between them and the ice, and the Questors cuddled up to what amounted to an improbably enormous hot water bottle.

Madlen nodded off almost at once, her brain overloaded with impossibilities. Cam tried to stay awake to savor this living dream—the feel of Dagrod's warm dry skin; the muffled thump of her huge heart; the gentle wheeze of her sides going in and out, in and out. . . . Bryn, half turned away from the others, drew frantically and surreptitiously, until yawns overcame him too.

In a pocket of light, under a ceiling of ice, in the eerie emptiness, three humans slept against a dragon's side.

CHAPTER THIRTY-FIVE

The City

They awoke to Dagrod squealing.

"What is it? Make it stop! I'm sorry! Make it stop!"

They tumbled onto the ice, looking blearily about for the source of her distress, and then Bryn spotted the backpack, lying on its side and vibrating wildly. He grabbed it, fished about inside, and then pulled out the dragon detector. It was registering right off the scale. He thumbed the switch quickly.

Dagrod collapsed beside them. "I'm really sorry," she panted. "I got stiff, but when I moved my leg your bag fell over and then it started making that awful noise, and . . . What *is* it?"

Bryn looked at Dagrod and then down at the thing in his hands. "It's, um, sort of . . . It's a dragon detector. For detecting dragons."

Dagrod snorted. "That's just stupid. Why don't you use your *eyes?* It's not as if we're invisible." Her fright had made her cross.

"No, well, apparently you give off a sort of radiation and if I wanted to know if you were around, or coming closer, or something, this would tell me. . . ." Bryn's voice trailed off, worried by the sudden shift of expression on her long face.

"Say that again?" she whispered.

Oh, help, he thought, *now I've done it.*

202

"It's nothing, really," he started to babble. "It's just a thing . . ."

"You said radiation—you said we give off radiation—you said it detects—?"

Bryn spread his hands. "Look," he said. "It just sort of happened. It was something else altogether they were trying to detect. Look, I'm putting it away now. I'm really sorry—"

But Dagrod had stopped listening. She had a strange, wondering look, and was murmuring to herself, "And I thought they were *fish*!"

"Dagrod?" said Cam tentatively.

"Look, there's someone who'd really like to see your device." The dragon sounded all at once full to the brim with suppressed excitement. "Would that be all right, do you think?"

"Er . . . sure . . . no problem . . ."

"Why exactly—," Dagrod began. But then, "No, don't tell *me*! Time to go—the City's not far now—time to go!"

It was a weird way for them all to wake up, and then the strangeness deepened, for the tunnel they were following suddenly ended.

They'd reached the outskirts of the City.

The space under the glacier had been carved out in a way that was more sculpture than construction. The children stared in amazement at chambers, streets, halls that could have held a hundred dragons; marketplaces and amphitheaters, playgrounds and parks; galleries and ramps that curved up toward the distant ice above; pillars, fluted and carved—it was an astonishing sight. Astonishing, and completely empty. There was no sign of life anywhere. There were no dragons.

"Where are they?" Bryn whispered. "Where've they all gone?"

"Nobody lives down here anymore," Dagrod replied. She

sounded matter-of-fact, but didn't raise her voice either. "We don't need the Lower City now. We're, well, dying out. Like I said, we can't seem to produce young, hardly at all, and the ones that make it to hatching are often . . . not right." She paused for a moment, looking down at the ice floor. Then she seemed to come to a decision. "Many believe we are being poisoned," she said. "An invisible poison . . . Some say it's the end of the Path. Some say it's the end of everything." She shivered. "Of course, they don't say that *out loud.* It's all whispers."

Whispers. Whispers. The empty spaces echoed her words.

Madlen leaned over to Bryn and said in a low, urgent voice, "Did you hear that, Bryn? It's affecting them too. They need us!"

He nodded, but said nothing.

He tried not to notice the strange looks Dagrod kept giving him as they set off again.

As they walked on, spiraling up through the glacier, it gradually came to Bryn that something was different. Then Madlen, pointing at the walls, asked him, "Is that the Northern Lights? I read about them someplace, but I was never sure what they were." And Bryn realized what had changed.

"No, the Northern Lights are in the sky," he whispered back. "This is different."

Ripples, sheets, curtains of light flickered in the walls as they passed. Shades of white within the glacial blue-green of the ice juddered and moved, almost as if alive. Cam came up beside them, and pointed.

"It's in the floor and the roof as well," it exclaimed. "I've never seen anything like it!"

The others nodded, and continued to stare as they walked along.

After a while Cam thumped Dagrod on the leg. "What's making the lights like that?" it asked her.

Dagrod looked down.

"We're near dragons now," she said. "And dragons light the ice. It doesn't matter what time of day or night it is—the part of the City we're coming to never sleeps. There's always somebody awake, and as long as a dragon's eyes are open, there will be light."

"That's so cool," said Cam. "But what I meant was, what's making the *flickering* lights?"

"What flickering lights?" Dagrod's attention was elsewhere. She kept stopping to rub at the sides of her head.

"What's wrong?" Bryn asked. "Got an earache?"

Dagrod wrinkled her big forehead and grunted. "It's the noise," she said. "Awful, isn't it?"

The humans looked at one another. Except for the sounds *they* were making as they walked over the ice, the silence seemed complete.

"What noise?" asked Cam.

"The *buzzing*!" replied the dragon irritably. Then she turned to them in surprise. "You mean, you can't hear it?"

They shook their heads.

"Lucky you," she sighed. "I really, really hate it. *Tsss, tsss, tsss.* It goes on all the time in the City. One of the reasons I get away as much as I can—that blasted *hiss, hiss.* If you let it, it can drive you crazy."

"Sounds like tinnitus," said Cam.

"Dragon ears are different from ours," said Madlen to Bryn.

He shrugged. "You think?"

The next moment he and the others found themselves being roughly shouldered into a cross-tunnel and crushed against the wall.

"Hey!" began Cam indignantly, but Dagrod hissed, *"Shut up!"*

Around the edges of Dagrod's body they could just glimpse what had caused her violent reaction. A small male dragon was passing by. Dagrod had explained to them how the sexes were distinguished, and this one's tiny crest suggested he was still very young. Nevertheless, Dagrod's hurry to get out of his path, and the way she lowered her head and eyes to the floor to show subservience, indicated he must be someone of importance.

The humans waited impatiently—and uncomfortably—for him to pass by. Only when she was sure it was safe did Dagrod release them from their hiding place.

"Who was that, the prince?" exclaimed Cam irritably.

Dagrod grunted. "Him? A prince? He's just my cousin Raon."

"So what were you squishing us for? And what was all that groveling in aid of?"

"I wasn't *groveling.* I'm a *female,* or had you forgotten? How do you *expect* me to behave toward a male? There are rules, you know. Oh, forget it. Come on. This way." Dagrod hustled them across the main tunnel and along a series of side ones. "I want to get Bry—all of you to the Keeper before anybody spots him. You."

"What do you mean?" asked Madlen as she scurried to keep up. "Who's the Keeper? Why are we hiding? You said before it was all right, us coming here."

"Oh. Yes. I'm sure it is. Probably. It's just . . . Let's see, what time is it? Right, the Keeper should be at the Teaching Hall."

The Questors exchanged bemused glances.

"So she's a teacher?" asked Cam, hoping to get some idea what was happening.

But Dagrod shook her head. "No, no, of course not. Only males can teach. By rights the Keeper should be male too, of course, but like I said, we live for a long time, and this one's been around forever. But as Keeper, she has to monitor all the lessons. She has to make sure what is being taught is according to Memory. It's History today. Turn here. And remember, when we go into the Females' Gallery, you're to keep quiet and STAY OUT OF SIGHT!"

CHAPTER THIRTY-SIX

History Lessons

*"... and Adagon looked about him and saw ...
nothing. No Worlds left to conquer;
no battles left to be fought. His honor burned
inside him, desperate to find its place in the
memories that would be. He was a dragon
in need of a deed."*

They were in the Females' Gallery of the large Teaching Hall. A screen of woven ice, so fine it moved at the slightest breath of air, hid them from view. In the hall below, a huge male dragon addressed a group of attentive young bucks. Dagrod had said it was a history class, but it certainly didn't sound like it.

"Where's the Keeper?" Bryn whispered to Dagrod.

"Over there," she answered. "But shh now. We mustn't interrupt the lesson!"

Bryn looked along to where she'd pointed. There was . . . *something* there, in the shadows at the far end of the gallery. He'd probably have taken it for a peculiar formation in the ice, but if you looked at it just right, it was possible to see that a long, knobbly dragon was indeed coiled up there.

Coiled up, and apparently fast asleep.

"So, unable to bear the thought of a life that was only ordinary, and a death at the end that was only benign, Adagon the Hero turned his back on the City and headed into the caverns and tunnels of the Under-Ice."

Bryn became aware of the deep voice of the teacher again.

"Adagon wandered there for many days, turning and circling through the mazing below the City, deeper and deeper in search of . . . something.

"When he found it, he almost didn't recognize it. It seemed a cave like any other, floored with rock and walled in by ice, and he was about to turn his back and go, when the light of his eyes caught something glinting in the dimness.

"Adagon moved closer and saw a great cone rising from the floor of the cave, and on top of the cone he saw a wondrous glittering, faceted Crystal, which drew him with an irresistible power. His desire for it could not be denied. He reached out a claw . . .

"'No!' came a voice, and even the fearless Adagon felt the touch of fear."

Something made Bryn glance over at his siblings. Cam was leaning forward, its face rapt. He smiled to himself. For a Dalrodian, this must be like walking about in a dream. Except that here the symbols chatted to you and took you home to meet the folks, and mythology was taught as history. *Right up Cam's street,* he thought . . .

. . . and right up Madlen's nose!

Legends and heroes and derring-do—none of it would have featured in a *Trentorian* classroom. She was fidgeting about as if her ice seat were hot. It was funny to see, but it was also going to draw attention to them, which had to be a bad idea. He reached past Cam and gave Madlen a shove and a warning look.

She scowled back at him, but took the hint and subsided, arms folded, into a sulky, disapproving heap.

"'Who are you?' the Hero called.

"And out of the shadows came a creature whose steps grated and scraped. Its scales were of basalt and its claws obsidian; its eyes gleaming mica and its teeth, black diamond, so sharp they could slice one thought from the next.

"It was a Lava Dragon and, from his size, Adagon judged him older than any other living thing."

Watching Cam and Madlen, thinking about what they were most likely thinking—seeing things through their eyes, in a way—something jolted inside Bryn's head. He couldn't just listen to the story, relax into it. He had to *pay attention* in a new way.

"'What is your name?' breathed Adagon in awe.

The Lava Dragon's voice echoed from the hidden roof and the cold walls. 'I am the Guardian of the Crystal and this place,' he said. 'And I tell you, it is not for those who can die. It is not for those who can be born.'

"Adagon frowned. 'You lie—it is for me!'

"'Leave,' the Guardian breathed. 'Leave!'

"And Adagon slammed his tail to the floor in a sudden rage. 'I will not leave!' he roared. 'Tell me—what is this place?'

"As the echoes of his words died away, the light in the Guardian's eyes flickered also, and he answered, 'This . . . is the Place of the Last Great Deed.'

"Adagon's heart swelled. 'Tell me the deed,' he cried. 'And whatever the price, I will do it.'

"The black dragon's voice was almost gentle, but his claws grated against the stones. 'You must take the Crystal I guard with my life.'

"Adagon paused, for he respected the other's great age. 'The cost for you is high, then, Old One, if I win.'

"But the Guardian's answer made no sense. 'The cost is greater for you, if I lose.'

"'So be it!' roared Adagon, patience at an end.

"At once the Lava Dragon was upon him. Slashing and biting, the two fought, day and night and into the following day. They circled and met, each clash powerful enough to shake the ground. The walls echoed to their roars. The floor was slick with their blood. The battle-fire in their eyes lit up the cavern to the distant roof."

The description of the battle, which normally Bryn would have quite enjoyed, suddenly seemed distasteful to him—*and* it seemed to be taking as long as the fight itself must have done— but the young males below were rapt.

"At last it was over. The Guardian lay on the stony floor. Adagon, barely alive, cut and gouged a hundred times, dragged himself over his opponent. He reached out for the Crystal, and, murmuring softly, 'The Last Great Deed,' he plucked it from its place.

"The moment the Crystal came away in his grasp, a deafening force exploded from the cone. Adagon was thrown against the wall, battered by a wave of noise, but he never let go of his prize. He felt himself weakening, as if his lifeblood were draining away. With a huge effort he dragged himself out into the tunnel, clutching the Crystal to his chest.

"How he made the tortuous journey back is not known, but finally he regained the City. He was brought lovingly into the Great Hall.

"'Adagon!' cried the King, aghast at the Hero's pitiful state. 'What have you done?'

"Adagon could not hear his King's words, or any other, but he guessed what he had been asked.

"'The Last Great Deed,' he whispered.

"At these words the Crystal fell from his claws, and rolled across the floor to the foot of the throne. The dragons felt its power drawing them, urging them to battle, calling them to glory.

"When they turned to look again, Adagon was dead.

"And ever since, the Crystal has fed our greatness. It is the source of our strength. We worship it as an emblem of the Path, and every time we take hold of it, we are made mightier than before."

There was a pause, followed by a great sigh of satisfaction that riffled round the room. Then, in a respectful silence, the class began to leave.

In the gallery Madlen started to stand up too, but Dagrod shoved her down again.

"Not yet," she insisted. Even though they weren't visible to the males, Dagrod had automatically adopted a subservient posture, head down, eyes down, until the males had all gone out. Only then did she straighten, and settle back again with a sigh.

"Well?" said Madlen, struggling to keep her voice down. "What are we waiting for *now*?"

Dagrod gave her a superior look. "You don't have any manners at all, do you?" she commented coldly. "The Keeper of Memory may only be a female, but she is *practically* a male in status, and you don't go around waking up *practically* male dragons just because you want to talk to them, now do you?"

Madlen flounced, and turned her back on dragons in general. Cam and Bryn grinned at each other, and made themselves comfortable against Dagrod's flank.

After a bit Bryn said, to nobody in particular, "You know, it makes you wonder what that old dragon meant. I mean, 'Last Great Deed.' I know it's supposed to be about the *ultimate* deed, but it could have been saying, '*End* of Great Deeds.' Game over. End of the road."

He didn't notice the mound that was the Keeper shift a little.

"Path," murmured Dagrod. "Dragons have Paths. *Humans* have roads."

"Whatever. But it's quite a sad story if you look at it like that, isn't it?"

Dagrod was quiet for a moment. When she spoke again, there was a puzzled note in her voice.

"Yes," she said, "I never thought of that."

"Or anything else, I imagine."

The voice from the far end of the gallery was completely unexpected. Everyone tried to jump up and turn around at the same time—and Dagrod's tail and Bryn's feet became totally tangled.

With a yell Bryn sprawled onto the gallery floor; the backpack was sent flying; the detector started squealing; his sketchbook fell out; and a sheaf of papers, caught on an updraft of air, fluttered about like large, agitated snowflakes.

He looked up to see one sheet being pinned to the ice by a long ink-stained claw.

The Keeper was awake, and staring at him.

CHAPTER THIRTY-SEVEN

The Keeper . . .

Uncoiled, she was unlike any dragon they'd
yet seen. She looked as if she had once
been hugely fat, and then some force of time had
stretched her out, elongating her until now she
seemed to go on forever. Her scales were dry and
dull; withered wings dragged a little along the
floor beside her when she moved; her snout was
long and twisted to the side. It would be easy
enough to discount such a dusty bone-bag, until
you saw her eyes.

"Treasonous words. A box that screams. And . . . these little
windows . . ." The great lids dropped, hooding her eyes for a
moment, setting the others free to speak.

"They're pictures!"

"It's just—"

"You see, I was fishing—"

"So," the Keeper said, rearing up suddenly so that the Questors—
and Dagrod—jumped back again. "You'd better bring your catch
along then, young . . . Dagrod, isn't it? Yes, of course it is. And
tell them to bring their artifacts with them. Not the sort of thing
to leave lying about." Her teeth showed slightly in an expression

the humans really couldn't read, and then she was gone.

"The Keeper has doors to everywhere," said Dagrod, noticing their amazement. "*We'll* be going the normal way."

"Going *where*?" demanded Cam.

"To the Library, of course. Where the Memory is kept."

The Library probably wasn't far from the Teaching Hall, but Dagrod took great care in keeping her "catch" unseen, using back tunnels and ducking more than once into an empty chamber while other dragons paced unsuspectingly by. At one point, however, they scurried past a pair of huge important-looking double doors. Bryn found himself wanting to slow down, but Dagrod wouldn't let him.

"What was that?" he whispered up at her.

"The Great Hall," she answered. "Where we keep the Crystal. Why?"

Bryn shook his head. "I don't know. I felt . . . something."

Cam and Madlen exchanged looks.

"Could that be it?" Cam murmured to its sister. "Could the Crystal be what he needs to find?"

Madlen lifted one shoulder. "Pretty inconvenient if it is," she whispered back. "We walk off with something like that, they're *bound* to notice."

"Yeah," said Cam. "Great."

The Library was bewildering. It was a labyrinth of low curving tunnels and unexpected nooks and crannies, strange corkscrew galleries, and confusing translucent walls, packed full of a seemingly random collection of books, scrolls, carved cubes, tapestries, and sheaves of strangely marked bones—all the ways dragons had stored information over the millennia.

"You took your time."

Even though they'd been expecting her, she still managed to make them jump.

It's like she's trying to prove something all the time, thought Bryn suddenly. *Keep us off kilter. Who does she remind me of?*

He felt something shift inside him. "We're here now," he said quietly. He spoke directly to her, as if no one else were there, as if what he really meant was, *I'm here now.*

For a moment she tried to stare him down. Then, with a curious ripple along her body that must have been the equivalent of a shrug, she said, "So . . . show me what you've got. Show me . . . *everything.*"

And now he didn't want to, out of sheer cussedness. Then the others saw him grin, as if something had all at once become clear. As he began to unload their belongings onto the table, he said cheerfully, "I'm not scared of you."

The Keeper went still, and watched him with those extraordinary eyes as if trying to eat him with them.

"Right," he said, giving the bag a shake. "That's the lot. Travel rations. First-aid kit. This box is probably not familiar to you." And he explained the dragon detector to her. "My sketchbook and drawing equipment. But I expect what you'll really want to know is why we're here in the first place." He took a breath. "We're on a Quest."

"WHAT!" It was Dagrod. She seemed horrified.

"We're on a Quest," said Madlen.

Dagrod's face crumpled. "You mean you're not . . . No, look, you fell through the ice, and then I *brought* you—*that's* why you're here . . . isn't it?"

Cam patted her reassuringly. "That's *how* we're here," it said. "But the *why* is a bit more complicated."

"You never said anything about anything like that!" Dagrod wailed.

"Er, you never asked."

Dagrod hung her head. "I didn't think, at first," she murmured. "And then I wondered . . . and I thought . . . I hoped, just maybe, you were here to help us."

The humans exchanged embarrassed glances. Then Bryn cleared his throat and tried to explain.

"We *are* here to help you . . . too. You see . . ."

As the story of the imbalance of the Worlds and the search for the mythic Objects unfolded, Dagrod's eyes got bigger and bigger. The Keeper showed no obvious reaction, though she twitched from time to time.

Even when he'd finished, the Keeper didn't speak right away. Instead, she turned her attention again to the objects on the table, touching them gently with her claws. With a delicate action, she flipped open Bryn's sketchbook and began laying out the sheets, peering at each picture with great concentration.

The others made as if to look too, then stopped, unsure of Bryn's reaction.

He stiffened, then he turned half away and lifted his hand in a gesture that was part permission, part defeat. Dagrod gave the portraits of humans a quick once-over, and then fixed on one of herself. Madlen and Cam moved gently from one picture to the next, aware of the privilege of seeing what their brother had always kept so carefully hidden.

"You couldn't draw *me*," the Keeper said suddenly. She twisted herself up, more than any of them would have thought possible, slit her eyes, and sneered at him down her warped snout.

Bryn turned back, but he didn't answer. He just looked at her for a long time, and then, still not speaking, he reached for his sketchbook and chose a fresh page.

It was a test of some kind—that much was clear—and Madlen, Cam, and Dagrod almost held their breath, willing Bryn to succeed. The Keeper, on the other hand, seemed determined to make his task as hard as possible. Along her great length, parts of her distorted and twitched as if with a life of their own. She changed shape like some sort of bad dream, as if she were defying Bryn to capture a likeness.

Finally, it became too much for Cam, who exclaimed suddenly, "Stop that! Hold still, can't you?"

But Bryn didn't seem to notice, or mind. In fact, he didn't look at the Keeper much at all after the beginning, and when he did, it was with such an abstracted expression that the others wondered what he was seeing.

Then he was finished.

The Keeper held out a claw to take the picture for herself, but Bryn shook his head, and instead laid it out on the table, where they could all see.

A dragon of flamboyant wings and ebony scales triumphed across a night sky, flaming silver against a full moon, so high above the mountains of ice that they were merely suggestions and barely real.

It was everything the Keeper held behind her eyes, hidden inside her twisted form.

"How did you do that?" she breathed.

"I draw what I see," he answered softly.

And for a long time nobody said a thing.

Then the Keeper turned her strange head toward Dagrod.

"Well," she said huskily. "You've done well, young female. You've brought me a Spaener."

CHAPTER THIRTY-EIGHT

. . . and the Spaener

"You think I'm a *what*!?" squawked Bryn.

The Keeper had disappeared deeper into the Library in search of documentation. Apparently dragon society had a very high regard for precedent. The old proverb "There's nothing new under the ice" was taken literally. No change in policy could be introduced that hadn't been tested in the past. However, the dragons' understanding of what constituted documentation was a good deal broader than anything *Madlen's* World would have recognized. Stories, poems, songs, as well as accounts of battles, dynasties, debates, and discoveries. Over the millennia, the Keepers had accumulated a distinctively draconic Memory.

"You're a Spaener," said Dagrod calmly. "It means something like 'seer.' You know, like a prophet. They're supposed to show up when we've come to the end of one Path and need to start on another. Otherwise, how would we know it was time to stop? All dragons are taught about the Spaeners."

"Dagrod! Get a grip!" said Bryn desperately. "This is *me* you're talking about. As you may have noticed, *I'm not a dragon*!"

"Oh, it doesn't have to be a dragon," Dagrod replied earnestly. "Could be anything. According to the Memory, one time it was even a puffin."

They stared.

"A puffin," Madlen said flatly. "You're trying to tell me that the great and mighty dragon nation took orders from a puffin."

"Well, no," said Dagrod. "Puffins can't talk. But, apparently, this one had the most penetrating stare. It was the time of the Short Rebellion, and Gor the Eleventh—well, that's what he became—he brought this puffin into the Assembly, and it *stared*. And it must have had the power to really see, because every dragon it stared at turned out to be a member of the cabal that was plotting to overthrow Gor the Tenth. They all confessed on the spot. It was incredible."

"No argument there," muttered Madlen.

"Of course, the rebellion was a very long time ago. No *modern* dragon would consider ending a Path before it was over."

There was a pause.

"It's usually a dragon," Dagrod continued. "The Spaener is, I mean. But this time it's you! And *I* found you!"

She beamed at Bryn shyly.

Bryn looked sick.

"But what about the Quest?" Madlen said aside to Cam. "Bryn's supposed to be looking for the thing, not messing about making a name for himself in dragon lore."

Cam chewed its lip. "Let's just hope he can do both," it answered softly. Then it perked up a bit. "And anyway, we've obviously come to the right place. If anybody's going to know what and where our mythic Object is, it's bound to be somebody who knows *everything*!"

"How wise, for one so short on legs. Currently, however, I have my mind on other things." The Keeper practically skipped up to them and tumbled a bundle of scrolls and cubes onto the table.

"Yes . . . yes . . . I can work with these. Your Quest/mythic-Object story is no use, of course. I could put my claw on a dozen versions but they'd just see it as confirmation of the Path we've already got. But the box, and the pictures, and a Spaener—now *that's* promising." She scratched her twisted snout enthusiastically, like a human rubbing its hands together in anticipation.

The Questors lifted eyebrows at one another.

"You seem different, Madam Keeper. More . . . cheerful?" suggested Cam tentatively.

The Keeper barked a short laugh. "Of course I'm cheerful! Do you have any idea how long dragons live?"

"No."

"Then you have no idea of the true meaning of the word 'boredom.'"

They stared at her.

"Look, I'm not just a librarian. Each new thing or bit of information that comes in interacts with all the other things in the Library, and I can see things in those relationships that mean something to us all. *I can make a difference.* But if nothing new comes in, what's my job? Guaranteeing everything stays the same.

"The thing about the Path of the Crystal, little humans, is the way it looks after itself. It's no coincidence that the Separation Treaty happened when it did. And that was only one of many ways we've closed ourselves off, small ways, innocuous ways, introduced so delicately that no one could object—"

"I don't know anything about a Separation Treaty. We never got taught about that in the Females' School," interrupted Dagrod.

The Keeper snorted. "Don't be stupid. Of course they're not going to teach you anything that might make you *think*!"

"What did you mean," asked Cam, "when you said the treaty wasn't a coincidence?"

The Keeper narrowed an eye. "Ah," she said, "the politician of the group. Well, think about it. If you have a status quo you'd like to *stay* status, what's a good way of going about it? Cordon it off—impose a quarantine—keep out anything new and different that might mar the perfection. See?"

Cam nodded. "Makes sense," it said.

"It would," said the Keeper. "That's human thinking for you." When Cam looked puzzled, the Keeper continued, "After all, the treaty was a human idea."

"Hang on," Bryn interrupted. "I always heard it was the dragons' idea."

The Keeper waved a claw dismissively. "Well, yes, it did originate from the City, but it was a *human* who drafted it for us—and suggested it in the first place too. Now who *was* that?" She pulled a book toward her and flipped through some of the pages. "What was his name? Or rather, is. He's still crawling about the place, on and off. Keeps a low profile, but I've sniffed him coming out of private meetings with Lord Rad and his kind from time to time—Here is it. Cor-dell. Alpine Cordell. Extraordinary name." She pointed to the bottom of a page. "I remember not much liking the direction it was all going in, even at the time. Seemed to me the more documentation we had of the proceedings, the less murky it might be later on. Important to have it all on record"—she winked at Bryn—"but I would say that, wouldn't I?"

"Cordell?" said Madlen. "Isn't he—"

"Yeah," said Cam. "*He's* all right, ma'am. I've seen him at The London House. He's just Secretary to the Council. They tell him what to do, and he does it. No sinister motives there—unless being gray and boring is sinister!"

The Keeper turned her extraordinary eye toward the Dalrodian.

"Are the young ever as clever as they think they are? I wonder."

Cam scowled. "What's that supposed to mean?" it said huffily.

The Keeper laughed and waved a dismissive claw at them. "Go away. I've got work to do. The Assembly sits tomorrow. Dagrod, keep them out of sight until morning. And then . . . we shall see . . ."

Then, noticing they were still there, she repeated gleefully, *"Go away!"* and disappeared into the far reaches of Memory.

"My lord?"

Lord Rad couldn't hide the shudder that the proximity of humans always gave him. Particularly when unprepared. This one, The London House one, had popped up from out of nowhere, right under his snout.

"My lord, a word. I have information. About some thieves . . . and a Quest . . ."

The human was always appropriately subservient, and, though he hated to admit it, he *had* been useful to Rad and his concerns. Perhaps that was putting it too strongly. He'd been not *un*-useful, might be closer to the mark. Best give the creature a moment. Nothing better to do.

"Well?" drawled the dragon lord. "You may proceed."

The human's bow was so humble that the thin smile on his face could not be seen.

"You found them where?!"

Back in The London House, the Preceptor lunged out of the chair toward him, but Cordell did not step back or flinch. He didn't repeat the information either. He knew he had been heard the first time.

The Preceptor turned away. "The dragon City. My, my. Haven't they made good time." The Preceptor's voice was ever so slightly unsteady.

Cordell said nothing.

"Perhaps leaving them to their own devices is not as efficient as I had surmised."

Cordell coughed. The Preceptor went very still.

"Well?"

"They have not been . . . completely left to themselves," Cordell murmured. "I have had a word. With a . . . friend."

The Preceptor walked over to the chair and sat down again.

"How delightful. Tell me all about it."

CHAPTER THIRTY-NINE

In Dagrod's Cave

"My little brother, the prophet," said Madlen,
cozying down. "Fancy that."

"Yes," Cam agreed. "I'd have treated him with more respect, if
only I'd known."

Bryn growled at them.

They had come by back ways to Dagrod's sleeping cave, and
the dragon had curled herself to form a warm slope for them to
lean against.

"Look, Dagrod, I admit I draw pictures." Bryn peered round
at her urgently. "But I'm not a prophet. I can't see into the
Future or *anything* like that. It's just this—"

He was interrupted by the sound of snoring.

Madlen laughed. "There you have it—Dagrod's answer. Can't
argue with that!"

"I'd no idea you had as much stuff as that, though," said Cam
thoughtfully. "I mean, you'd whip your book out, draw something, and then it was away again before anybody could say
'Hey whatcha drawing?'" It looked over at its brother. "You're
actually very, very good, aren't you? Pity about your World's
prejudice."

Bryn didn't seem to know what to do with himself. He got

up and began to pace; then, finding himself facing an ice wall, he kicked it.

"And it's all so unnecessary," Cam continued calmly.

Bryn stared. "Unnecessary? *What's* unnecessary?"

Cam looked over at him. "All the fuss," it said. "If you didn't decide on your sex right away, you'd have tons of time to grow up, find out what you're good at, what you like doing, let yourself sort of evolve into—"

"I don't want to be a girl!" Bryn yelled.

There was a tight pause. Then Madlen spoke, her voice quiet. "I'm a girl," she said. "I can't draw."

Bryn glared at her. "That's not the point," he growled.

Madlen looked down at her hands. "Maybe," she murmured. "Maybe not."

"But it's not flipping far off it," commented Cam, and turning its back on the others, it snuggled into Dagrod's warmth.

"Cam doesn't understand," muttered Bryn.

"No, well, it wouldn't," said Madlen, still studying her hands.

"But you do, don't you?"

"Me? Understand about other people making up your mind for you, telling you who you are? Oh yeah, sure. Full of understanding, me." And Madlen, too, curled up and closed her eyes.

Bryn couldn't sleep. It wasn't that he wasn't tired enough—he was exhausted. But every time he shut his eyes, he could still see the way the walls and ceiling flickered with light. He felt as if his whole body had begun to pulse in time with it. It was as if he'd become a two-legged version of the detector, but without an off switch.

He rolled over again, trying to find the magic position that would let him escape into sleep. A minute later he shifted onto his back, slowing his breathing, forcing his eyes to stay shut, thinking sleepy thoughts. . . .

It was hopeless.

He sat up, and moved as quietly as he could away from the others. He pulled on his boots, and crept out of the room.

He didn't notice the two sets of eyes that watched him go.

CHAPTER FORTY

The Touch of the Crystal

There was a silvery twilit sheen to the corridors.
Bryn felt very small in the wide tunnels; he stayed
close to the wall as he walked along. The
restlessness inside him had seemed
unfocused when he was trying to sleep, but now
that he was up and on the move, he felt
a purpose solidifying in his mind.

He was going to the Great Hall. He was pretty sure he remembered how to get there. He'd be careful. No one would see him. He wouldn't get himself or Dagrod or the others in trouble.

But he had to find out. He had to see the Crystal for himself.

And then, he was there. He wasn't sure what he would do if the huge double doors were locked, but it wasn't a problem. They slid apart with the lightest touch, frictionless on the glassy floor. Bryn slipped inside and pushed them shut behind him.

Then, for a moment, he stood and stared.

The Great Hall soared. White ice, veined with silver, carved and shaped so that the vaulted ceiling seemed to float, resting only for courtesy's sake on the fluted columns and curved walls. Even in the dim light of dragon-sleep, the size and height and luminosity lifted the heart. To be capable of constructing such a space was almost inconceivable, but to be able to imagine it in the first place . . .

And then he forgot about everything except the Crystal, glinting there at the far end of the chamber.

It was faceted like a diamond, as clear and brilliant as the ice pedestal that held it up. It was a cage of freezing light that flickered and pulsed. It drew him, and he walked the length of the Hall. It was calling to him, to an empty place inside him, and it promised him such things. . . .

It was the perfect Quest Object—beautiful, powerful, mythic. It made Madlen's pathetic little hatchet look pretty sick, that was for sure. How could he not have known immediately that this would be it? He could see himself already, back at The London House, revealing the Crystal to the Council, to Mrs. Macma-honney, to Kate. He'd be the Hero, while the others would still be just children. It wouldn't really be stealing, because Heroes don't steal—they *find.*

Without pausing to think, Bryn reached up and took it from its pedestal—and the instant the Crystal met his skin there was an icy almost electric shock that exploded up his arm and into his brain. He staggered and blinked hard to clear his sight. Then . . .

It was as if Bryn were recognizing himself for the first time. He saw himself as he'd always wanted to be. He was so much taller than he'd ever realized, and stronger. He was power-ful, a warrior, and anybody who said otherwise would regret it. He knew just what he'd do to them, to all of them, one after another. He'd throttle the life out of them. For every sneer, he'd squeeze, and for every taunt, he'd squeeze, and for every failure, he'd—

Who was that? There was someone trying to sneak up behind

him, someone trying to catch him unawares, but he was too smart for them, he was too—

With a shriek Bryn dropped the Crystal, spun on his heel, and attacked. He had his hands around that someone's neck and was tightening, oblivious to anything else, oblivious to Cam yelling in his ear, to Madlen's hands scratching at his, Madlen's face reddening in a grimace of fear as his grip on her throat—

Reality flooded back into his brain and he flung himself away from his sister. She collapsed, dragging air into her lungs, staring at him in horror. Cam had grabbed up the Crystal as the only weapon at hand and was now standing over Madlen, with the Crystal raised above its head, ready to protect her from him.

"I . . . Are you . . . ? I didn't . . . No!" Bryn panted; then when Cam thrust the Crystal at him in a warning gesture, he flinched away and curled in on himself on the floor. "Put it back," he sobbed. "Get it away from me!" He pointed toward the pedestal, and then buried his face in his hands, shuddering.

Cam looked at him, and then at the Crystal, uncertain at first that it was safe to give up the weapon. But there was nothing in Bryn's huddled figure that suggested he was about to erupt again. Besides, the Crystal was disturbing to hold, unpleasantly demanding in a way the Dalrodian didn't understand. It trotted over to the pedestal and plopped the thing unceremoniously back into place.

"Right," it said firmly. "Just what was *that* all about?"

It was some time before Cam could persuade Bryn to even look up, let alone speak to them.

"I'm fine, really!" Madlen kept insisting. "I was only scared for a second. We thought you knew we were there. It's *our* fault for scaring *you!*"

Finally Bryn was coaxed into trying to explain. He told them about his restlessness, the sense of time passing and the Quest still to be done, and his decision to see for himself if what the Great Hall contained was what they were seeking.

"The . . ." He waved a hand toward the pedestal, but kept his head turned away.

"The Crystal, yes?" prompted Cam.

Bryn nodded. "As soon as I saw it . . . It's so beautiful," he said huskily. "Just to look at it made me feel . . . I don't know how to say it. It made me feel I could do anything, you know? I was really strong, really powerful . . . and then it made me do that awful thing to you."

Madlen made an impatient gesture. "You didn't know it was me!" she protested. "It doesn't count."

Bryn looked sadly over at the marks on her neck.

"I didn't know it was you," he said in a small voice. "But I knew it was somebody." He scrubbed wearily at his face. "It counts." He began to swear quietly into his hands. Then, "And it didn't *make me*," he said, muffled. "That's a lie. The Crystal didn't make me try to kill you. It just made me feel as if I could. I always thought I'd be too scared, too soft."

Cam put its hand on his arm. "There's *could*," Cam said, "and there's *would*."

Madlen came up and patted him on the other arm. "And there's *bed*," she said. "And that's where we should be. Now!"

Bryn grinned weakly, and let them lead him away.

CHAPTER FORTY-ONE

<u>Dragon Assembly</u>

The three Questors were still deeply asleep when Dagrod burst in on them.

"Get up! Get up!" she trumpeted. "The Assembly has been called. They're already gathering!"

Shoving and chivvying, she got them up, out, and to the entrance to the Great Hall. Then, like an oversize sheepdog herding diminutive sheep, she separated Bryn out from the others and pushed him toward the big double doors.

"We'll be in the gallery," Dagrod whispered loudly. And when he just stood there, she frowned and urged him, "Go ON!" before hustling the others away.

"Do as the female says."

Bryn almost jumped out of his skin. An elderly dragon lord had come up behind him. He towered over the boy, but seemed more curious than aggressive.

"Heard about you, human! Long time since we had one of *your* sort about. Should make for an interesting Assembly!" The lord wheezed out a chuckle, and then looked pointedly at the doors.

"After you, sir?" quavered Bryn.

The dragon wheezed again, and shook his head.

"After *you*, Spaener," he rumbled, as the doors opened from within.

Bryn never knew how he got his legs to move, but somehow, shakily, he managed it. As he entered, he found that the Great Hall was even more astonishingly beautiful than before, lit now by the reflected colors of hundreds of dragon eyes, as great heads turned, and emotions interacted and changed. The luminescence reached up to the heights, and even the few shadows that remained had flickering colors to them. At the far end of the chamber, one of the ornate thrones was no longer empty: The biggest dragon he had yet seen—the King—sat there, and next to him was the Crystal.

Bryn looked away from it quickly, and realized that his entrance had been noticed. Gulping convulsively, he walked the gauntlet of staring faces to the foot of the throne and gave a clumsy bow.

"Sire," he squeaked, and then could think of nothing else to say.

There was a pause, in which he didn't dare look up. Then, "Keeper?" The King spoke over his head.

"Sire?"

Bryn could hear the Keeper's voice clearly from the gallery. Evidently the builders had been masters of acoustics as well.

"This is the Spaener?"

"Yes, sire."

"And you would present him to the Assembly?"

"I would, sire."

"Proceed then, Keeper of Memory."

Bryn felt a claw on his shoulder. One of the dragons near the King was indicating to him to stand aside, which he was only too grateful to do.

The Keeper stood up. She spoke from the gallery, as befitting a female, but it was clear that she had the male Assembly's respect nonetheless. There was barely a fidget during her long and detailed review of past Spaeners and their effect on the Paths of dragon-kind. Even the puffin was mentioned.

"And now," she said, "a new Spaener? We have followed the Path of the Crystal faithfully, and now it is time to find another way? Is that what this human and his artifacts mean to us? I have searched the Memory for precedents, and this is what I have found."

This is it, thought Bryn, but even as the Keeper drew breath to speak, another voice cut across the expectant silence.

"Why don't you ask the human why it's *really* here?"

An enormous copper-colored dragon separated itself from the crowd.

"Lord Rad?" said the King. "You wish to speak? *Before* the Keeper is finished?"

The dragon lord bowed low, acknowledging the criticism, but he did not withdraw from his position on the floor.

"Very well." The King indicated his permission, and the Keeper reluctantly sat down. Bryn felt the blood drain away from his face as Lord Rad bowed once more and then, with exaggerated slowness, straightened. But for a long moment the dragon ignored him and just looked at the floor, as if deep in thought.

"Why *is* the human here?" Rad began to pace the Hall, wondering aloud. "Is it out of its deep-felt desire to aid dragon-kind?" The lord tilted his head coyly to the side. "Did it say to its little self, 'What *shall* I do today? I know! I'll go to the City and tell the Dragon High Assembly how to do its job.'" His voice dropped down from whining mimicry to a deep warning growl.

"No. The creature has desires of its own. It planned to *steal* the Crystal . . . for itself."

There was a shocked gasp from the assembled crowd.

"That's a lie!" cried Bryn, fists clenched.

"Oh?" Lord Rad's syllable dropped, like a malignant toad, into a pool of sudden silence. For the first time he was staring directly at Bryn, and the loathing in his eyes terrified the boy. "So you can tell me in all honesty that you've never been in this place before, then, can you? You never came to the Great Hall, alone, in the dead of night, uninvited, unobserved? You never crept the length of our most sacred Assembly chamber, hugging the shadows, sneaking as close as you dared, and reached out your little hand toward the Crystal, *our Crystal*, with thoughts of theft seething in your human mind?"

Bryn was white-faced. He felt as if he couldn't breathe.

"It wasn't . . . I didn't . . . not, not exactly . . ." He stuttered to a halt, and hung his head.

Watching from the gallery, Madlen couldn't bear to see him looking so guilty, so defeated. She leapt up.

"It's not true!" she shouted furiously. "You're just twisting it! And anyway, he wasn't alone! We were there too!"

As soon as she'd said it, she knew she'd made a mistake.

She could feel the shock in the air. Madlen cursed herself for forgetting the taboos against females. She'd spent her whole life following the rules and *now* . . . !

Very slowly Lord Rad swung his head round toward the gallery.

"Ah yes," he drawled. "The female. And . . . the other one. Now what is the term for a grouping of this kind . . . a collection of humans who are after something that doesn't belong to them? Is it a gang of thieves? Liars? Tricksters? No, no, these humans are *Questors*."

"How do you know this? My lord?"

Everyone's attention turned back to the gallery.

"As the Keeper of Memory"—and she put a slight emphasis on the words, to remind him of her status—"it is essential that *all* information come to me, to be recorded and stored in the appropriate fashion. I have no record of *you* coming to me, to tell me about Questors or Quests or the threat of theft. A number of questions arise from this. One of these is, are you in possession of any *other* information I should have? And another, as already asked, is how did you find *this* out?"

Cam was impressed with the way the Keeper had shifted the moral low ground back to the lord so neatly and, without needing to actually lie, had hidden the fact that she had much of the information already.

"She's *very* good at this," Cam whispered to Madlen.

"Yeah, but how *did* that Lord Rad know? We didn't tell him!" she whispered back. "I thought The London House was supposed to be keeping us a secret!"

Rad's copper skin had darkened, but Bryn spoke before the dragon could find an answer.

"I *was* going to . . . take it," he admitted hoarsely. "I thought it was what we needed—what the Worlds needed, to bring them back into balance. *It's what we're supposed to do.* You understand about Quests—you *must*! I thought I'd found what we'd been sent for. But I was wrong." He hung his head wearily. "I really wanted the Crystal to be it, the thing we were looking for. It seemed so easy. How could I blow something so easy? I just had to walk in, and take it." He drew a ragged breath, then let it out in a wail. *"But it wasn't it!"*

This was clearly not what Lord Rad had been expecting to hear.

"Are you saying the Crystal is *not* the object of your Quest?" he blared.

Bryn shook his head miserably.

Then the King spoke. In spite of its depth and volume, his voice was not ungentle. "Are you sure? It is an object of great power."

Bryn shook his head again.

"But . . . how could you know?" the King persisted.

Barely above a whisper came the reply. "Because of what I did. After I picked it up."

"Explain, human."

Bryn looked up into the King's eyes and, almost pleadingly, tried to. "When I had it, the Crystal, in my hands, I felt completely different. I felt like I could do anything. I felt like a Hero."

Around him, great heads nodded in recognition. They'd felt it too.

"Go on."

"I'd never felt like that before. It completely swept me away— and then, and then, I found myself with my hands round my sister's throat."

There was a stunned silence, and then a low moan from the gallery.

"What did you just say?" whispered the King.

"I tried to take the Crystal and I tried to kill my sister."

"WHAT!"

The Hall erupted into hubbub, both above and below. Bryn staggered back from the force of shouted questions and exclamations.

"Leave him alone! Don't make him say it again!" yelled Madlen, and when no one listened, she almost sobbed, "It's not true anyway, not really."

But there was something about the uproar that was strange. Instead of horror and outrage on the faces of the dragons in the gallery about her, Madlen was detecting excitement all around her, even joy. And on the floor of the Hall there was confusion.

"What's happening?" Madlen yelled at Dagrod, but before the dragon could answer, the King bellowed for quiet.

"Keeper?" he said as soon as it was still. He sounded incredulous. "What does this mean?"

The Keeper uncoiled herself slowly and deliberately. When she spoke, her voice was low-pitched and subdued. "The story of Nad and his sister, Randon, is taught to every dragon child. How he killed her, mistaking her for his enemy, Arnd, because of an enchantment. Who here does *not* know the tale of their tragedy?"

She paused, as if in thought, or perhaps to let something simmer and sink in. Then, looking about the chamber, she asked another question.

"What is a Spaener," she asked, "but one who sees what is hidden? Has this human seen, without understanding, the ultimate end of our Path? Has this human, without volition, acted out the essence of the Crystal?" She lowered her head submissively. "I am only the Keeper. What the Memory holds, I present. It is my lords' decision, of course. But"—and she looked from under her brows at the crowd below, about to make a final point, the glint of victory already in her eyes—

She got no further, interrupted by another dragon lord who surged forward and roared his scorn at her and the others. *"This is treason!* An acknowledged thief as Spaener? He was told to say these things. He has been *schooled—"*

The Keeper leaned far over the Gallery railing to bellow her denial. "*That is not so!* I had no knowledge of the human's attempt on his sister. . . ."

Other voices joined in the storm, some agreeing that it was shocking, degrading to even listen to a human, others urging that it could be true, an end could be coming. For some time Lord Rad let the battle rage, and then, when he judged the moment was right, he cut across them all with his words:

"*Is this where our honor has ended?*"

There was a stunned silence, and then, "I can answer that."

A new voice had spoken, a dark contralto, and it drew the attention of every being in the room. Unnoticed, the Queen had arrived at the entrance to the Great Hall. She did not attempt to enter—the throne beside the King had been empty since the Path of the Crystal had been established. She just stood at the door, bent down—but not in submission. She was holding something with great care in her claws, shielding it with her body.

"Sire." She looked up, and spoke to the King, her voice carrying effortlessly down the length of the Hall. "Our child has hatched. We have waited a long time for a new life in the City, and now she is here." The Queen took a breath. "She is here. And she holds the answer to Lord Rad's question. *This* is where our honor has ended." And the Queen straightened, and held the tiny dragon up for all to see.

The baby was beautiful, even to human eyes, but for the terrible withering of her leg and wing. Bryn looked from the child to the mother and saw how she was drowning in a storm of love and pain.

The King left his throne. He came to her and gently took the baby from her. There was a long moment of silence. Then, without turning back to the room, the King spoke.

"Hear me. No dragon can go to the cave of Adagon's Deed.

The noise is too great to bear, and live. So this is my decision. The human is to be given the Crystal. I do not believe the cave's defenses will affect him. The Crystal is to be put back. What Adagon began, let the human finish. In this way the Path . . . is ended."

The King's voice was hardly above a whisper, but his words reached every part of the chamber. Then the King and Queen passed on, and the great double doors boomed shut behind them.

In the shocked stillness a growling noise, barely controlled, could be heard. It came from Lord Rad. He was shaking with fury, and his eyes were slit as if for battle.

"Put it back?" he grated. "What Adagon did at the cost of his life, what we have built all these years of *our* lives upon, is to be undone? And like *this*?" The words seemed to choke him.

An old dragon stepped toward him.

"You must," he said. "It is the end of the Path. It is the King's express command. Even if the Assembly would, it could not disagree."

Around the room great heads nodded in agreement, and there was a low rumble of voices.

"You must."

"The end of the Path."

"You must."

Lord Rad finally bowed his head, as if to acknowledge defeat. There was a sigh of relief from the others and then, tactfully, they began to withdraw. They moved quietly despite their bulk, and in a very little time they were all gone, until only Rad and Bryn remained.

The boy shrank into himself, trying to be invisible. He didn't dare look up. There was only silence in the room now, but it was a silence that grew and grew—until it exploded into a shriek of rage. Bryn flung himself aside just as Rad slammed his tail up, over, and down, directly onto the pillar of ice. It shattered into a million pieces that clattered across the marble floor, a glittering carpet of crystalline shapes, grabbing the light and scattering it about in countless sparks and flares.

And, somewhere in the midst of it all, was the Crystal.

Lord Rad was breathing heavily, and his voice was hoarse and wild.

"Let the human have it. Let the human have the Crystal, *our* Crystal, our honor. You can have it—*if you can find it!*"

Stunned, Bryn stared at the chaos strewn across the floor.

"But . . . that's impossible," he said.

"Impossible?" sneered Rad. "But aren't you the Spaener? Aren't you the one who *sees*? It won't be a problem for *you*. Why don't you just *look*?"

"I can't find the Crystal. I can't," repeated Bryn in a voice that cracked partway through. "No one could, not even a dragon, not just by looking."

"But a dragon can do more than just look."

Bryn jerked. It was Dagrod. It was a sign of the new times that she had come into the Great Hall, braved the Forbidden Place.

Lord Rad swung round to face her, at first not believing her audacity, then cold with scorn. "You! What can *you* do? You're just a child, a female, little more than a worm. You're *nothing*."

"I'm . . . I'll . . . You . . ." Bryn could see the fear taking over her, the courage oozing away—he understood it all so well— but then with a great effort she lifted her head, and looked Rad in the face.

"I may be nothing," she croaked, "but I can still do *this*!"

And, taking a deep breath, Dagrod flared.

Cam had been right—it *was* a totally amazing sight. Her flame was a rich umber edged with gold, and the ice fragments on the floor vanished into a veil of mist, like dew beneath the sun.

Then, with a gentle breath, she blew the mist away, and picked up the Crystal.

"Here, Bryn," she said. "Put it back."

And from the gallery came the strange noise of dragons, unseen, clicking their applause.

CHAPTER FORTY-TWO

<u>Putting It Back</u>

"This is the route Adagon took, as far as we can work out. Mapping of the Under-Ice has been sporadic, but I have done my best to collate the findings."

The Keeper handed Bryn a sheaf of overlapping transparencies made of paper-fine ice and showed him how each level was represented on a separate sheet. It was clever, just the sort of thing that would normally have intrigued him, but now he only nodded his thanks.

The tunnel leading into the maze under the City had been closed as a Forbidden Place. Willing claws had broken the seal, and then hurried away. Not surprisingly, no one had been eager to hang around.

Now Dagrod, the Keeper, and the Questors were all that remained. There was an awkward silence.

"I'll be compiling a list of mythic Quest Objects on your return," the Keeper said brightly.

Bryn nodded.

Then Madlen spoke. "And we believe him, the King, when he said that about the cave not harming humans?"

After a moment the Keeper nodded. "Most probably we do," she said.

And with that they had to be content.

Bryn had asked for and been given a small pouch made of stout leather, and the Crystal was now securely tied into it.

"I'll carry it, if you like," Cam said suddenly.

The Keeper started to speak, but Bryn interrupted.

"You're not coming," Bryn said abruptly to Cam.

"Why not?"

Bryn and the Keeper spoke at the same time. "You can't."

"There's no symmetry in that." The Keeper spoke as if stating the obvious, and, to the others' surprise, Bryn was nodding in agreement.

"I'm what's needed, not you two," he said hoarsely. "If Adagon was the Hero, and he started the Path, it's a coward that's needed to end it."

And he was gone, almost running in his eagerness to leave them behind.

The Keeper shook her head slowly.

"That's not the symmetry I had in mind," she said.

Dagrod looked confused. "What did he mean?" she wailed, but no one tried to explain.

Cam sighed, and settled down against a wall. The Keeper curled herself elaborately nearby. Madlen stood, staring after Bryn, making her horrible hum.

There was nothing more they could do. Theirs was the hard job of the ones left behind.

As he followed the map through the tunnels, Bryn kept hearing the words of the story in his mind. How Adagon had come the same way in search of his destiny, and then dragged himself back again, deafened by the great noise, bleeding and broken from his battle with the Guardian. *What would that feel like,* he wondered, *to know you were dying, and going on anyway, back up all those tunnels of ice, clutching the Crystal—my Crystal?*

He'd asked for the pouch to protect him from contact with the Crystal on the way, but now, without thinking, he reached for it in his pocket. Instantly, even through the tough leather, he could feel the cold electric buzz, the power rush. He pulled his hand away quickly, and took a deep breath to steady himself.

It shouldn't be long, he thought. *Any minute now, I should start hearing the roaring noise they talked about. Not much farther. It must be the way the tunnels keep swerving about. That must be why I'm still not hearing it.*

And then, suddenly, he found he was there. He stumbled to a halt just inside the entrance to the cave, unable to believe that it was a chamber not of deafening clamor, but instead one of an utter silence. He checked the map, to make sure he hadn't turned two sheets over by mistake, but no, this seemed to be it.

He flicked the switch of the device to be certain this was the source of the radiation, and immediately dropped it onto the ground. The thing was vibrating too hard to hold, and whining like an attack of wasps. Bryn left it where it lay, and stepped farther into the chamber.

The floor was stone—bedrock, the ancient body of the World. It was dark granite, rough and jagged, as the story had described. Toward the center, it warped up into a vent, rising several yards into the air. And from the top of the vent, pulsing like a severed artery, was . . . *something.*

It was an energy, discernible through the distortion of the air, and from the way his skin prickled, the way his blood throbbed in time to its rhythm. He knew that geysers of boiling water exploded out of the ground, but this geyser was icy cold. And while water will fall back to the earth it came from, this kept going. In the eerie stillness it fountained up to the ceiling and then seemed to just carry on, penetrating it, silently, unrelentingly. Bryn could sense it, pulsing up through all the yards of ice, into all the walls and rooms and passages of the City above, into all the living cells of all the living dragons.

It struck him just how far underground he was, and just how much tonnage of ice hung over him, waiting to collapse. He felt a kind of inverted vertigo, and for a moment he couldn't catch his breath. He staggered, and pitched forward, crashed down onto his hands and knees—

—and screamed. The pain first flowered under his palm and then blossomed through his entire body. Looking down, he saw blood pooling darkly on the rock. Shaking and sick, he saw how he'd sliced open his hand. A dragon's obsidian claw, lost in battle, wedged into a crack, cutting-edge up.

Bryn curled in on himself, moaning, cradling his hand close to his chest. Only the pain was real, and he had no defense against it. Every wall in his mind was flattened before it, and all the hidden fears and held-in shame rose up to meet it. He whimpered. The sound echoed in the silence, and then it began to change. It began to morph into another sound, a sound that was not coming from him. Dull, rasping, hardly above a whisper, but growing all the time, it came from the rock around the vent.

With a huge effort, Bryn lifted his head. He stared in horror as the rock began to shift, separating and changing its shape into a huge head with a great snout and an enormous eye.

An eye that was slowly opening.

CHAPTER FORTY-THREE

<u>The Eye and the Claw</u>

That dull, dead eye fixed him to the floor like a spike. There was a horrible gasping, panting sound that he half-knew must be coming from him.

Stone ground against stone as the Guardian lifted his head.

Thief! Fraud! it seemed to sneer. *Fight me, coward!*

Involuntarily, Bryn's hands clenched. Blood pulsed out of his wound like the poison from the vent above, so that his eyes blurred and he staggered on the edge of consciousness. He cried out, shaking his head to try to clear his sight, but when he was able to focus again, he found that the dragon had gone.

Bryn gulped. It hadn't gone—the shape was still there—but it was only stone.

He was going crazy; he felt guilty and ashamed. The desire to get away, anywhere away, beat about his head, but he was so slowed by pain and the storm of emotions battering at him that he just lay there, crying.

In the end it was exhaustion that helped him. He was used up, too tired to feel any more. He just wanted to go to bed.

But first he had to put the Crystal back.

Every movement was an effort. Panting, he managed to

half sit up and drag the leather pouch out of his pocket. And then it got worse—stupidly, unbelievably worse.

He couldn't untie the knot.

He tried to use his teeth, and his feet, but without two functioning hands, Bryn couldn't get the Crystal out of the sack. He knew he had to. He couldn't just stuff the bag into the vent. It was up to him to reunite the bare rock, the unveiled Crystal. He had to.

Then he remembered the claw. Obsidian—razor sharp. The pain pulsed up his arm. If it could *hurt* him like that, it should be able to *help* him.

He peered wearily about the cave floor. There it was, still wedged into the crack, with his blood darkly wet on it. He anchored the pouch with his foot and very, very carefully prized the claw free. The outer curve of it was smooth and safe to hold. Bryn gripped it with his good hand.

One slice, and the Crystal tumbled out onto the rock.

All he had to do now was pick the Crystal up, climb to the vent, and use the Crystal to seal the vent. All he had to do was the easy part—it was nothing—but he was just so tired. His hand throbbed, and his coat was soaked with blood where he'd been nursing it. When his mind wandered toward the thought of how much damage he'd done to himself, Bryn felt sick. *My hand! My hand!* he cried silently. *Don't go there,* he answered himself. *One thing at a time. What are you waiting for? Don't screw up now.*

Clumsily, Bryn shoved first the claw and then the Crystal into the front of his coat. He needed his good hand free. As he straightened up, his eyes blurred again and his tongue went dry. *Don't faint!* he thought urgently, but luckily the giddiness passed.

He began to climb. Even in the icy air, he was sweating. This close, the fountain of energy throbbed dizzyingly, and he could feel the power of it pulsing through his bones. Soon he was crawling. He narrowed his eyes and dragged himself onto the top.

At last he leaned against the summit of the vent and, panting, reached into his coat.

The Crystal came out smeared in blood. It wasn't beautiful anymore. It was just a bit of stained rock. He'd wondered what it would do to him to touch it again. Would it make him feel like a Hero? Would he be able to bear to give it away? But now that the time had come, he felt nothing. Just a great weariness, and a wish for it all to be over.

Bryn reached out his hand, and dropped the Crystal into place.

The chamber shuddered gently, once, and then it was as if the light had gone out. Not that it darkened—but the pounding blazing icy fountain that had powered up with such deadly strength—it was as if *that* had never been.

Bryn looked about him for a moment. He didn't notice that the device, on the floor by the entrance, was finally still. With a little sigh he slipped back down the slope, loose-limbed, unconscious.

DALRODIA

CHAPTER FORTY-FOUR

<u>Bryn Wakes Up</u>

It was hot. He felt horribly uncomfortable, as if he'd fallen asleep in an awkward position and forgotten to move. His mouth was dry, and his eyes ached when he tried to prize them open.

"Where am I?" he croaked.

Someone rustled up from the foot of the bed.

"Well, what do you know," said a familiar voice. "People actually do *say* that."

"Madlen?"

"That's me." She stood beside the bed, looking down at him.

She seemed different, but he was too muddled to think how. He blinked stupidly.

"I'm under oath to fetch Serena the moment you stir," she continued. "So wait here. I mean it, don't you dare go away again."

She floated off. *Go away again?* Bryn thought. *What's that about?* He could feel himself starting to drift toward sleep, and was only dimly aware when a large woman suddenly appeared from out of nowhere. She fussed at him irritatingly, making him drink, and messing with his pillow, but she smelled quite nice, and before he could properly protest, he *was* asleep.

When he next woke, Cam and Madlen were both there in the room. They'd been ordered not to tire him out, apparently, but that didn't stop them trying to fill him in on what had happened after the cave.

It didn't stop Madlen, anyway. Cam seemed preoccupied and restless.

"When we found you, we thought you were *dead*!" Madlen exclaimed. "You'd certainly bled enough!"

Bryn didn't want to think about that. "But how did you know to come looking for me?" he asked instead. "I mean, how did the dragons know the vent had been sealed?"

Madlen laughed. "That was so weird," she said. "You remember Dagrod complaining about that buzzing in her ears? You know, she mentioned it when we first arrived at the City, and she kept rubbing at her head and stuff?"

Bryn nodded.

"Well," continued Madlen. "There we all were, sitting around and worrying, and Dagrod and everybody was pacing up and down and it was all really tense but boring at the same time, you know? And *then*, the dragons suddenly froze. They just stopped, midpace, with these goopy expressions on their faces. And Cam said, 'What's wrong?' and they said, 'It's stopped! The noise has stopped! Can't you hear it?' Which, if you think about it, is not a truly sensible question. Apparently, the tinnitus was how the dragons perceived the energy leak!"

Bryn stared at her. "They were *hearing* it?"

"Yeah, and you know what is even weirder? When you plugged the vent, the lights went out! I don't mean all the lights, but the ones like the aurora—you know?—all at once they weren't there anymore! And when *I* said, 'Where'd the flickering lights go?' *Dagrod* said, *'What flickering lights?'"*

"They'd never seen them in the first place," said Cam, showing interest in the conversation for the first time. "We *saw* the radiation—but they *heard* it." It shook its head. "Just goes to show, doesn't it?"

"Just goes to show what?" said Bryn.

Cam shrugged. "Dragons aren't like people?" it suggested, and lapsed back into moodiness.

"Well *that's* profound," snorted Madlen.

Bryn leaned back against the pillows. "But there's another thing I don't get. What am I doing *here*?" He wrinkled his forehead. "It's not like there aren't any doctors on Kir."

"Take too long to get you to them," said Madlen.

"Yeah. I guess. But how did we get *here*?"

Madlen hooted and Cam started to turn red.

"What a performance!" she said. "You should have seen it, Bryn! Cam marched right up to the Keeper and *demanded* you be sent to the Holder palace on Dalrodia for immediate medical treatment, just like that, like, I don't know, it simply *expected* to be obeyed. And it worked! The Keeper bustled off and got another map and—would you believe it?—there was a tunnel to here! Sealed, of course."

"A tunnel to another *World*?"

"All very top secret, apparently. Dagrod's eyes got so big I swear they were going to fly off her face. Seems this tunnel dates back to before human times—'pre-infestation,' as the dragons so elegantly put it. Anyway, they were sealing it up again almost before we'd got you inside, and then, I don't know, there was a sort of shift, and we were someplace else. Here, actually, only on a lower level. A deserted bit, but security is so tight . . ." She looked embarrassed. "All I did was sneeze, and a million alarms went off and there were these big hulking guys piling in. I think at first they thought we were invading animals, all covered in fur like that—and pretty stupid animals too, with an air temperature of about four hundred degrees!"

"Did you know you talk in your sleep?" Cam said to Bryn in the interests of changing the subject.

"What a stupid question!" Madlen scoffed. "How could he possibly know what he does when he's asleep?"

Bryn ignored her. "I talk in my sleep? Cool! What do I say?"

"Mostly you talked about *that*." Cam pointed at the dragon claw.

It was on the small table beside his bed. He picked it up and stroked the smooth side of it with his thumb.

"You know, I almost think I remember that. Did you try to take it away or something?"

Madlen nodded.

"I didn't want to lose it," he continued. "It makes me feel better, even though . . . Kate was right. You just *know*. It's almost like the Quest Object finds *you*, instead of the other way round."

Madlen gave a half gasp, half squeak.

"I knew it! I knew it!" she squealed. "I told you that the claw was it. I *told* you!" She turned to Cam, then stopped. "You're still not convinced, are you?"

Bryn looked at it. "Well? Come on, what's the trouble? Spit it out," he said.

Cam looked miserable. "Well . . . I feel like a poop, but . . . I can't help wondering, just a bit, if maybe you're thinking the claw's the second Quest thing because . . . it's all you've got. Sorry."

Bryn thought for a minute.

"Yeah, well, you *are* a poop, but"—and he nodded at the claw in his hand—"*this* isn't something you need to worry about. I don't want to sound all pompous and mythic, but this is just something I *know*. It's like it's *outside* worry, like that bit of The London House, you know? It's like it's . . . it's sitting in the middle of a sort of puddle of calm." He grinned. "Like a frog in a pond in the summertime. Do you have frogs?"

Cam shrugged. "There are sand frogs. I don't suppose they worry much."

"What a World!" murmured Madlen, and suddenly Bryn yawned.

"Sorry!" he apologized. "No idea where *that* came from!"

"*I* do!" It was Serena, on cue. "Now, then," she said to Bryn. "No need to look as grim as all that! I'll be very careful, I promise." Serena sat on the bed and took his bandaged hand between her own. He gave her a weak smile, but she didn't notice. She was paying attention to something else. For a long time she just sat there, breathing. Then, from nowhere, he felt a warmth in his hand that hadn't been there before, and a strange, slight shifting in his bones.

Serena sighed deeply. Her eyes came back into focus, and she gave him a smile and a nod.

"Right," she said, getting up to leave. "You'll do. Now scamper off, you two, and let the boy slee—"

"No," Bryn interrupted. "Wait, Serena—I need to know . . . my hand—is it going to be—?"

"He's an artist, you see," Madlen butted in. "It's his drawing hand."

Bryn closed his eyes for a moment, automatically mortified, but then he opened them again and nodded. "That's right."

Serena sat down again and looked directly at him.

"It's a fair question," she said, "and I'll give you a fair answer. It was a bad wound. I'd be lying if I told you otherwise. And it'll be a long road to it being the way it was, and that's the truth too. *But* with care and careful exercise and plenty of rest and *no drawing* for a good long time to come—"

Bryn leaned over and kissed her on both cheeks.

"Serena," he said solemnly. "I love you."

Her blush was monumental. "Now, now, none of that! People will be talking about us!"

"Let them!" he declared.

CHAPTER FORTY-FIVE

<u>Ivory</u>

Cam was desperately worried, too worried to talk to the others. It could hardly bear to admit what it feared even to *itself.* But at some point soon the words would have to be said out loud.

Ivory—its mother, the Lady Holder of the whole World, the sure and certain center of its entire life—Ivory had gone mad.

Everything that was happening pointed to it. What else could it be? The only other possible explanation was that she was evil—consciously, willfully wicked—and that was inconceivable.

Wasn't it?

Cam's uneasiness about Ivory had started almost at once. The first chance it could get—after Serena had taken charge of Bryn, and Madlen had been settled into a guest room—Cam had dragged its mother away and poured it all out—all the things that had been happening, the unbalancing of the Worlds, the Quest, its longing for Ivory and home. And Ivory had done everything right. She'd hugged Cam and called it Little Lizard, just as she used to, and exclaimed and gone "Ah!" in all the right places, and the reunion had been everything Cam had been missing, and yet in the end Cam felt . . . unsatisfied.

Unsatisfied and grumpy, and aware of being unreasonable as well.

She'd noticed, of course. Cam had never been able to hide anything from her. And Cam could see she was hurt.

"You need to rest now," was all she'd said, though. "And tomorrow I've got something to show you."

And, even then, something felt *wrong*. Even then.

She'd come to Cam's room early with good news about Bryn.

"Serena insists he's out of danger, and she's very proud of *you* for getting him to her so quickly!" She smiled. Cam could smell the perfume she always wore, cool and warm at the same time. "Will you come with me? I've something I want you to see."

As Cam had stood up to follow her, she'd put a hand on its shoulder.

"Cam," she'd said. "I don't want you to think that no one but you is aware of what's been happening, that there's no one else trying to make things right. It's too much, and you're too young, and the fate of the Worlds is too heavy a burden for children to shoulder alone."

"I'm not as young as I was," said Cam a little huskily.

"No. Of course not. But I want you to know that adults have been engaged as well!"

She'd let Cam go then, and had led the way into the body of the cliff. Cam thought it knew every nook and cranny, until they came to a door that had never been there before.

Ivory placed her palm against the access panel. Then she looked across at Cam.

"You know, I never had the heart to take you off the access program," she said with a sad sort of smile.

Cam was startled. Then it remembered that, to Ivory, it had been away for ten long years.

She had already started moving off.

"Ivory, wait. Tell me where we're going!"

She slowed, but didn't turn her head. When she spoke, her words had an almost mechanical quality to them, as if she were repeating something learned by rote.

"I'm taking you to see the drill head. We're attempting to access the water table. I believe that is what will save the World."

Simple words, but they caused Cam to stop short and grab Ivory's arm.

"What are you talking about?" It could barely speak. "Everybody knows that's suicide! Everybody knows once you tap the base water table, you'll be destabilizing the entire geology of the World. . . . The earthquakes! You're already doing it! I heard about a tremor while we were at The London House—out Tantalan way. We're having earthquakes because you've *already* destabilized—"

Cam let go of her and stepped away until it was backed against the wall.

"But what about the desalination plan? The cloud cropping idea? Artificial water production? *None* of them worked? You've ditched them all *already?*"

Ivory just looked at it. "You forget how long you've been away, Cam. Below a certain level of surface water, desalination would have been pointless. Farming rain clouds was also an idea that assumed a certain level of moisture to seed from. And the dreams have all pointed explicitly away from every route but one. The water table. Drilling began not long after you left us."

"You had a dream that told you to drill?"

"More clearly than you can imagine! And not just one!" Ivory's pale cheeks were flushed. Cam hadn't seen her so excited in a long time. She looked almost . . . frantic.

And it was all so *wrong.* Dreams weren't supposed to *be* clear, not at first glance, and they did not give specific instructions! True dreams made you work for their meaning; it took years of training on top of a natural aptitude; true dreams . . .

In spite of the heat, Cam shivered. "Tell me about it."

Ivory's smile was a little tremulous. "You've no idea how good it is to hear somebody say that!" she said. "It's been so long since I've been able to discuss things with anyone. Not really since your father died. Before you left, I was holding on, waiting for you to be ready to train, hoping your father's blood would—"

Cam put its hand on her arm again, gently this time.

"There's not time for all that now, is there?" it said. "Everything's different. You've just got me as I am."

Her smile was heartbreakingly sad. "I've missed you badly all these years, Camlet. And I'll tell you something I'm not proud of—I've hated that woman for having you when I didn't." She laughed, a dry sound. "Perhaps that's why I've got so old."

But Cam wasn't ready to talk about Kate. *One thing at a time,* it thought. *I can do this. I can get this clear. I have to get this clear.*

"How did you know where to dig?" Cam asked.

Ivory shook herself, getting a grip. "The information was all there," she said more firmly, "but so buried in the archives I would never have ordinarily stumbled on it." Ivory shook her head in wonder. "If the computer hadn't crashed when it did . . . It was when I was reinstalling from the backups that this file title just leapt out at me. 'Geological Survey Chart of Fault

Access to Subterranean/Base Waterbed.' Then, of course, it was gone. I couldn't believe I'd actually seen it at first, and it took ages to stop the installation, scroll back. I was afraid I'd gone too far, not gone far enough . . . but there it was. Who knows how long it had been there, squirreled away in the computer's memory, completely forgotten by us. Makes you wonder what other treasures we have without knowing!"

"Makes you wonder," Cam repeated. *There must be another explanation.* The words kept circling round its brain. *There must be another explanation.*

The air was getting hotter as the tunnel sloped deeper down under the cliff. Cam wiped a sleeve across its face. Ivory noticed the gesture.

"The workers suffer. We've had to improvise individual air filters for them to wear, since the quality's so bad, but there's been no efficient way to combat the increased heat. I don't remember how many degrees per foot down, but—"

"What's that noise?" Cam interrupted. The clamor had been growing steadily as Ivory was speaking.

"That's the drill head. It's quite loud."

They turned a corner and there it was—a cavern that pulsed with the noise of machinery at full throttle; men shouting to be heard; dollies of dross from the shaft trundling across the littered stone floor to a lift that disappeared through another shaft in the roof, the dross to be dumped on the surface far above. Metal—stone—dust—heat, battering at what was only flesh and blood, an unequal struggle.

"It's awful!" Cam bleated inadequately, but Ivory was already striding ahead to meet the Foreman, and didn't hear.

She had almost reached him, when a horrible Klaxon began to sound, cutting through the clamor with a new note of panic and despair. The Foreman swung away, heading for a structure in the center of the area—he and every other soul in the place.

"An accident!" shouted a man Cam grabbed in passing. "There's been another accident down the shaft!"

Cam and Ivory stood on the outskirts of the crowd. All work on the site had been abandoned, and in the comparative quiet they could clearly hear the lift laboring up the shaft toward them.

The sound stopped, and everyone rushed forward to drag open the doors. The blast of heat and stink made Cam reel even at that distance, but the workmen didn't appear to notice. They pulled the survivors out of the lift and helped them to the medical stations with practiced efficiency. The last man had to be carried. His friend tried to follow him, but came to a trembling standstill at the edge of the crowd, and stood there swaying, bewildered. Ivory went over to him at once, and he stared at her, as if not sure what he was seeing.

"The cooling system broke down again. He stayed behind to secure the dig face." The man's whole body was shaking uncontrollably. "He made us go back to the lift first, and he stayed behind. I should have stayed but . . . I was . . . I couldn't . . ."

Ivory took his filthy hands into hers and looked into his eyes.

"Go and rest," she said. "You're not afraid. You didn't do anything wrong. The heat sickness is speaking, not you."

She gestured to one of the workmen, and he took the man from her with great gentleness. She didn't move. But before Cam could speak to her, the Foreman came back.

"I'm sorry you had to see that, Lady," he said, wiping his face and looking anxious.

Ivory shook her head. "I sent them down," she said simply.

"The men know the risks. They wouldn't go if they didn't

trust you; if they didn't believe the work was worth it."

Gravely, Ivory tilted her head and inclined it slightly—and Cam was once again overwhelmed by her gracefulness and her unerring ability to find the right gesture, the right phrase. Without saying a word she had told the Foreman how deeply she appreciated their faith in her; reassured him that their faith was well-founded; made him, even more unshakeably, her man. Even though Cam knew down to its bones that Ivory was *wrong,* the drilling was wrong, their confidence in her was wrong, still Cam couldn't help but admire, and wonder to itself, *How does she know how to do it?*

Will I ever be able to, half so well?

CHAPTER FORTY-SIX

<u>The Research Department</u>

"So they've put you in the Research Department," Mrs. Macmahonney said. "How very stupid of them."

Kate groaned. "I know! Everybody knows it's fieldwork I'm good at—"

But Mrs. Mac shook her head. "No, I mean, how very stupid of them to let you loose *in the one place they shouldn't*!"

In the Basement of The London House, the reluctant researcher gave a tiny inadvertent yip.

"Find something?" Her Supervisor came over quickly, but the new recruit's screen was blank.

"No, sorry," she said. "It was nothing. Cramp." And she rubbed at her calf apologetically.

"You're not used to sitting still so long," the Supervisor explained kindly. "Tell you what, why don't you pop out to the kitchen and see what's happened to our morning coffee? Tell Mrs. Macmahonney the troops are gasping. Give your legs a stretch at the same time."

"Thanks. I will!"

He didn't notice her palming the disk at all.

❋ ❋ ❋

"HA!"

Kate sashayed up to the kitchen table and, with a flourish, laid a small disk down in front of Mrs. Macmahonney. Mrs. Mac looked from it to Kate's flushed face and back down again.

"When you say 'HA,'" she said, "can I take it that you mean . . . ?"

Kate nodded, grinning like a grinny thing.

As Mrs. Mac carefully inserted the disk into the toaster, Kate hung over her shoulder and told her all about it.

"Of course he was too smart to leave any kind of record of where he'd been in the body," she said. "And of course he'd hidden his computer files, though I found some, but then they were so locked up they were worse than nothing. BUT he *wasn't* smart enough to remember the way the backwash lights up the path echoes of mind-travel."

The toaster popped. Mrs. Mac took the lid off the slightly cracked butter dish sitting beside it, then lifted out and uncurled a roll of read-out.

"So we still don't know what he's been up to, but by all that's short and furry, *we know where!* He's been poking his horrible nose into Dalrodia's business, here, and here."

"Messing around in some poor soul's mind."

"Not just any poor soul—look at this!"

Kate looked. "He's gone for the Holder? But surely she'd *notice!*"

"Not if she were asleep at the time," said Mrs. Mac, leaning back and fixing Kate with a grim eye. "He's been directing her dreams."

Kate whistled. "But, then, they're not safe where she is! Who knows what he might tell her to do to them!" Kate was starting to get breathless. "They've got to leave—*now*!"

"We've got to get word to them some way that no one else will notice," said Mrs. Mac, tapping the table speculatively with one finger.

"Lord Bullvador—," began Kate, but Mrs. Mac shook her head at once.

"Cordell would find out," she said. "No, we need to be *beneath* his notice, like in the Basement."

"Research?" Then Kate's voice changed. "Research . . ."

"It's my guess you won't be the only one ferreting," said Mrs. Mac. "Cam's bound to be doing some research of its own. We'll slip in a message anywhere we think it might look."

"I'll get on to that, then. But what if Cam doesn't use a computer?"

"Then we fall back on The One Great Truth."

Kate looked puzzled. "I don't remember that. What is The One Great Truth?"

Mrs. Mac looked gnomic and tapped her nose. "Everybody has to eat," she said.

CHAPTER FORTY-SEVEN

"It's really, really nice here, Cam," said Madlen.

Bryn had been declared fit to be up, and the three were gathered in Cam's elegant suite of rooms.

Cam didn't answer.

"I really like the way you live," Madlen persisted. "It's cultured, you know? And gentle and witty and . . . *pretty*!"

"And it smells nice," added Bryn helpfully. When Madlen turned on him, he raised his good hand in defense. "What? It does smell nice. It smells lousy on my World, when it's not actually frozen, of course. Obviously, *ice* doesn't smell—"

"Ivory's gone mad," grated Cam suddenly.

There was a shocked silence, then, "She's—," began Madlen.

"You—," began Bryn

But Cam just shook its head, and told them about the drilling, its sense of wrongness, *everything.*

"Only a crazy person would do that to the World," Cam finished.

The others exchanged appalled looks.

"But, well," Bryn tried, "maybe when we've found the last

Quest thing, and taken it back to the Council, and they've done . . . whatever, then it'll be okay again. Yeah? She won't be crazy anymore and your World'll be all fixed, and—"

"It's too late."

"What do you mean? The land's too messed up by the sun—gone past the point of no return sort of thing?"

Cam just shook its head. "It's not the land. It's us. *We're* what's gone past the point of no return."

"You don't know that!" exclaimed Madlen. "Look, couldn't you get hold of a bit of Dream Apple and eat it and, you know, dream up the answer to it all? Or at least where we're supposed to be looking for the Quest Object? It'd be a huge help."

"No. I'm not old enough. It doesn't work on emergents. And besides, there's no reason to think I'd know how to interpret it if I could. Takes training."

"And you can't ask Ivory to help because she's . . ."

"Mad. That's right."

"Okay, you're really going to have to help us here," said Bryn. "Explain the whole dream thing—*slowly*, okay? And then we'll be in a better position to judge what's what."

"Yeah," said Madlen. "I mean, I know what a dream is—you know, the way the brain sort of fires randomly when you're asleep, that sort of thing? What I don't see is how you can run a World on the basis of them."

Cam took a deep breath. "Okay, I'll try. This is how it works. Dreams are visions. We interpret them, to tell us how to order our actions and how to understand what's going on. Holders are the Inner World's official dreamers, and we have access to the Corym."

Blank faces confronted it. Cam tried again.

"See, in order to dream with really proper significance, the dreamer must first eat the Corym fruit. It's a tree that's unique to this World, and it's also uniquely tuned to Dalrodian DNA. Well, Holder DNA. Long ago there were lots of Corym trees all over the World and anybody could eat and dream. But some people were just better at it than other people, and then it sort of started to run in families, I guess, and then, gradually, they got to be called Holders. . . ."

Cam trailed off, and looked at the others anxiously.

"So . . . ," said Madlen slowly, "the way it's ended up is, you get to make the rules if you dream, and you only get to dream if you're a ruler. Is that it?"

Cam looked depressed.

Bryn said quickly, "It's no different anywhere else, Madlen, is it? Let's stick to the point here. Why do you think Ivory's crazy, or having crazy dreams, or whatever it is you think?"

"Look, I'll show you." Cam went to the monitor on the desk. "I've been doing some research. Ivory said her dreams told her to drill down to the waterbed. I've checked, and that's exactly what the dreams do! They show our people doing just that, no doubt about it. There's absolutely no other way you could possibly interpret those dreams."

"And . . . that's bad," said Bryn tentatively.

Cam groaned in frustration. "YES IT'S BAD! It's wrong. It's not a real dream. Here, look at this." Cam turned to the computer and called up a file. "As far as I can see, this is Ivory's last *sane* dream. She had this dream not long before I left. Since then they've been getting gradually more and more *wrong*."

The others gathered round, unsure what to expect. What they got was like a movie. Ivory was doing the voice-over, describing in words what the computer had re-created on the screen. The three watched and listened.

"This is what I dreamed, as truly as I can say. . . .

"I was standing on a hill, looking down on a place where people were making a city. Time was speeded up, so that I could see walls and buildings rising and falling, built and decayed and knocked down for new houses and public places and temples and schools, so fast it was like watching ripples blown across sand. The people moved too fast to even see, except as blurs in the streets and alleys. And then trees shot up, all over the city, of every sort, and I was so caught up in watching them that I didn't see the city walls melt away for the last time. But then I realized that the city was over and only crumbling ruins remained. The trees lasted a little longer, but then they died and dried in the wind. The wind petrified them, so that they became like jagged teeth in a skull when life is long gone."

Her voice was desolate.

"And that, I thought, was the end of the dream. So I started to turn away, feeling so tired, so sad, and then movement caught my eye once more." They could hear her voice brighten. "It was the trees. I'm almost sure I saw them . . . walking! It was only a glimpse, because the dream really *was* over, but I believe I *did* see them walk!"

Cam pressed the pause button, and turned to the others. "That's a proper dream. It's not OBVIOUS! I mean, it's obvious it's the Forgotten City she's seeing—that's an ancient place out in the desert—there's no mistaking *that*. But there's nothing saying, 'Go do this!' It has to be thought about and lived with and understood. And you need to be wise and experienced to do that. Oh cripes, do you understand a word I've been saying?"

Cam was reaching out its hand to slam shut the file, when all of a sudden a message box popped up.

"Eh?"

The message was short, and clear. It said,
LEAVE NOW!

It's getting worse, thought Ivory groggily. *I never used to sleep in the day so much.*

The Corym was running low again. *First free day I'll get the plane out,* she thought. *I'll take Cam—and the other two—they should see the Well. . . .*

She didn't even remember taking the apple this time, but when she lifted the box on her desk, it certainly felt lighter than before. She sighed, and pulled her computer over into position, ready to get her dream filed. Then her bleariness vanished, and the dream flooded back into her brain. In horrible unavoidable clarity it came back to her what she had to do.

"Oh, Cam!" she whispered into the emptiness. "Little Lizard, I'm so sorry!"

"I haven't got a clue about that," Cam was saying, "but we have to *go.* We're not going to find anything here. I mean, you know how you both knew you had the right thing because it felt right?"

They nodded.

"Well, *nothing* feels right here."

The other two sighed, thinking of the soft beds, the lovely rooms, the food . . . but they didn't disagree.

"Got any idea where it is?" asked Madlen.

"Not really. But I know where we're going to start looking."

"Where?"

"We're going to the Forgotten City. Maybe we'll even find the footprints of the trees Ivory dreamed about."

"And if we don't?"

"Oh, *I* don't know!" said Cam, exasperated. "Maybe we'll go look for the Woman of the Mountain. They say she knows everything, so she should know enough to help us."

"What Woman of the Mountain is that?" asked Madlen.

Cam flicked a hand. "No, forget it, she's just a story I remember. From when I was little."

There was a plate of curved cookies on the table. Without paying much attention, Bryn snagged a handful and stuffed one into his mouth.

"Stories can be—," he started to say, when he suddenly spat the cookie out again. "Yuck. There's . . . paper in this cookie!" he exclaimed.

"Of course there is. They're fortune cookies. . . . Bryn? . . . Bryn!"

Bryn held out the slightly chewed bit of paper. Cam took it, and read the message aloud.

"LEAVE NOW!"

Madlen was busy opening the rest of the cookies. The message was the same in all of them.

"Wow," she murmured. "That settles it, I guess!"

"Yeah," said Bryn. "Even Fortune Cookies Anonymous wants us out. Unless you think—"

"Somebody's trying to kill us again!" quavered Madlen, pushing the bits of paper away from her.

But Cam just grinned. It held up the plate, and showed her what was printed on the bottom.

PROPERTY OF THE LONDON HOUSE—RETURN TO KITCHEN

"Mrs. Mac!" the three chorused—then jumped guiltily when a loud knock came at the door. Frantically they stuffed the plate and messages under the bed as Cam called, "Come in?"

The door opened.

It was Ivory.

CHAPTER FORTY-EIGHT

<u>Tagged</u>

"Sit down, children."

They did so, looking around the unfamiliar, unpleasant room.

The Palace was surrounded by a sprawling Service Sector known as the Area. Ivory had led them into a part that even Cam had never visited before, and now she stood and looked at the three with an odd expression on her face.

"I've brought you here because I'm going to have you tagged."

Madlen and Bryn were no wiser, but Cam gasped as if someone had just landed a kick in its gut.

Taking a breath, Ivory plowed on.

"It's for your own good—"

Cam stood up so fast its chair fell over. "*Good?* What does shaming your own child have to do with its *good*? Or, that's right I forgot, I'm not your child, am I . . ." Cam stopped, choking on the words. "This isn't good. It's evil."

The others had never seen Cam in such a state.

"Um," said Bryn tentatively. "Tagging?"

Ivory seemed unable to speak. Cam, its hot eyes never leaving her face, answered them.

"You wouldn't understand. You probably won't even have heard of what they do here, because it isn't something we *like* Other-Worlders to know." Cam paused, took a breath, and continued. "You might think, looking around, that all is well in Dalrodia. What a perfect World. Everybody knows their place. Everybody's happy where they are. So of course there is no crime. Happy, sane people don't commit crimes, do they, so anybody who does must be *in*sane. And insane people need to be watched. All the time."

"That's right, young Holder. Watching and checking, that's how it works."

The Tag Master's entrance had taken them by surprise. He moved very quietly for such a large man. He had obviously been heavily muscled in his younger days, but the muscle had gone to fat now. His Dalrodian clothes strained across his paunch; the features of his face had become blurred by fat; and his mouth was wet and red.

"I'd heard we had visitors. Other-Worlders." He took a small step toward Madlen, and then seemed to remember himself.

"Lady." He turned and bowed, belatedly, to Ivory. "It is an honor. How may I serve you?"

Ivory's nostrils twitched slightly, but otherwise she showed no reaction.

"You are right, Master. These two are visitors. Guests. Please explain our system to them."

A look crossed the man's fat face, just for an instant, and it suddenly seemed to Bryn that there was a frightening intelligence behind those piggy eyes.

"Well, well. An honor."

And the Tag Master showed them how Dalrodia controlled its people. He called down a big screen with a map, with hundreds of little moving lights scattered across it.

"We like to know where our Tagged are, young sir and madam. Always. Especially in recent times, recent *difficult* times."

"But . . . there are so *many*!" Madlen murmured, turning to Cam, but obviously Cam too had had no idea.

Then the Master showed them the cufflike wrist tags, with the integral needle on the inner side.

"I slide that," he said, "ever so gently, into a vein and I have access to everything I need. Adrenaline levels, mainly. The Tag Master's friend," he said, and leered at them. "It goes up, and I think, Is the individual in question having a lovely healthy jog in the fresh air, or is he—or as it might be, she—doing something . . . inappropriate? So I send in the Checkers. Just to be on the safe side. It's all for their own good, oh yes, no doubt about that. We wouldn't do it otherwise, would we, now?"

Ivory's face paled at the echo of her words coming from his lips, but she managed to control her voice when she spoke.

"Thank you, Master. And now, I would like you to tag them."

The man's eyes lit up strangely, and his teeth showed.

"Not a social visit, then," he murmured. "Well, well. And I have this right—you wish me to tag the young Holder here? The Other-Worlders too?"

Ivory inclined her head, and looked sick.

"My, my . . . at once, Lady."

He made quite a show of swabbing their skin with antiseptic, and then injecting a little anesthetic, before inserting the needle. And in fact it didn't hurt, much. The wrist tag itself was surprisingly heavy, though, and hard to ignore. And Cam's registered a too-high adrenaline level almost at once, causing an alarm to go off and two burly Checkers to storm into the room on the double. Cam quickly dropped its sleeve over the tag, blushing furiously.

"False alarm, false alarm," said the Tag Master, and waved them out again.

"A minor adjustment," he said to Cam, and taking a small diagnostic pad, he passed it a number of times over Cam's wrist. Cam looked aside, refusing to acknowledge his existence.

Then it was done.

"This has been difficult . . . for all of us." Ivory looked small, suddenly, and strangely far away, as if seen down the wrong end of a telescope.

She's under terrible pressure, thought Madlen. *She's not as strong as I thought,* thought Bryn. *Mother!* thought Cam.

"I'd like you to go to your rooms now and rest. I have business to finish with the Master."

Mystified, and suddenly weary, Madlen and Bryn followed Cam out of the room.

"Tag Master."

"Lady."

"I want them on a private frequency. This one. You will take no action at any point without first consulting me. I will be assigning my own men to look after them."

"But, Lady"—the Tag Master's bow somehow managed to be obscenely familiar—"*I* am your own man."

Ivory shuddered. She placed the slip with the frequency code, and a purse of something heavy, on the table.

Then she turned and walked away.

"I'm only going to say this once. I was wrong. She's not mad. She's evil."

They had returned to Cam's suite in silence. They'd eaten the food they were brought in silence. Then, when the dishes had been taken away, Cam spoke. They'd never heard Cam sound so cold and controlled before. So *still.*

"But, Cam—"

"Wait, though—"

"We haven't time to argue," Cam cut them off. "The system allows a twelve-hour cooling down period, to allow the Tagged to become accustomed to what's happened to them, to let the adrenaline levels even out. We want to be well away from here by then. We stick to the original plan. We go to the Forgotten City. We try to find out what my . . . that dream meant." For a second the deadness in its voice wavered, then Cam was back in control. "First, we rest while we can. Then I need to get some things organized. And then . . ." Cam held up its hand, palm forward. "It'll be time for an unscheduled power cut!"

        .

In a corridor of The London House

"Have you located them?"

"Dalrodia, Preceptor."

"And still intact?"

"Essentially, yes, Preceptor. The boy sustained an injury—"

"Will he die of it?"

"Unlikely, Preceptor."

The figure swore, briefly but with venomous creativity.

"But I have arranged matters so that they should continue to be easy to find."

The Preceptor gave a grudging nod. "That will do. Things now are coming to a crisis point in the Council. I may not be at leisure to speak with you again this side of the finish, so pay

*attention. The time for finesse is over. I need—I require—them
dead. See to it."*

*Cordell showed no surprise. He inclined his head, and
turned to leave.*

*At the last moment the Preceptor put a hand on his sleeve to
detain him. It was an intimacy that was uncharacteristic—and
unwelcome.*

"See to it," the Preceptor repeated, "but do not be seen . . ."

*Cordell waited a moment, but there was nothing more. The
Preceptor, reluctantly it seemed, let him go.*

Kate leaned over Mrs. Macmahonney's shoulder. Mrs. Mac was
at her big stove, staring intently into an enormous frying pan.
The room filled with the smell of hot extra virgin olive oil.

"Water."

Kate hurried off and filled a glass from the tap. Mrs. Mac took
it from her, delicately dipped three fingers, and flicked them
over the pan.

The droplets immediately sizzled into steam.

"Not yet," she murmured, and dipped her fingers again.

Again the water vanished. But the third time . . .

"Got 'em!" said Mrs. Mac triumphantly.

Three tiny perfect globes of water danced in place over the
hot oil. The two women peered anxiously into the pan.

"Still sitting tight. What are they *waiting* for?" Kate had just
started to say—

—when the three droplets began to move.

CHAPTER FORTY-NINE

<u>Out into the Night</u>

The desert at night astonished Madlen and Bryn. They had really seen it before only off in the distance, in the battering glare of the day, under a brassy sky more like a lid than anything else. But now—

"I never knew it was ever not hot on your World!" said Bryn, snuffing up the dry cool air appreciatively.

"And the stars!" exclaimed Madlen.

Away from the ambient light of the Area, the black sky exploded into brilliant speckles and sweeps of stars. The constellations were the same as those the other two were used to, but the brightness and clarity were . . . Other-Worldly.

"It's because there's no moisture in the atmosphere," explained Cam, "so nothing much gets in the way." It paused, adding quietly, "I'd forgotten it was like this." For the first time the deadness began to leave Cam's voice.

Escaping the Palace had been surprisingly easy. Cam had required supplies and sonks (Dalrodia's desert beasts, used for riding and load-carrying), and what a high-caste required, it got. Then, just after dark, Cam had accessed the power grid, programmed in "First Grade Maintenance Shutdown" and pressed "Enter."

"Thank goodness Ivory got sentimental about not taking your print off the programs!" Madlen had commented nervously.

Once they'd led the animals well past the perimeter, Cam turned to its siblings.

"Right," it said. "Up you get."

The other two looked alarmed.

"No way! I've never ridden *anything* before! I thought we were going to walk!"

"Hey, don't forget I'm one-handed here!"

"Have you ever sat on a sofa?" Cam was not impressed by their panic. "If you can do that, you can ride a sonk."

The animals certainly *seemed* harmless. They looked a bit like blobby mules wearing snowshoes and outsize hairy overcoats.

"Look at it this way," said Cam, climbing aboard one. "It's maybe four hours riding, all night to walk, and the Checkers will be heading after us the minute the power's back up. Your choice."

They caved in.

The Forgotten City dated from a time in Dalrodian history that seemed unimaginably distant to most of the World's present inhabitants. Nobody knew for sure whether the petrified forest, which existed on the same site, came before or after the city. And did the iridescent fossil trees prove that the World had had a different climate in its past, or didn't they? *Had* there once been surface water on Dalrodia?

By the time they arrived, however, the three Questors couldn't have cared less about any of it. They slid off the sonks, who appeared to be able to fall asleep where they stood, and unrolled their blankets in the shelter of a ruined wall. Cam made a fire with compacted fuel it had brought, and was about to offer to heat some food, when it was interrupted by snoring sounds. Madlen and Bryn were asleep, two blanket bundles in the darkness.

Cam smiled at them, and did the same.

In the Forgotten City a golden mole swam under the surface of the sand, listening for prey. In through a ruined window it surfed, and across an indoor dune, then out a doorway where no door had hung for millennia. Unaware of its approach, the desert cricket began its dry, scraping song. The mole surged, and the night was quiet again, while the constellations continued their slow swirl across the sky.

Cam stirred. It was having a dream. As it lay with its cheek pressed against the ground, it heard irregular thrumming, as if the earth had become an orchestra of drums, all played with muffled sticks. In its sleep Cam thought, *How interesting. The symbolism of the drum suggests the heartbeat of the World, and yet I can definitely hear* many *beats, which might mean many Worlds. . . .*

The wind began to whisper. It sounded just like two people talking. Cam could almost hear the words.

"What if they're bait? What if it's a trap?"

"They've *never* tagged their own before."

"Maybe they stole the clothes and the high-caste gear. Maybe they're honest Tagged."

"Can we take that chance? I say kill them now, before the Checkers arrive."

"So you *do* think they're trying to escape—"

"Quiet!"

What does it mean? Cam wondered. *What a wonderfully puzzling dream!*

Then, all of a sudden, Cam woke to the feel of a cold blade against its throat.

"Move," said a voice conversationally. "Or make a sound. Either suits me. Then I can kill you."

CHAPTER FIFTY

<u>The Deserted</u>

Cam froze. In the dying firelight it couldn't see more of the speaker than a black shape. Then a last bit of fuel caught and flared— and Cam saw eyes glittering in the depths of a desert man's hood.

"What, no inadvisable screaming or attempts to overpower me and escape?" The voice sounded disappointed, then perked up. "Never mind, the night is young."

What sounded like an animal, but probably wasn't, called softly.

"Come on, then." He pulled Cam up, spun it neatly, and tied its wrists behind its back. "Join your friends."

As Cam began to stumble forward, someone coaxed the fire back into life. By its light, Cam saw Bryn and Madlen, bleary-eyed and bound like itself, standing uncertainly. And surrounding them, at the edge of the light, how many desert people? Half a dozen? Twenty? Whenever Cam focused on one of the hooded figures, they seemed to melt back into the dark, or shifted to another part of the shadows.

"So. What's the catch this fine night? What have we come

upon, so far from all those cozy Holder cliffs and palaces? Here's a picnic gone wrong, don't you think?"

Whoever was speaking was circling them in the dark, like a hyena circling a wounded animal, alert for the weakness that will finish the battle. Cam tried to follow the voice, straining its eyes, turning round and slipping in the fine sand, until it realized it was being played with. Then it just stood, head up, and waited.

"A high-caste emergent. *With a tag*. A high-caste woman. *With a tag*. And a high-caste youth—sands, you can't be long out of emergence, eh?—*with a tag*."

Cam winced at each "tag," a reaction that did not go unnoticed.

"What's the matter, little one? Embarrassed because your loved ones put you up for tagging? Well, don't worry. Embarrassment isn't life threatening. Neither is humiliation. Or shame. You can trust us on *that*."

"They've got nice clothes, Dair. Can we kill them now?" It was Cam's captor speaking.

"What, before we've asked them if they mind?" The voice that came from the other side of the fire was a woman's, and sounded weary. "That wouldn't be very polite, would it, Vath."

"Oops," said Vath cheerfully. "Silly me. Do you mind? See? They don't mind. *Now* can we kill them?"

The man he'd called Dair sighed. "This isn't the Area, Vath. Nobody kills anybody until Ur clears it. You may be a newbie, but I suggest you learn the rules. And shut up till you have."

He turned back into the darkness. Someone else had arrived, and a low conversation passed between them. Then, with an abrupt movement, Dair threw back his hood.

"It's all right, they're alone," he said. "Ailm's done a full scout.

We'll eat, assuming our friends here had the sense to pack provisions, and then we move out. Keep them close meantime."

There was some subdued bustle, which ended in a meal that smelled . . . not bad. One of the men brought some for them.

"Eat," he said, not unkindly.

"I'm not—," Madlen began, but Bryn nudged her sharply.

The man nodded in approval. "Never say no to food, Lady," he said. "You'd know that if you'd ever gone without."

He made her feel ashamed, without her quite knowing why, and she did as she was told.

Cam ate on automatic, all its attention on the troop around them. It tried to hear their soft conversations and learn their faces. Something was niggling at the back of Cam's brain, something it couldn't quite place—and then it *could*, so suddenly it jumped.

"What's the matter, little high-caste? Something bite you?" It was obvious the troop had been studying them just as keenly.

"That's it—your *names*!" said Cam. "You're named after trees!"

Madlen and Bryn stared blankly. This obviously took the desert people by surprise as well.

"Fancy the child knowing the old names for trees!" exclaimed one.

"But why?" Cam insisted.

"Well, see, we do it because irony is highly valued among us lot—," began a man.

"That's 'cause it's cheap!" interrupted another.

An older woman spoke across the laughter. "We name ourselves after symbols of hope," she said firmly.

Cam scrambled to its feet, excited. "Then I have to tell you—there's been a dream *about you*! My—the Lady Holder dreamed it. A dream about . . ." Cam's voice trailed off into silence.

The desert people had turned away.

"We've no interest in *Holder* dreams," someone said with scorn.

Cam sank slowly back down onto the sand.

Then, in the silence, somebody else asked a question.

"Why did you come out here, child? What did you think you were running *to*?"

It was, at best, a neutral voice, but it sounded to Cam at that moment almost like kindness. So it gathered up its courage, and began to tell them the story of the Quest. Cam told it well, but Madlen and Bryn, watching anxiously, couldn't tell how Dair's troop was reacting. Their faces were hidden in their hoods, or shadowed in the dim light. One thing was clear, though. The three were in their hands. The desert people could be invaluable allies in their search for the final Object of Power. Or they could just as easily slit the children's throats.

But, in the end, the gulf between one end of the caste system and the other was too great for their captors to feel any common cause across it. Cam was too obviously not one of theirs, and neither were Cam's concerns.

If the big picture had gone crooked, it was somebody else's job to straighten it.

"Now, see the troubles you get into when you get ideas outside your place," a voice jeered.

There was some grim laughter.

"You'd have thought messing up *one* World would be enough for 'em."

"What do you think *we* can do about it, child. We've got nothing!"

"What about the Corym, high-caste? Isn't that mythic enough for you?"

"Yeah. Take 'em a Dream Apple—you'll have no trouble getting one. The Lady Holder'll be glad to share—just ask!"

All around them were mocking voices in the dark. Cam's head hung down. Madlen and Bryn were afraid it was crying, but before they could move to comfort it, it looked up.

Cam's face was deathly pale, but it was in control. It had been listening, and thinking hard, not weeping.

"It's not the Corym," Cam said quietly. "If it were, I would know. That much is clear to me. It's just that . . ."

"It's just that what?" someone prompted.

Suddenly Cam looked intensely young, and lost. "It's just that nothing else *is*."

And the tide of sympathy might have turned in the Questors' favor, but at that moment the lookout hooted from the city's edge, and the focus of attention moved back to the realities of the known World.

"Time we were gone," said Dair.

As the troop began to move about in the darkness, organized and virtually silent, Bryn turned to the woman guarding them.

"Where are we going?" he asked.

But before she could respond, Dair began to call out his orders in a soft voice.

"Ailm, get their tags off, and keep back as many as you need for a trap. We'll let Vath exercise his bloodlust a bit, eh? Suil, Nuin, and Onn, you take the high-castes. I want to get them to Ur by dawn. Coll, you bring the sonks on after. Let's go."

"Stick out your wrists," said the woman, producing a fearsome tool, half blade, half pincers, from somewhere in her robe. "This'll hurt."

It did.

Once the tags were cut, she simply dropped them into a heap on the sand.

"Checker bait," she said, and spat. "Come on."

They followed her down an empty street and around the corner of a wall—and suddenly there was an overwhelmingly musky smell, deep grunting sounds, and a sense of big bodies in the dark. The woman lit a small hand torch and they could see eyes glinting. Lots of eyes.

"Ever ridden a camelion before?" she asked casually.

"I'll take that one," said a man, pointing at Madlen. He then reached across and untied the nearest camelion. The thing snarled and swung its head round with terrifying speed. Madlen gasped at the sight of fangs glittering in the moonlight, but before the creature could rip the man's face off, he had kicked it viciously, grabbed an ear, and swung himself out of reach onto its back.

Madlen tried to back away. "I can't do that!" she squawked.

But the woman pushed her forward. "Forget it. If Onn can stop showing off for a second, you'll find he's quite in control. You just have to climb up and hold on. Nothing fancy."

Madlen could see now that there *was* some sort of rein and bit system on the creature. Taking a shaky breath, she stepped closer.

At the last minute Onn loosened his grip a fraction, and the camelion instantly tried to get to her. Just before its teeth could connect, he reined sharply back again, and leered down into her horrified face.

"Now, now, Blossom," he said to the grumbling beast. "Don't you know it isn't polite to play with your food?"

"Give over, Onn." The desert woman sounded weary and bored. "Here." And she gave the reluctant Madlen a leg up.

The man was chuckling to himself as he shunted her into a more central position on the camelion's neck, but then he stopped paying attention to her at all. As the group headed out into the open desert, the mood shifted in humans and beasts. Stealth, silence, vigilance—the senses stretched and alert, the mind open to those instincts and intuitions that would keep them all alive that little bit longer.

Cam was silent too, its eyes fixed on the camelion's broad head, its fingers gripped convulsively in the animal's thick harsh hair. Once, its rider—she was young, not long past emergency—reached her hand over Cam's shoulder and touched where the tag had rubbed its wrist.

"What did you do?" she asked, her voice barely above a whisper.

Cam shook its head. "Nothing. I didn't do anything." Cam paused, and then, "What did *you* do?" it asked, just as quietly.

"Same," she replied.

Bryn heard their exchange, and wished he could give Cam a comforting shove.

After that, nobody spoke, as three Questors rode with their captors toward the dawn.

CHAPTER FIFTY-ONE

Stranger

It was still dark, but Ivory had barely slept.
Anyway, it was a peaceful time to get a
few hours' work done, before the rest of the
Palace woke up. Serena would be fussing round
her as soon as she discovered she was
out of bed, but for now . . .

Without knocking, a stranger entered the room and walked up
to her desk. Ivory was too astonished to speak.

"I haven't time for our usual mode of communication," the
stranger said.

She pulled herself together and stood up, frowning, regal.
"What do you want?" she demanded. "Who are you?"

"Who am I? And to think of all the nights we've spent
together! Madam, I am desolate."

The color was draining from her face, and the hand she put
on the chair-back trembled slightly.

"A simple manipulation of the Interpretive Program was well
within my abilities, Lady, but I preferred the more, ah, personal
touch. You and I have had such *pleasant* dreams together. . . . In
many ways, directing the destiny of Dalrodia has been remark-
ably easy—the least onerous of all the Worlds. Discrediting

the rule of the Holders has been hardly a challenge at all."

"Who *are* you?" she said again, but he ignored her question.

"It's been mostly a matter of faith, hasn't it? As the drilling went on, and the earthquakes got worse, and your World spun closer and closer to the sun, you—still—had faith. Such a useful lever. History mentions it again and again. But, of course, if once we start learning from history we might also start running out of mistakes to make, and then where would we be? Now, dear Lady, perhaps we could get to the point? Where are the children?"

"What children?"

The man clicked his tongue as if she were being naughty.

"Oh, I could just go to the Tag Master," he said. "Of course I could. But you know, I'd really rather get the information from you. I'd hate for you not to feel how much a part of it all you've been, all the way through. I was almost going to say I couldn't have done it without you, but of course that wouldn't be true. But I'm sure I wouldn't have *enjoyed* it so much without you."

He was advancing on her all the time. As she backed away, her eyes flicked from side to side, looking for an escape.

"You realize I'll kill anyone who comes through that door," he said conversationally. "Just in case you were thinking of calling for help."

Ivory stopped. She'd run out of room, backed against the wall. She lifted her chin.

"I don't know where they are," she said without a quaver.

"I think you do," purred Alpine Cordell. "And I think that very soon I'll know too."

Serena was grumbling to herself as she approached her Lady's office—"Working already. What kind of a night's sleep do you call that? You'll make yourself ill."—when the stranger brushed past her. There was nothing particularly noticeable about him. He looked like another of those London House messengers—but why so early?

For some reason she broke into a run.

"Well, Lady—"

Ivory lay beside her overturned chair, curled in on herself and shuddering as the pain continued to wash across her, as relentless as a tide. With a great effort she raised her head and spoke. "I didn't tell him," she panted. "I *didn't.* He just ripped into my mind and took it."

"Pigeon. Lady," Serena crooned, desperate to comfort but unsure where Ivory could be touched without more damage.

"I've been wrong. I've been so wrong—and I betrayed them . . . us. . . . I've betrayed us all. . . ."

Ivory wept.

Alpine Cordell had never visited the Area before in body, but he knew exactly where he was going. It was his job to know. The Worlds had no secrets from him, no seedy corner or shameful surprise he hadn't already discovered. From any distance he could smell despair and the misuse of power among the powerless. It drew him like perfume.

The Tag Master did the bulk of his work at night, and so was already at his post when the stranger walked in.

"What can I do for you, Lor . . ." The Tag Master's voice drained away at the sight of Cordell's face.

"I want these three, this frequency."

The Tag Master took the information slip with inexplicably shaking fingers and looked at it.

"That is not a normal band, Lord," he quavered, trying to rally himself, but the stranger simply curled back his lip a little. A smile? The Tag Master was used to entreaty, despair, terror from others; he was *not* used to the feel of cold sweat down his own spine. "Er, I should . . . consult the Lady Hol—but maybe not . . ."

He turned to the machinery and did as he'd been told.

"Here, my lord. The ones you require are just here, in a place known as the Forgotten City. They eluded us last night during an unexpected power cut, but we know exactly where they've gone. Normally the Checkers would have retrieved them and be . . . returning them by now, but the Lady Holder insisted I do nothing without consulting her, and I hardly liked to disturb her in the night."

"She has already been disturbed," said the stranger. "She knows I am here."

"Ah. Well. As you see, this is where they are. See? Just here. Lord?"

He pointed eagerly at the display but the stranger ignored the finger and continued to stare instead into the Tag Master's face.

"You will take me to them."

The Tag Master paled. "Transport. A guide. An escort, of course," he babbled. "I will organize these for you at once, Lord. Of course. At once."

Again the lip curled.

"Perhaps I have not made myself clear. *You* will take me to them."

"Me?" the Tag Master whispered hoarsely.

The stranger nodded. "Now," he said.

It was never sensible to leave the shelter of the Area after a Storm Warning had been announced. Also, a motorized land vehicle was one of the less reliable forms of transport for the treacherous desert terrain. And travelling without a substantial escort was inviting major trouble from ambush or, at the very least, becoming stuck without enough manpower to get things started again.

"We are leaving immediately," the stranger had stated. "I will not be involved with animals of any description. There will be no escort or attendants except you."

No one pointed out to the stranger that these were not sensible requests. No one had the nerve.

Not long after the crawler had trundled out of sight, the electrics of the border fence flickered. One of the guards stuck out his tongue to taste the air, wrinkling his nose at the metallic tang.

"That's no ordinary storm," he grunted.

His colleague-at-arms nodded.

"Somebody ought to go after those idiots in the crawler. Somebody ought to warn them," said the first guard in a non-committal voice.

His colleague agreed.

"Somebody ought to go on out and lay down their life in order to save them. The fact that if they'd had the sense they were born with they would never have gone in the first place isn't an issue."

The power juddered again, and failed.

The first guard sighed. "That maintenance shutdown certainly didn't help much, did it?" he said, reaching for his mug of tea. "Oh well, too late to do anything about them now."

His colleague agreed.

CHAPTER FIFTY-TWO

The Woman of the Mountain

It was still dark when the troop arrived at the main camp, which was hidden among the broken rocks and ravines of the foothills. The three children were taken down from the camelions and then, for the moment, ignored.

Madlen leaned closer to Bryn. "You okay?" she asked in a low voice. "Your hand okay?"

Bryn made a face, but then nodded. "It aches. I'm not exactly giving it rest like Serena said to, am I? But I don't think it's opened up again."

"Follow me." Dair had come up behind them. "It's time."

He led them to a large low tent and, lifting the entrance flap, motioned them inside. In the torchlight they could see the tent was crowded with desert people, silent, cold-eyed, and suspicious.

The Questors huddled uncertainly, just inside the opening.

"Don't be fooled," Dair murmured as he brushed past them. "Just because Holder justice says they are thieves and murderers and rapists doesn't mean some of them aren't."

As he watched them work this out, Dair's grin broadened without reaching his eyes.

"That's right," he whispered. "You don't know the truth about me, either."

And then he was gone. The crowd parted respectfully for him, until they had formed a sort of corridor leading to the far corner of the tent. There was something there, like a heap of clothes on a rug. Dair leaned down to the heap—and it moved.

"What's *that?*" whispered Bryn, and was immediately cuffed across the head by a man standing near them.

"Mind your mouth, high-caste," he growled. "Show some respect for the Woman of the Mountain."

The children stared at one another with sudden wild hope, but before they could speak, Dair looked back over his shoulder and beckoned for them to come. Someone gave them a shove forward, and they walked nervously past rows of hostile faces.

Then, as they came closer, the thing on the floor lifted its head. A woman, unbelievably ancient-looking, peered up at them.

Cam bowed. Bryn and Madlen did the same, awkwardly.

"Lady," said Cam at its most formal, "we are Questors. We—"

"I know what you are." The woman's voice was a thin whisper, as if it had come from a long way off.

Cam blinked, and continued.

"Then you know what we're looking for? Can you help us?"

The old woman nodded her head slowly, and the three felt their hearts leap.

"I have nothing for you," she said, and then, bizarrely, she smiled at them. As if she'd given them a great gift. As if she'd given them *the answer.*

"No. You don't understand—," Cam began, but the old woman had already turned her attention away from them. She beckoned to Dair, and the leader crouched down beside her.

"Well, Ur?" he said, his voice respectful, yet gentle. "What do you say?"

The old woman screwed up her face until there was nothing but wrinkles left to see.

"They're wrong," she whispered. "They shouldn't be here."

"You mean . . . they're spies?"

The old woman shook her head. Wisps of dry white hair fell across her face. She was becoming agitated.

"Not *spies*! Can't you see for yourselves? They're *wrong*! Too soon . . . or do I mean too late?"

Dair stroked the hair carefully back from the old woman's face.

"We are your children, Ur. You'll have to help us. Why shouldn't they be here?"

Ur looked at him with her pale eyes.

"They don't belong."

"Two of them, certainly, come from other Worlds," he agreed. "They say so, and they look it. But the small one's pure high-caste, Mother."

"Not pure," she said at the same moment that Cam said, "Half."

Dair looked confused, but then brushed it aside. "I'm asking the wrong questions." He seemed to think for a moment, absently stroking the old woman's arm as she rocked back and forth. Then, "Mother, listen to me. Where *should* they be? Not here, but where? We'll take them there, wherever it is, and you'll feel better then."

She had started to shake, and her skin had a cold sheen of sweat on it.

"Storm's coming," someone called softly from the tent's opening. "Could be that."

The old woman peered round Dair toward the speaker. "The *Future*'s what's coming," she snapped. "And I will not have it meet them *here*!"

"Don't worry, Mother. We'll take them away. But you must tell us—*where* shall we take them?"

A flare of power gripped her huddled body so that her hair stood out like a corona and her eyes shone out of her wizened face. "The Well. The Well of Light. I can see drops of blood spattered. . . . I can see the blood in baskets. . . . I can . . ."

But the flare was brief, and ended almost before it began. The old woman subsided onto her pile of cushions and rugs, and croaked wearily at them, "Go away. All of you. Get out."

There was a rustle of fabric as the mountain people began to file out of the tent. Dair and the children had turned to follow them, when Ur shot out a clawed hand and grabbed Cam's clothes.

"LEAVE NOW," she said.

Then she let go, and turned away from them all. Cam made as if to speak, but Dair shook his head, and motioned them away.

At the entrance the leader stopped beside a woman and looked up at the sky. It was paling toward daybreak.

"You said storm, Beith," he said quietly. "How soon?"

The woman sniffed at the air and then half-opened her mouth as if to taste it.

"Half a day," she said. "Maybe less. You'll have time to use the back route, if you hurry. Though . . ."

"Well?"

"It would be quicker just to kill them."

Dair snorted, and looked back at Ur squatting on her rugs like a malignant sheep.

"I'll chance the storm!" he said.

❋ ❋ ❋

The sun was almost at its highest as Alpine Cordell and his sweating, disheveled companion ground into the Forgotten City. Leaving the crawler, the Tag Master led the way on foot, tracer in hand, farther and farther into the ruins. At last, he panted to a halt.

"They're there, Lord, beyond that wall. I'll just wait here, shall I?" he whispered hoarsely.

But no chance. The Other-Worlder gave him a look, and he forced himself forward in what was meant to be a ferocious lunge, but was actually more of a stagger.

"Right then, Runaways," he blared. "I've got you now-w-w-arghhh!"

Instead of three sniveling children, the Tag Master found himself faced with half a dozen desert men. He swung round in time to see more sliding in behind him.

Eyes bugging, he stared at the circle of silent, ominous hooded figures, then down at the little heap of wrist tags lying in the sand.

"Er," he said.

"Cretin." The Other-Worlder spat the word as he joined the Tag Master—and then pushed past the nearest desert man and started to address a rock.

"There has been . . . a delay," he said to it. "I have not yet been able to kill them."

What? thought the Tag Master. *Who's he talking to?*

The desert people drew back a little, spooked as well.

The Other-Worlder ignored them all.

"I have had to use normal tracking and transport because of the power flux on this World, Preceptor. Otherwise I would obviously not have chosen to do so." A pause. "Yes, Preceptor.

As you wish. For the duration of the storm. In which case, my work could in fact be done for me, as they may well not be within range of adequate shelter. . . . Till then, Preceptor, I will . . ." Before he'd finished speaking, the stranger had faded away. There was no sign of him.

The desert people did not waste time in amazement. As one, they turned to face the Dalrodian.

"Well, Tag Master, that just leaves you," one said.

The Tag Master had turned a gray-green color. "You kn-know me?" he asked.

"Oh yes. You are certainly known. *Thoroughly* known."

The Tag Master wasn't even sure which of the hooded figures was speaking.

"But this isn't a good place to renew old acquaintances," one of the figures said. "As the stranger mentioned, a storm is coming. You, of course, have the right to shelter with us. The desert code is adamant on such things. 'In the time of the storm the stranger is sacred.' After the storm, of course, the rules are not quite so clear."

The Tag Master stood there, gulping, as dust devils started to swirl about his feet.

CHAPTER FIFTY-THREE

The Well of Light

The sky was cloudless, and bleached by the glare
of the sunlight, and in the heat, the
children had "sonk-slept" most of the way.
Cam's comparison of the animals to sofas was,
thankfully, proving true. And if the three showed
any signs of sliding off, one of the desert people
was always there to shove them back onto
an even keel again.

It was close on noon when Dair called a halt. They had been travelling along the base of an immensely high cliff for some time. Madlen and Bryn, blinking and yawning, could see nothing that made this stretch of rock different from any other, but Cam seemed to know where it was.

"The lift won't be working," Cam said, "but I've got access to the stairwell." It turned to Dair. "Thank you for your help." Cam bowed, not as low as to Ur, but enough to surprise the desert man. Then it walked towards the cliff face.

When Madlen looked round a moment later, the desert people had disappeared.

"I don't see how . . . ," Bryn was beginning to say, when Cam lifted its hand and slid a small section of rock to one side.

It palmed the sensor plate, and a door in the rock rumbled open in their faces.

"Obviously we don't normally take this route," Cam said as it waved them into the cliff. "We fly in, up top. But you always need bunkers and safety exits, stuff like that."

The door to the outside closed as it was speaking, and the lights came on. The other two gazed about, looking stupid. Before them was the entrance to a lift, firmly closed, and the beginning of a flight of stairs.

"Uh, you were kidding, right? About the lift," said Madlen. "It really *isn't* a question of *walking,* right?"

Cam looked at her. "It really is. The lift's only activated from the top," Cam said, and started to climb.

"How . . . much . . . farther?" gasped Bryn. Madlen was beyond speech. How many hundred steps had they climbed? She'd lost track.

"Almost . . . there . . . ," panted Cam.

They'd seen other doors, presumably leading off into the cliff, but had just plodded on past them. Until now.

"Here." Cam put its hand to the access pad, and once again it was recognized. The door glided open. "It's along . . . there." Cam pointed down the corridor, and slid to the floor. The others collapsed beside it, and for a long time the three were completely occupied in trying to catch their breath and letting their hearts catch up with them.

At last they were only wheezing a little. They heaved themselves up off the floor and headed for the Well of Light.

They hadn't far to go. Madlen had just started to think, *I wonder why they call it the Well of Light,* when the answer hit her between the eyes.

"Wow."

They had entered a roughly circular space, carved out of the rock and reaching up, up, all the way to the outside world. It was an immensely deep shaft, and should have been as dark as the bottom of any ordinary well, and yet the area was filled with natural daylight.

"They do it with mirrors," said Cam.

Looking up, the others could see light flooding down from the surface, broken into its rainbow colors and reassembled as it passed, bouncing back and forth, from one huge, angled sheet of glass to the next.

"The Well of Light," murmured Madlen.

"And this . . . is the *Corym somniferum*," said Cam, as if making a formal introduction.

There was a raised bed, full of good dark soil. And in the soil . . .

That's it? thought Madlen.

Bryn nudged her. "Try to *look* impressed," he muttered, and Madlen quickly rearranged her face.

"I guess I was expecting silver branches and purple leaves or something," she whispered back. "Not some stunted bit of scrub!"

"Yeah. Well, us stunted types are full of surprises." He skipped aside just as she tried to kick him.

Cam wasn't paying any attention to them. It was just staring at the little tree, the last lone Dream Apple in all the Worlds. Then it gave itself a shake.

"The Corym orchard used to be up above on the plateau. But the winds and the storms kept getting worse and the sun was burning them up. So we moved them here."

"Them?" asked Madlen.

"It's been so long. There were still three trees when I was here last—"

Cam's words were cut off by a sudden, heavy, deep noise. The stone floor ruckled weirdly under their feet, making them stagger and gasp.

The three peered about wildly, and by sheer good luck, Bryn happened to look up.

"NO!" he yelled.

The mirrors were beginning to crack. Time seemed to slow as they all stared up into the Well. The sheets of glass shivered like the hide of an animal, and then began to split, huge jagged splinters of light pulling apart from one another with a sound like teeth shattering. The black gaps between widened, and widened, until suddenly everything speeded up again and a lethal rain plummeted toward them.

They hurled themselves toward the tunnel entrance at the last second, landing bruisingly in a heap on the stone floor, with all the breath punched out of them. Behind them the shards hit with a sickeningly slick slicing noise.

In the sudden dimness Cam could hear someone whispering, "Oh no, oh no" over and over. It was a moment before Cam realized the voice was its own.

Bryn cleared the dust out of his throat. "Everyone all right?" he asked hoarsely. He was on his feet again and pulling Madlen up. Cam nodded and dragged itself upright against the wall.

"What *happened*?" Madlen whimpered, just as Bryn gasped, "The tree—oh, Cam—*the tree*!"

It was hard to see in the Well now. The distant sky was a brassy patch far above. Very little light reached them where they stood. As their eyes adjusted, though, a crystalline phosphorescence from the walls did offer some illumination. It was an alien kind of light, and it revealed a scene that was nightmarish and surreal.

The subterranean bed had a new crop. Spiky fragments of glass punctured the soil, some as tall as a man, others barely showing, ready to shred any unwary foot. In the center, where the tree had stood, only scraps of raw wood remained, broken branches, a shattered trunk.

And all around, like drops of blood, the fruit lay scattered.

"Ur!" gasped Madlen. "She *knew*!"

"How—," began Bryn, but Cam shook itself, and took charge.

"Come with me," it said.

There was a side cave a little way back along the tunnel, where gardening equipment was kept. The quake had tumbled the orderly array of tools into a heap on the floor, but Cam waded in, heaving spades and forks and pruners aside.

"Here, take these," it said, tossing some bags at the others. "There should be baskets, too, if they're not smashed. You start."

Madlen and Bryn looked at each other.

"Um?" said Bryn.

Cam sat back on its heels.

"Look," it said, trying to sound patient, and failing. "We haven't much time. The Well is probably going to collapse. This will mean several hundred tons of rock on top of the last crop of Corym my World will ever see. It seems sensible to try to collect that crop *before* this happens, rather than after."

"Right," said Madlen.

"On our way," said Bryn.

But when Cam caught up with them, a salvaged basket under each arm, they were still standing in the doorway.

"It's just . . . not getting our feet sliced up," Bryn explained apologetically.

Cam thought for a moment, then nodded to itself.

"Here, use these," it said. There were some small paving stones stacked against the wall. Cam took one over, dropped it on the lethal soil, and went back for another.

"Portable path! Clever!" said Bryn, following suit.

The fruit was surprising to touch. It was hard, for one thing, and felt almost ceramic. It was also warm, and gave off a strong scent of lavender and something else. They could easily have been overwhelmed by the perfume, which sang to all their senses of sleep, sleep—but the thought of more tremors worked wonders at keeping them alert.

"That's it, Cam." Bryn straightened up. He'd slung his bag over his shoulder to keep his good hand free, and now it was bulging with fruit.

"All clear here," said Madlen, her basket full.

Cam set down the second heavy basket for a moment and looked about. It was true. All the Corym had been gathered up, including the shattered fragments. Their hands and clothes were stained with spilled red juice, so that they looked like extras from a massacre.

"I'd say it's time to go."

They humped their loads down the corridor toward the stairwell.

"And now we're going to go down, down, down, and discover a nice safe bunker," grunted Madlen as they puffed along, "and have a shower maybe, or a long soak in a bath—"

The floor shook again, and bits of the ceiling dusted down. Their pace picked up considerably.

"Tremors—they come in twos, right?" muttered Bryn nervously.

"I'm pretty sure it's supposed to be threes—," Madlen started to correct him, when the big one hit.

It was impossible to keep their feet as the rock rolled in irregular waves and sideways jolts. The noise battered at them, rising up from deep underground, and the air grew foggy and thick with rock dust. Choking and gasping, they staggered forward, and skidded to a stop at the stairwell door.

The drifting dust parted, to show the wreck of the stairs leading down. That route was closed, impassably blocked by splintered stone.

The only way left was up.

CHAPTER FIFTY-FOUR

<u>The Plateau</u>

The hot wind hit them as soon as they climbed out onto the high plateau. It battered them with grit, and sucked the sweat off their skin without making them any cooler.

"Mummy-maker," said Cam.

"What?"

"That's what we call this wind. They say it can draw out the last drop of moisture from *anything* and mummify it."

"Ever seen one?" asked Bryn, running a dry tongue round his mouth. "A mummy?"

Cam shrugged. "Saw a rat once. It might have been a fake, though. Still, it looked a lot like you—"

Madlen butted in. "Cam," she said, scratching at her arms, then her neck. "I think I'm allergic to this juice stuff. My skin's crawling."

"Now you mention it . . ." Bryn joined in, scratching his nails through his hair.

But Cam waved a dismissive hand. "Storm's coming. Always does that. Come on. We need to get the Corym to the hangar."

Bryn shouldered his sack and looked around.

"*What* hangar?" he said.

Cam was already off, staggering under the weight of its baskets and bags, apparently heading off into the broken wilderness. Then, slowly, Cam disappeared.

The other two hurried to catch up, and found Cam at the bottom of a wide, shallow ramp. At its base huddled a low building with a metal roof and large, tightly shut double doors.

"Come on, palm print, work your magic!" Cam muttered.

With a screech the doors parted slightly.

They dragged themselves and their cargo through the gap, and into the gloom beyond. Cam rummaged about for some lamps and lit them. The wind still whined and quested round the narrow opening of the doors, but their sanctuary was comparatively still.

Madlen slumped down on the floor. Bryn went to nosey round a number of interestingly plane-shaped things under tarpaulins, and Cam headed for an office area to one side of the hangar, where the meteorological records and reports should be.

When Cam came out to them again, the expression on its face wasn't hard to interpret.

"Oh, great," said Madlen wearily. "More good news."

Cam shook its head. "Not really. It's a haboob."

They didn't respond.

"A very bad sandstorm," Cam explained.

"So we'll need to stay put here till it's over, right?" Madlen looked wistful.

Cam sighed, and shook its head again.

"When I lived here, you know, ten years ago, already the haboob had become bigger, more frequent. But—here, look for yourselves." And it thrust a sheaf of weather readouts at them.

Bryn glanced, and shrugged. "I don't speak Weather," he said. "You'll have to translate."

"Okay." Cam thought for a moment. "Wind doesn't come

simple, but I'll try to explain. This'll have started as an electric storm, way off in the desert. It's had plenty of time to pick up speed. And then, when you might think it should be wearing out, a pattern of downdrafts inside the storm starts. Gust fronts form."

"Downdrafts?"

"Gust what?"

Cam sighed again.

"Air blows down, all right? *Fast.* And when it hits the ground it blasts up a bunch of sand and dust, and then it pushes all that forward, *fast,* and now there's this wall of grit maybe a mile high, and it basically sandblasts everything in its path into nothingness." Cam drew breath. "That's an *ordinary* haboob, and there's a *monster* one on its way."

"So, we sit tight?" offered Madlen again.

"If we stay here," replied Cam, "we have every chance of being killed in a number of interesting ways, including being buried alive or blown away."

"So, we run?" suggested Bryn.

Cam tapped the readouts.

"This thing's travelling speed is predicted at over fifty miles per hour. Last time I checked, that's faster than me."

"So we *fly* out?" Bryn's eyes sparkled in the lamplight.

"Don't be stupid!" Madlen snapped. "None of us knows how to fly a plane!"

"I do." Cam's voice was flat. They could see it was holding itself unnaturally still, as if afraid of something inside escaping.

Bryn let out a whoop. "That is so cool! We grab a plane and we outrun the storm and . . ."

But Cam was shaking its head. "We're not flying away from it," Cam said, and a little excitement leaked through. "We're flying *over.*"

CHAPTER FIFTY-FIVE

<u>Over!</u>

Madlen was appalled. As Cam wandered around, checking under tarpaulins, Madlen waved her hands about and spluttered.

"This is crazy! Why don't we just throw ourselves off the cliff and be done with it?"

"It'll work, Madlen. I *know* it'll work!" Bryn was just this side of jumping up and down. "Flying, now *that's* an adventure!"

"Besides, it isn't just us we're trying to save," said Cam quietly, coming out from under yet another tarpaulin.

Madlen stared at Cam for a long moment, and gave in.

"This is still crazy," she said hoarsely, turning to the shrouded shapes. "Which one?"

Bryn leapt into the air shouting, "Yeehah!" and Cam allowed itself a pale grin.

"This one'll be fine," Cam said. "It's what I'm licensed for. Private two-seater."

"What do you mean, two-seater?" fussed Madlen. "Last time I looked, there were *three* of us."

"One of you gets to be luggage," Cam said.

"You!" Madlen and Bryn chorused instantly. "No way!"

"I could do with some help here," Cam interrupted.

For a while everyone's attention was focused on the work at hand: uncovering the plane, making sure it was fueled up, loading the sacks and baskets of Corym into the tiny storage space behind the seats. Then, suddenly, Cam stopped.

"Hear that?" it said in a small, tight voice.

The others peered about, trying to pinpoint the source of some new menace. But there was nothing, not even the whine of the wind forcing itself in through the crack in the doors. No sound at all.

"We've run out of time," said Cam, dropping down from the cockpit. "You two help me open the doors."

"But . . . ," Madlen began, then stopped. *It's not the moment to try to understand meteorology*, she scolded herself. *It's the moment to get out of its way!*

As they dragged the heavy doors apart, Bryn glanced up at the sky—and swallowed nervously. "You can't tell me that's normal," he said, pointing, "even for *this* World!"

"Well, you know the old saying," Cam called back over its shoulder as it ran for the plane. "Green sky, better fly!"

"You just made that up!" Bryn sprinted after it.

"Even *old* sayings were young once. Get in!"

Bryn rushed round to the other side, wrenched open the door, and began to pull himself up and in—only to discover Madlen, firmly ensconced in the passenger seat, grinning at him.

"In the back, Suitcase!" she crowed.

Bryn growled, and crawled past her.

"There's no room!" he complained, but the others ignored him.

"Here goes," muttered Cam.

The engine caught on the second attempt. Cam eased the plane forward, through the doors, and, a bit jerkily, on up the ramp. In the eerie green light, the plane started the long taxi to the end of the runway, travelling away from the cliff edge.

As they rumbled along, Madlen noticed little dust devils beginning to form beside the runway. *Wind's back, then,* she thought. *Now, what do they call those eddy things?*

Suddenly Cam turned in the pilot's seat. Its face was greeny-white and urgent. "I can't not try!" Cam said, sounding desperate. "You see that, don't you? I know I'm not Ivory . . ."

Madlen stared. "Of course you're not Ivory. Who says you *should* be?"

Cam looked ashamed. "She'd know what to do," it muttered.

"Don't be stupid. *You* know what to do. What you're *doing* is what to do!" Madlen insisted, a little obscurely. "Best bet, remember? Best shot, clearly stated in the *Questors' Handbook* nobody bothered to give us!"

"But—," Cam began, when Bryn interrupted.

"Look, kid, I'm folded in half back here and there's sacred fruit digging into my butt, so—do you think we could GET ON and discuss how good an idea it is when it's all over?"

"Yeah, listen to your luggage," said Madlen.

Cam nodded, turned the plane, and braked. It muttered to itself a little as it checked switches and dials, and then began to ease the stick forward.

The sound the engine was making deepened. They could feel the plane fighting against the brakes, like a bird tied to a perch. Madlen glanced across and saw that Cam was tensed and vibrating slightly in just the same way.

"Let's fly," she said, with hardly a quaver in her voice, and patted Cam on the arm.

Cam disengaged the brakes, and the little plane trundled

bravely forward. Sand sporadically hit like shrapnel against the windscreen, and Cam set the bristled wipers going.

"Willy-willies!" cried Madlen suddenly. "That's what they're called."

Cam grinned, but didn't take its eyes off the runway ahead.

"Come on, my beauty!" Cam called to the plane as it gathered momentum. "Hutt! Hutt!"

The runway sped under their wheels. The edge of the cliff galloped toward them. The wing tips juddered excitedly. Cam held on till the last second and, just as they fell off the cliff face, pulled back on the stick.

They all screamed as the g-force bit in earnest. For an instant the desert lay, spread out before them, immediately below the front windscreen. Then, with a swoop and a whoop, they were out of the fall and beginning to climb.

In a long curve, Cam brought the plane back over the airstrip again.

"I need to ride the thermals," it shouted in explanation. "We need height."

Below them a lower layer of wind had arrived, and they watched in fascinated horror as, one by one, the hangar roofs began peeling off. It was uncanny, seeing them ripped away without hearing the scream of metal. For a second the stored planes were visible, laid out in rows beneath them, and then it was as if a huge finger had reached down into each building and started to stir, round and round, faster and faster, as wings splintered and bits spewed up into the air.

It was a mesmerizing display of destruction, with all the reality of cinema. Then—

CRACK!

A stray piece of a cockpit grazed the body of their plane.

"More height!"

Nobody argued.

"I can see all the way to those mountains now!" yelled Madlen.

"Where?" Bryn shoved her head aside and peered forward. "Lemme see. I don't see any mountains!"

"Wait till we come round again. . . . Look—there!"

A great smudge stretched across the horizon. It was peculiarly blurry and hard to focus on, as if fog or clouds were getting in the way.

They stared, puzzled.

"That's not mountains." Cam's voice was high-pitched. "That's the sandstorm."

"That's sand?" bleated Bryn.

"A wall of sand. Over a mile in height. Moving at more than fifty miles per hour. I *told* you," yelled Cam.

"You told us," murmured Madlen, appalled. "But telling isn't the half of it!"

The plane began to buck sharply, irregularly, so that the three kept banging their heads on the roof. The sun was obscured by infinitesimally fine dust that smeared the sun's light and at the same time made it seem to loom, impossibly large, impossibly close. The greenish cast of earlier was replaced now by a kind of acid white, like overexposed film. With the colors of their clothes and skin leached out like that, they looked like a crew of ghosts.

"That's the best we're going to get," Cam yelled.

"What?"

"The thermals. All used up. It's the straight climb for us now."

And as the plane came round one last time, Cam leaned it

away from the plateau and out toward the open desert.

The leading edge of the haboob stretched right across the horizon, as far as the eye could see. And it was growing, higher, and higher . . .

"How far away would you say that is?" Bryn called from behind the seats. "I mean, just how big *is* it?"

Cam shrugged. "Hard to say. If I knew how far away it was, I could take a guess at how high it reached. And the other way round, of course. Basic trig—"

"Never mind that! How long before it gets here?" interrupted Madlen.

"Long enough!" Cam yelled reassuringly, and gave the others a thumbs-up of encouragement.

It's up to you now, beautiful, it thought to the plane. Cam could feel itself reaching out, to the wings, to the engine, to the prop, willing them to be strong and fleet. *You can do it.*

"Can't you go up any steeper?" Bryn yelled.

"No. Too steep a climb makes her stall."

The haboob raced to meet them. They could see it more clearly by the second, how its leading edge bulged and tumbled, the dust the color of rusty blood. Incongruously, the sky above the storm was still bright blue. That was the sky they were aiming for, but it wasn't getting any closer.

It was as if they were sinking, and not rising at all.

Cam had the stick as far back as it would go, the throttle wide open. Every muscle in Cam's body was rigid with concentration.

"Cam?" quavered Madlen. "Cam?"

For a long moment Cam didn't speak. Then Madlen could see its confidence drain away.

"No," Cam said. "We're not going to make it. We're too slow, and too weak, and too heavy."

Suddenly Cam slammed its fist into the dashboard so hard it left a dent.

"I won't do it!" Cam yelled. "I won't kill you for them!"

The others stared, frightened and confused.

"Throw the fruit out—there's a hatch on the floor. Throw it all out!"

"But—," Bryn tried to protest.

"DO IT!" Cam screamed.

They sped across the desert, a rain of Corym in their wake. The plane lifted as it lightened, reaching for height like a climbing plant reaches for the sun. But all the while the wall of darkness rolled closer and closer, eating the sky as it came.

"That's it, Cam! We've done it. We've done our best!"

But the same thought screamed in each mind:

Was it enough?

CHAPTER FIFTY-SIX

Elsewhere

In another place, Mrs. Macmahonney was staring at her blender.

"Kate?" Her voice was hesitant, but it brought Kate to her side in an instant.

"What is it?"

Mrs. Mac didn't answer. The liquid in the blender was turning color. It was darkening, and the blades were picking up speed. The sound they produced was becoming shriller and harsher. Mrs. Macmahonney began pressing buttons urgently, and dragged on the lever, and then leaned over and wrenched the plug out of the wall.

No effect. If anything, the noise got worse, more frenzied, and the blades screamed.

Then it blew up.

Mrs. Macmahonney and Kate were thrown backward onto the floor. A black-red liquid, like old blood, spattered over the wall, and one of the blades imbedded itself in the table leg, inches from Kate's head.

"GET THEM BACK!" yelled Mrs. Macmahonney. "NOW!"

CHAPTER FIFTY-SEVEN

The Desert

A young man paused to stretch his back from the digging. His name was Ebb. He had lived in the desert all his life, and though this storm had been well worse than any he'd experienced before, it was still one of many, and the routine of the aftermath remained the same. He and Nari, his wife, had already repitched the tent and brought their belongings back to it from the shelter of the caves. The animals were still tethered there, to keep them out of the way for a time, but they were thirsty. He needed to get the wellhead dug clear of sand soon, so that he could water them. It would be good to get some of the grit off his own skin too, he was thinking—when he saw the plane.

Ebb was amazed. *Whoever'd fly through a storm like that must be mad!* he thought.

The plane was coming in to land on a stretch of flat ground a little to the south. Ebb watched intently. The lineup was only a little shaky. Just before the wheels touched down, the pilot pulled the nose up. It had the makings of a decent landing—until, at the very last moment, the wind threw a vicious cross-gust. It caught the plane's underbelly and flipped it effortlessly onto its back.

Ebb gasped. Shouting for Nari, he threw down his shovel and began to run. Then, "Thank goodness!" he panted.

A figure was crawling out of the stricken plane, and another, and a third.

Madlen got to her feet. She was out of the plane and firmly on the ground, but the sky still whirled and her stomach was in revolt. She closed her eyes and tried to breathe deeply, calmingly. It only made things worse.

Then people began to arrive from out of nowhere. It made no sense for there to be people here at all, and when they started to talk to her, she found she couldn't concentrate on what they were saying.

"They want to know if we're injured." That was Cam's voice, nice and familiar, though it sounded odd. There was a thin line of blood running down its forehead. It asked, "Are you injured?"

"Er, no, no," said Madlen. "I don't think so. Bruises and stuff, but, no—"

She turned away and was sick on the sand. "I think I'd like to lie down for a bit," she said when she'd finished.

"I'm Nari. I'll take you," said one of the people, speaking slowly and carefully. She was a small woman, pretty and dark. Madlen felt too tall, too big all over, but when she stumbled, Nari had no difficulty holding her up.

"You're very strong for such a little person," mumbled Madlen. Her brain was so shaken up, she just said whatever lay on the top.

But Nari didn't seem offended. "Thank you!" she said with a beautiful smile.

Madlen concentrated on putting one foot in front of the other.

Finally they reached a low tent and Madlen crawled in, deeply thankful to be out of the remains of the wind, and off her feet. Nari settled her at once on a pile of rugs to one side and brought her a cup to drink from. Sleep was fast taking her over, when Madlen suddenly struggled onto one elbow and plucked at Nari's sleeve.

"The others are okay," she muttered. "Right?"

Nari patted her as if she were a child, and said, "You're not to worry. They are unhurt, the other high-castes. Now you rest."

Madlen lay back, sleep blurring everything around her. *That's good,* she thought, *the others are okay. The other . . . high-castes . . .*

She frowned, and slept.

Bryn was bruised and confused and deliriously happy. He partly understood how great the loss of the Corym was; he partly couldn't believe their luck at still being alive; but mostly, he was filled with the joy of flying.

It had been so . . . not like anything else. Maybe the danger they'd been in had added some essential spice, but he didn't think it was just that. He wanted to do it again, not in the storage compartment next time. He wanted to be doing it *himself,* with *him* as the pilot. It had been . . .

Bryn sat on the sand and cradled his bandaged hand, trying not to grin, while Cam talked to the stranger.

Cam was not seriously injured. There was no overwhelmingly strong physical pain it could use to wrap round the horrible coldness inside.

"There is a communication center a few hours from here." The man—Ebb—was speaking. "It's too late today, but tomorrow I will take you there. Meanwhile, I hope you will come to my tent and rest?"

Cam nodded mechanically.

"And the plane?" the man asked. "What would you like me to do with it?" He meant *Do you want me to cover it? Should I try to turn it over?* But Cam said, "Keep it," in a dead voice.

"K-keep—," sputtered Ebb, astonished, but the high-caste emergent was already turning away.

After he had handed the strangers over to Nari in their tent, Ebb stood outside for a minute, thinking. He wondered, just for a moment, what it would be like to *be* high-caste, to live on the cliffs, to have dreams, to have wings—to have wings even to give away! He smiled. He knew better. Those kinds of things weren't for the likes of him.

Then his youngest, Tem, walking now for less than a week, fell over onto its nose and howled. Ebb laughed to himself, and scooped it up. The child snuggled in.

Well, he thought, *I might not have wings, but I do have a wellhead to dig out.* He set the toddler back on its feet, and went to do just that.

A little time later, Nari came out of their tent, collected Tem, and left to see to the animals. Over her shoulder the child saw a figure, appearing suddenly as if from nowhere. The figure looked around, and then hid behind a rock. Tem thought about this for a moment. Then forgot about it.

After a while the figure reappeared and crept toward the tent. It was cloaked, and held something in its hand that might or might not have been a weapon. There was something disturbing about the way it seemed to blur in and out of focus. Something sinister . . .

The figure ducked in under the flap of the tent.

It was hours later, and too dark to work anymore, when Ebb crawled under the tent flap at last. He'd cleared the wellhead, and the beasts had been seen to, and that was all this day could ask of anyone.

"Our guests?" he said softly to Nari, as he started to strip off his shirt. She'd lit just the one light, and it was pleasantly quiet and dim indoors.

"Gone," she said.

"What?" His voice was muffled in his shirt, but he managed to fight his way out of the folds. "They're what?"

Nari shrugged. "I don't know how. I'm not even sure when. I just know they were here, and when I came back a while ago, they had left."

He could tell she was angry. He reached across and took her hands in his. She tried to pull away but he held on.

"Well?" he said gently.

She stopped fighting and looked at him, hurt.

"They didn't say thank you," she said. "They didn't say good-bye and they didn't say thank you. Tem has better manners and it's barely one."

Ebb pulled her over to sit beside him, and she leaned into his shoulder. He put an arm round her.

"It seems rude, I don't argue," he said. "But I'm wondering"—she started to pull away again but he tightened his hold—*"just wondering,* though, whether they might have reasons. Two of them—did you notice?—weren't even Dalrodian.

And if they come from a different place, maybe they might have *different* manners."

She shook her head vigorously. "No," she said. "Saying thank you is manners for everybody."

"Well, you're right, of course," he said, and so she felt obliged to take the other side, as he knew she would.

"Maybe they had to leave in such a hurry that they just didn't have time . . . ," she began.

"There's always time for good manners," Ebb said pompously.

Nari punched him on the arm, none too gently.

"I wouldn't have thought they were any of them fit to go far," she said. Then with a sigh she got up. "Well, wherever they are, they're nothing to us, and I've food to serve. Get washed *now,* you sonk, and come and eat."

Ebb grinned, and went to wash.

He didn't hear her when she said, very quietly, as she reached for a plate, "I hope they're all right."

THE LONDON HOUSE

CHAPTER FIFTY-EIGHT

<u>Returns</u>

"What's wrong with them?" Kate shrieked. "What's happened?"

Ben leaned against the wall of the kitchen, looking like pale death. The three children lay in a heap about his feet.

"Still breathing," he panted. "Not harmed, Kate, I swear. It wasn't something you'd have wanted them doing while conscious."

Mrs. Macmahonney was on her knees, anxiously checking pulses and pulling back eyelids.

"Leave off!" yelled Bryn, curling instinctively around his bandaged hand. The others also began to stir and complain.

Kate threw herself into Ben's arms, nearly knocking him over, wailing incoherent thanks.

A peculiar expression came over his face, but then he shook his head reluctantly. "No time. Get them upstairs."

The moment she pulled away from him, he slid to the floor and shut his eyes. "I'll catch you up," he murmured, as Kate and Mrs. Mac dragged the three onto their feet and pushed them out the door.

Outside the kitchen everything had changed. They were in a corridor when they should have been on a stair, and there was no clue which way they should be heading.

"Come on," said Mrs. Mac, frantically peering back and forth. "Come on, come on."

Cam was swaying slightly.

"Wait, this is all wrong!" it said. "We have to go back. *I* have to go back!" When the adults just looked at it, shaking their heads, its voice grew shriller. "Don't you understand, you made a mistake! You've pulled us out too soon! *The Quest isn't complete!*"

Cam threw the other two agonized looks, but there was nothing they could do.

"They'll *have* to let us go back," Madlen whispered.

Bryn gripped Cam's shoulder. "Yeah," he said. "The second this crisis thing is over, we're straight back to Dalrodia and this lot can go and—"

Mrs. Macmahonney coughed sharply and Bryn subsided.

"Just *what's* going on?" Madlen turned on her.

"We pulled you out."

"I'd gathered that," she said rudely. *"Why?"*

"Too dangerous," said Mrs. Mac.

"But the storm was *over*!" said Cam.

"Not there," said Kate. "Here. It's getting too dangerous *here*. So what do we do? Oh, right, we bring you back." She laughed, and then choked it down, as if afraid of losing control.

"Gotcha!" cried Mrs. Mac, lunging at the wall opposite. It parted before her like the Red Sea, becoming another corridor. She bustled them along it.

"This way!" called Lady Mary from the far end. "I'm holding the door for you."

"Bless you, lass!" Mrs. Macmahonney sounded surprisingly grateful.

The Questors exchanged worried glances as they followed after her.

Almost before they were through it, the door slammed shut, clipping Madlen's heels. Lady Mary didn't apologize. She didn't even seem to notice. All around them the chamber was in a complete state. The acrid smell of too much energy discharge caught at their throats. Whoever'd set up the chairs wouldn't be using them again, since nothing much remained of the furniture but oddly sinister-looking heaps of melted material. Mrs. Mac tutted at the sight and flicked her wrist, but nobody really noticed the way she made them disappear.

As Lady Mary moved to join the other Prelates, the children were shocked to see how rumpled they'd all become. Lord Metheglin, Lord Bullvador, Lady Vera, Lady Mary, Lady Beatitude—they all looked haggard and hollow-eyed and . . . diminished.

The Council members, for their part, barely recognized the three children in the battered, wild-haired figures before them now. The children were the same people of course, but they wore their tattered, exotic finery with a difference. Lady Mary was distracted enough to begin to say, "My, how you've grow—" when someone *else* exploded into the room in a flurry of grit and gale.

It was Alpine Cordell.

"Where have you been?" bellowed Lord Bullvador.

"It's *him*!" cried Kate and Mrs. Mac, immediately pushing the children behind them.

"You're late," said a voice that no one quite recognized.

And Lady Beatitude stepped away from her colleagues and joined the Secretary. All the crazy vagueness fell away from her like a sloughed skin, and her pretty features hardened.

"I told you to get rid of them," she grated. "You didn't. And you've got *sand in your hair*!"

The man stiffened. "Fieldwork can be trying, Preceptor," he said, but Lady Beatitude was already turning her shoulder to him.

"It isn't important," she said.

"Preceptor. Your humble servant." His bow expressed many things, but humility was not one of them.

"Why is he calling her that?" Kate turned to Mrs. Macmahonney, eyes wide.

"Bea!" shrilled Lord Metheglin. "What's going on!"

"Oh, *really.*" Lady Beatitude turned her face insolently toward him. "You don't need me to spell it out for you, do you?"

There was a sharp intake of breath, then, "Don't overplay your part, dear," said Lady Mary quietly. "It's not . . . professional."

The color drained from Lady Beatitude's porcelain skin, and then flooded back again. "Heaven forbid," she said, tight-lipped. She flicked a finger at Cordell. "Call up the Lady Mary's Questors' file."

A gesture—and the hologram appeared in the center of the chamber, in all its original beauty, the figures luminous with qualities and virtues, the lines of light that joined them glowing. The whole image spun slowly before them in its stately dance.

"And then along came our Bea, loopy harmless Bea, *who had been overplaying her part for years and years,* to work a little magic of her own." Lady Beatitude's voice was harsh. It grated on them.

"What did you do?" demanded Vera.

"What did I do? As I remember, I did very little. . . . Cordell, *my* Questors' file."

A shadowy image of Lady Beatitude stepped away from the Prelate's body, moved forward, and silently dipped its hand in the hologram. The figures bleared, the colors muddied.

"But—but you could have no idea what effect that would have!" Lord Metheglin was shocked. "They could have had any number of physical or mental defects. You couldn't possibly have known how they'd turn out!"

Beatitude smiled. "Except for one thing," she said. "I knew they wouldn't be perfect. You needed perfection. I just made sure you didn't get it."

She turned her head, and looked at the three.

Looked *into* the three.

It was horrible. Without warning she was inside their heads. She was jury, and judge, and there was no appeal. They were being considered down to the depths of their beings, *tested*— and found wanting. Her contempt for them was so complete, so debilitating, so bleak . . .

"Oh well, if it was *perfection* the old dears were after, thank goodness loony Bea *did* stick her finger in!" It was Mrs. Mac, in a loud stage whisper. Lady Beatitude jerked, turned on her with a hiss—and the three Questors drew ragged breaths, alone in their heads again. They huddled closer.

Lady Beatitude sneered, but didn't renew the assault.

On Alpine Cordell's lips there might just have been the flicker of a smile as he removed the hologram.

For a moment no one spoke. Then, "Tampering with the children was not an isolated act, was it?" asked Lady Vera. She addressed Cordell directly, as if she couldn't bring herself to speak to Beatitude.

Again the flicker of a smile.

"No. Oh no. The Preceptor's activities began much, much

earlier," he said. "Then, sometime later, my . . . *recruitment* took place. Lady Beatitude felt there were too many dimensions for *one* to direct. Though, interestingly, diverting energy from the balance did not prove all that difficult. And the Worlds . . . *cooperated* a good deal."

"*What?*"

Cordell nodded. "Oh yes. It was in their natures! Trentor, for example. It was bound to throw up some sort of character like the child Frederick. All that institutionalized autism couldn't fail to produce results. Kir, having two separate sentient species, muddied the waters a little. Once we ascertained which to concentrate on, however, the path became clearer, though not having multiple nostril pairs made it tricky at first to get the dragons' attention. And Dalrodia—well, with a caste system like that, there was very little to do. It was simply a rotten apple ready to fall into our palm. I believe I just made a joke."

No one seemed able to speak at first, or to meet one another's eyes.

"You tipped the Worlds out of balance, on purpose, and then stood back while they grew more and more out of sync." It was Lord Bullvador who summed it up.

There was a sigh from the others, as if in resignation that what should not be thought had now been said.

Beatitude applauded. "Oh, very good. Got it at last. You know, a surprisingly *tiny* degree of instability was all that was required. I simply didn't pull my weight one day, when our happy Prelate family was engaged in yet another act of mindless maintenance. Nobody noticed at the time, but from then on . . . And one of the wonders of inertia is its relentlessness. One . . . little . . . shove . . ."

"You must have been pretty worried, then, when we decided

on the Questors," Lord Metheglin blustered unconvincingly.

Lady Beatitude snorted. "Of course I wasn't worried! After I fine-tuned them, they were bound to fail. All they had to do was run true to their breeding—perfectly equipped, by design, to boldly go and get themselves killed. Well, imagine my surprise when they couldn't even manage to do *that*! In spite of all my assistance, they survived and still brought home the bacon. *The culmination of the Traditional Option. Quests. Questors.*" She spoke as if the words tasted foul to her mouth. "*The Objects of Power.* Of course I'd a plan in place to cover even that possibility, unlikely as it seemed. I 'encouraged' my colleagues to 'encourage' the children to seek out particular kinds of Objects. So what did the Council (under my tutelage) want the Questors to return with? After all, the data banks are full to bursting with mythic symbolism. What Objects of Power seemed fit to them?" Lady Beatitude showed her teeth in a grin. "The Ribbon of Abstract Thought. The Crystal of Courage. The Fruit of Dreams." She snorted. "Straight out of a kiddies' computer game. Just the sort of sentimental slop they *wanted* to see. And now they can. Show them, children. Show the Council the Objects of Power you have brought."

The three Questors instantly felt a horrible constraint, a grinding mental pressure. It made them want to do *anything,* just to make it stop.

"You first, boy," said Beatitude. "Give it to me. Give me the Crystal."

With a great effort Bryn shook his head. "I haven't got it," he wheezed.

"Don't even think of lying to me," said Lady Beatitude coldly. She seemed to be listening for something—and the sense of someone rummaging inside Bryn's mind intensified.

"But you're not!" she shrilled, just as Bryn cried out, *"I'm not! I'm not! Leave me alone!"*

With a speed that took them all by surprise, Lady Beatitude lunged at Bryn and ripped the dragon claw out of his pocket.

She drew in her breath, harsh and sharp, and blindly thrust the claw away from her. It clattered to the floor, and Bryn scrambled after it.

Beatitude swerved abruptly toward Madlen, who automatically put her hand up to her throat. The woman wrenched the string from her neck and stared at the little axe, panting.

"No," she muttered, flinging the necklace back in Madlen's face. *"No!"*

Then it was Cam's turn. With a visible effort Lady Beatitude regained control over herself. She moved closer, towering menacingly over the Dalrodian.

"You, at least, will not disappoint," Lady Beatitude said huskily. "You're Holder stock, half at least. You will have been able to see the obvious."

Cam felt her pushing, shoving through its mind.

"Tell—me—where—it—*is*!"

For a tiny second Cam saw her face waver, as if it were coming out of focus. But before the search could start again—

"Cam, it's in your pocket," Mrs. Macmahonney interrupted. Her voice was very quiet, and sure.

For one wild wonderful moment, Cam thought that somehow, magically, it would reach its hand into its pocket, and there would be something there. *Anything* there. From out of nowhere, the final Quest Object. It hadn't all been a waste; Cam hadn't failed, alone of all the Questors, to bring back anything at all. It would be ALL RIGHT.

The Dalrodian reached its hand into its pocket, and for a long moment no one breathed.

Then, with a great sigh, Cam brought its hand into the open and held it out for all to see.

Empty.

CHAPTER FIFTY-NINE

<u>Reversals</u>

And Lady Beatitude began to laugh. There was a hysterical edge to her laughter that frightened the Questors almost more than anything that had gone before.

"That's it, is it?" she cackled. "These are the Objects of Power that will save the Worlds? A trinket, an old claw, and . . . nothing? Is that the best you can do?"

"On the contrary," said Lady Mary in her quiet voice. "I find the children's selections extremely . . . enlightening."

"Yes. Indeed," said Lord Metheglin. "It almost makes one wonder if we may have made just the smallest miscalculation."

Lady Mary and Lord Metheglin looked at each other thoughtfully.

"From the beginning," Mary said, "you'll remember it was our understanding that the Quest would be a search for the *most,* the *greatest,* the *epitome.* Each World's strength writ large."

"Just the things for Questors who were the most, the greatest . . . ," said Metheglin. "Traditional Heroes and Heroines for the Traditional Option. But—"

"But," Mary said, "what if, all along, it was not the *pinnacle* of each of the Worlds that was needed, but the exact *opposite*?"

There was a moment of intense thought as everyone in the room considered this extraordinary statement, but it was Beatitude who got there first.

"What?" She was breathing heavily, and suddenly looked old. Then she rallied. "What difference does it make?" she mocked. "It won't work anyway. It's far too late *now*! You haven't a hope of undoing what I've done. None of your precious plans and mighty efforts had a chance against *me*—"

"But *why*?" Lord Bullvador interrupted, sounding honestly puzzled. "I don't understand!"

Lady Beatitude looked up at him, sideways, a curious expression of longing and slyness on her face. "Oh, Bull. You never should have brought me back after the accident. It was cruel. Don't you remember how exciting I used to be? Don't you remember how I used to make your heart race? Isn't that why you wanted me on the Council in the first place? Everybody knew—"

He said nothing, but his face paled.

"What do you mean, we never should have brought you back?" cut in Lady Vera. "You were dead, Bea, as near as dammit *scattered.* How can you say we shouldn't have tried to save you?"

Lady Beatitude turned to her, every gesture of her body portraying the sorrow of the unjustly accused. "Did you *ask*? What do you know about me? What do you know about how I suffered? You never liked me, none of you, only Bull did." Tears came prettily to her eyes, a single one trickling gently down her smooth cheek.

The atmosphere was thick with embarrassment and guilt, surprised out of hiding by her nobility, her dignified grief. Even the children were ashamed, deeply, achingly, hopelessly.

"What a pan of tripe." Mrs. Mac's voice made everyone jump. She stood there, fists on hips, her jaw stuck out, frowning fiercely. "I can't believe supposedly intelligent people like you are wasting your time listening to this, pardon me, crap. Do you not know twisted when you meet it?"

"I can make them think anything I want!" Lady Beatitude spat, her face suddenly contorted, ugly.

Mrs. Mac nodded. "Maybe so. Maybe so. You've huge power, Bea. Even now, when it's all falling apart."

"I don't have to talk to you!" Beatitude turned her back and spoke to the Prelates. "Well? And what are you going to do about it? Dock Cordell's pay? Send me to my room without supper? You don't *know* what to do when an oh-so-holy Prelate goes bad, do you! Deary me. *Not* an everyday event!"

"No, not everyday," said Lady Vera. "But of course there are precedents." She paused. "You could hardly think you were the first."

Lady Beatitude stared. It was obvious she had thought just that.

"Oh no," Vera continued. "You're not unique. Nothing new under the sun, as they say. Sadly true." She spoke almost absentmindedly. Something strange seemed to pass between her and the other three Prelates, a not-quite-visible exchange of glances, a decision made. Without Lady Beatitude's noticing, there was a shift in the room, a drop in temperature, a feeling of the walls moving in.

And then the walls *did* move. Perhaps not the actual walls, but the shadows within them. The darkness started to come closer, and began to spin round the lighted center of the room, slowly at first, but picking up speed. Lady Vera talked on.

"It's so difficult to be truly original."

Lady Beatitude's eyes narrowed.

The shadows whirled silently round them all, impersonal, deadly, and black.

"There's nothing you can do to me," Beatitude snarled. "I'll get out of any cage you can think of. Because I'm smarter than you—*smarter than all of you*!"

The walls of shadow were spinning faster now. It was almost as if their pace responded to the growing hysteria in Lady Beatitude's voice.

How can she not see it? Madlen wondered.

It's fear. It's taking her over, thought Bryn.

Poor fool. Poor fool. It was Ivory's voice in Cam's head. It was Cam's voice as well.

There were flecks of foam on Beatitude's lips. She was edging away from the Prelates, tiny steps, almost imperceptible, steps that brought her closer and closer to the spinning dark, but she was oblivious to the danger. She was hunched and crabbed now like a caricature of the wicked witch.

"Why, Bea? Why?" Lord Bullvador whispered to her.

Her voice scraped and snarled. "You want to know why I did it? Do you? I'll tell you. I did it because I c—"

—and the wall took her. It swallowed her up, and there was nothing left in the place where she had stood.

There was a moment of utter, breathless silence. Then, "I warned her about overplaying," murmured Lady Mary.

"Where *is* she?" Madlen whispered.

"Scattered." It was Alpine Cordell who spoke. His dry voice jarred on their stretched nerves. For once, e*veryone* was noticing him. He shrugged. "I make it my business to always know the precedents."

"Then . . . you know it is your turn next," said Lord Bullvador.

Alpine Cordell stood for a moment, his eyes fixed on a point just above their heads. It was, as always, impossible to guess from his face what he was thinking.

"Mr. Cordell!" prompted Lady Vera in her most commanding voice.

The Secretary began to walk toward the wall of shadow.

"My turn?" he was heard to say. "Really? I think not."

Before anyone could speak he had raised his hands and entered the spinning darkness. The shadows parted before him like curtains and then, as he passed, closed in behind. As if drained of its energy, the spinning wall slowed and stopped, and became only shadows again. But Alpine Cordell had disappeared.

"Goodness!"

"Well, I'll be . . ."

"Meth?"

The Prelate concentrated for a long moment, then shook his head. "I've no sense of him. Not in the House. Nowhere in the Worlds."

"Not even . . . scattered?"

"No."

"Flipping hell," Lord Bullvador said, remembered the children, and coughed.

Suddenly someone broke into the light at almost exactly the same spot Cordell had just left it, so that they all jumped back, startled. But it wasn't the Secretary returning. It was the Agent, Ben. If he'd looked bad before, he looked worse now.

"I had to come and tell you. We've done . . . everything we could," he panted. "It's not enough. We cannot hold."

There was a moment when only his ragged breathing could be heard, and then Lord Bullvador bowed his head.

"All right, Meth," said Lady Vera. "It's time."

Without a word Lord Metheglin turned and walked away. No one moved or spoke. Then the sound of his footsteps could be heard, returning through the darkness.

As he emerged into the light, they could see he had something in his hands.

CHAPTER SIXTY

Revelations

The object Lord Metheglin carried was draped in a dark velvet cloth. Lord Bullvador brought a small table from somewhere, put it down, and stepped back.

Metheglin laid the object on the table and, with a curious gentleness, drew the velvet cloth away. The Questors, Kate, and Ben craned forward to see what this wonder might be.

They saw a box, wooden perhaps, and black with age.

"What is it?" whispered Cam.

"It's just an old box," said Madlen, disappointed.

Lady Mary spoke without taking her eyes off the object.

"A *very* old box," she said quietly. "There has been a Council to care for the Three Worlds for a rather amazingly long time, my dears, and the box is far older than *that*. Watch now."

Lord Metheglin took a deep breath, and closed his eyes. The light in the room drew in, concentrating on the box. No one dared blink or hardly breathe. The shadows crowded behind them as if trying to look over their shoulders, to see what was to happen next.

Metheglin was speaking now, but so softly no one could hear the words. He began to move his long thin hands, tracing shapes in the air that glittered for a moment on the eye, like sparklers in the park. At first nothing changed, and then, silently, and with an odd old smell, the blackened box heaved itself open like ancient toothless jaws.

Inside were three more boxes, one a ruddy cherrywood, one deep mahogany, one the palest beech. As if in answer to Metheglin's murmuring voice and the gestures of his hands, the three boxes rose up until they were free of the casing.

They hung there, waiting.

"Questors."

The children jumped at the sound of Lady Vera's voice.

"Go on."

Hesitantly, they reached out their hands. There was no question in anyone's mind which of the boxes to choose. They plucked them out of the air and held them gingerly, Bryn the cherrywood box, Madlen the mahogany, Cam the beech.

Madlen looked up to ask what they were to do next, but it was already happening. Like miniature versions of the casing, the three boxes also opened their mouths.

"Put in what you have found."

Madlen slipped the string over her head and held it above the box. She let it and the tiny axe slide through her fingers. The necklace lay against the dark wood, shimmering slightly.

Bryn cradled the box against his body and used his good hand to pull the dragon's claw out of his pocket. He paused, then placed it gently into the rich warm interior.

Cam looked at the box in its hand for a long moment. It sensed a rustle of movement outside the circle of light, as if someone had involuntarily reached out, and as suddenly changed their mind.

It didn't matter. Nobody else seemed real just then; nothing else seemed important. Only the box.

Cam could see every line of the grain in the wood, and smell the very faint aroma that the living tree had left behind. It reached out its hand, and turned it, open-palmed, over the empty box, and felt the energy pour from one to the other. Then it closed its hand and let it drop to its side.

The box no longer seemed empty.

There was a soft, sourceless sigh, and the three boxes closed. Lord Metheglin's voice was heard again, speaking just below the level of comprehension. The boxes moved back above their casing and sank, seamlessly, into it. The black lid closed with a minute click . . .

. . . and that could so easily have been the end of it. Magic and miracle enough. Certainly the Prelates weren't expecting anything more. Lord Metheglin had already stepped forward with the velvet cloth to cover it all again. But before he could do so—

The casing changed. From an ancient, opaque black, it cleared now into a rich deep orange color. It began to glow, as if from an internal light, and it appeared translucent. In its depths something stirred as if alive, but what it was they couldn't see.

"Amber," somebody breathed. "I never knew it was amber."

A wonderful warm smell filled the chamber. And then it all faded—the light, the warmth, the scent, and there was nothing left but the ancient black casing, giving no hint to what it was or what it contained.

Metheglin covered it reverently with the velvet, and carried it away. Nobody stirred until he had come back again.

Then, as he reentered the circle of light, the spell broke with an almost audible snap. Bullvador, Mary, and Vera clustered round, beaming and thumping him on the back.

"Well done, Methy!"

"That was splendid!"

"Good job!"

Lord Metheglin managed to look suitably solemn and modest for about a second. Then, grinning wildly, he did a dance that showed off his skinny legs and sent his robe swirling.

"It's done! We did it! Did you see that? Fabulous! Hurrah!"

"Anybody'd think *they* were the Questors!" muttered Mrs. Mac to Bryn, but there was no sting in her words. He smiled happily back.

"So, it's all right now?" squeaked Cam. "We did it, right?"

"I don't understand!" Madlen wailed. It was all too much.

The adults instinctively responded to the note of incipient hysteria in her voice.

"Well, now, of course you don't. How could you?" cooed Lady Mary.

"Steady on, girl!" Lady Vera sounded a bit panicky.

"Meth! Explain to the children at once!" boomed Lord Bullvador.

"Why of course. Of course. It's very simple, really. Here, I'll call up the file on epic symbols." Lord Metheglin, pink-faced, tidied his robe and then busied himself with his palmtop. "No . . . no, not that bit. . . . Right, here we go."

And he began to read aloud.

"'Objects of Power tend to have a strong metaphorical significance, far beyond the apparent actual value that could be assigned them.' . . . Blah, blah . . . Specifics, please . . . ah . . . 'The Hatchet or Axe, for example, is the weapon of choice of the Hero/Heroine who wishes to set free all those entrapped by spells.' See? And then . . . 'The Claw of a Dragon is a symbol of balance—one side cuts, the other heals.' Perfectly simple . . .

'And the Rich Woman's/Man's Empty Hand is the sign of the one who has given up everything for others.'"

Lord Metheglin beamed at them all indiscriminately.

"See? Miss Madlen's World was enslaved by its own 'institutionalized autism,' if I may borrow a phrase from our departed, um, colleague. So the correctly significant Object of Power required would *not* be the *pinnacle* of that process—the Ribbon of Abstract Thought—but instead its opposite. Impassioned action, as symbolized by the, er, diminutive axe. Master Bryn's World was in need of healing to balance the unduly violent heroics, and young emergent Cam's World needed to face the end of the current political paradigm and so what was required there was *not* the Fruit of Dreams as was our original postulation—"

"In other words," interrupted Lady Vera, "we goofed."

"All right, all right. Yes. Though I wouldn't have put it just that way," huffed Lord Metheglin. "I admit we were *mistaken* in inclining to the 'pinnacle' approach, as opposed to the slightly less obvious 'opposite-to-equalize' approach, which has in point of fact proved to be—"

Lady Mary turned to the three children. "It's just as well our poems were as challenging as they were. Otherwise you might have been misled."

The Questors looked blank.

"What poems?" said Bryn.

"We never saw any poems," said Cam.

Kate coughed. "Um, sorry. Apparently they . . . never arrived."

"WHAT!"

Lady Vera guffawed and patted Metheglin heartily on the back. "And you put all that effort into them, didn't you! Poor Meth!"

"Well, actually, Bea did a lot of the work . . . ," began Lord Metheglin. His voice died away as he realized what he'd just said.

In the embarrassed silence that followed, Cam's whisper was easily heard.

"But what about the future? I want to know what's supposed to happen *now*."

"Ah," said Lord Metheglin. "Well. I'm glad you asked me that question. It's a very good question and it does you credit. It really does—"

"Oh, Meth, stop drivelling!" interrupted Lady Vera. "Just *tell* the child!"

Lord Metheglin drew himself up. "I was not drivelling!" he said indignantly. "I was simply trying to encourage a young inquiring mind in its, um, inquiring—"

"We don't know," said Lady Vera flatly, turning her back on her irate colleague. "There are any number of computer models to choose from, of course. You're welcome to review the data. It's filed under "futures.dowehave1.doc." But I suspect we'll be taking the Traditional Option on this one too."

"The Traditional Option?" said Madlen, nervously.

"Yes—you know—'Wait and See.'" Lady Vera nodded once, firmly.

"It's going to be ever so interesting," chirped Lady Mary.

Madlen, Bryn, and Cam looked at one another, and at Kate, and burst out laughing.

As his colleagues were busy staring anxiously at the uncontrollably giggling and snorting Questors, Lord Bullvador took the opportunity for a quiet word with Mrs. Mac.

"We'll need a replacement," he said, leaning down to her.

"Four isn't exactly a mythic number in these cases, as of course you know. So I was wondering . . . ?"

He looked at her hopefully.

"No chance," said Mrs. Macmahonney loudly.

The others looked over, and came to join them.

"Eh?" said Lord Meth, "What's wrong *here*?"

Bullvador heaved an irritated sigh. "Nothing's wrong," he muttered. "Everything's grand. I was just speaking with Mrs. Macmahonney about the empty place on the Council. It's not important."

"Not important!" bugled Lady Vera. "Not important! Really, Bull—"

"Of course, there's always Nigel." Lady Mary's deceptively gentle voice cut across her colleague's.

There was a general horrified gasp.

"You cannot be serious!"

"Mary!"

"Oh *no*!"

The noise they were making managed to cut through the giggling.

"Who's Nigel?" hiccuped Madlen to Kate, who was wiping her eyes.

"He's the Periodic Gentleman," she whispered back. "Used to be this very powerful guy, then he took early retirement. Now he's a sort of loose cannon at the House. They tell us to stay well out of his way, but they don't tell us why . . ."

"YOU CANNOT PUT NIGEL HETHERINGTON ON THE COUNCIL." It was Mrs. Mac. She was standing there, fists on hips, eyes sparking, effortlessly the center of attention.

"But, madam," murmured Lord Meth as if butter wouldn't melt in his mouth, "what else can we do?"

Lord Bullvador shot him a grateful glance, which he quickly changed to a concerned frown when he realized Mrs. Mac was glaring at him. There was a moment's silence.

"Oh, all *right*, then," she conceded crossly. "ON ONE CONDITION."

"Anything, dear lady, anything," cried Bullvador expansively, though the other Prelates looked worried. "Name your terms."

"One term," said Mrs. Mac. "One condition."

"Which is?" asked Lady Vera.

"We meet in the kitchen. I'm not having meals disrupted just because the Worlds need saving all the time." She glared around at them, defying anyone to object.

"Er . . ."

"Well, but . . ."

"Um . . ."

"That's fine, then. It's settled. Now if you don't mind, I've got a House to feed."

Mrs. Macmahonney strode out of the room like a stubby colossus. Nobody got in her way.

"What a woman," murmured Lord Bullvador, and then blushed.

As they came out of the Council chamber, Ben put a hand on Kate's arm.

"All right, then?" he asked.

Kate's smile was gigawatt.

"All right," she said.

"Kate?" It was Madlen calling, and Kate moved away without another glance.

But Ben was still watching, and Bryn was watching him.

"Personally," he murmured as he came up beside the Agent, "I think you should ask her out."

Ben twitched. "Her? What? Who?"

"Look, if it's permission you need, consider it given." Bryn grinned slyly up at him. "By the man of the family."

Then, with a squeaky giggle, the mighty, manly Questor trotted off down the corridor in search of food.

CHAPTER SIXTY-ONE

Attic Conversations

It was later on, and the three had been sent up to the attic bedrooms, by order of Mrs. Mac. Nobody'd argued.

When Kate came in, Madlen hadn't turned on the light yet. She was standing in the dusk beside the bed, looking up through the skylight at the stars.

"Amazing," said Kate quietly.

Madlen turned. "The stars? Yes, they are," she said.

"Er, no. I meant you." Kate blushed suddenly and flopped down on the bed. "Don't mind me. I'm new at this family business."

"Me too." Madlen grinned. "Maybe we could practice on each other?"

"I could try being terribly strict and proper, and you could slam doors, and throw things, and say how unfair it is that nothing ever happens to you," suggested Kate.

"Sure. Sounds like fun! And then we could get over it . . . and you could show me how you do that makeover thing on yourself in midair!"

"That is a deep dark secret," Kate began solemnly. Then she laughed. "Of course I'll show you how. It's just a matter of . . ."

❋ ❋ ❋

In the next room Bryn was aware of the pleasant murmur of Kate's and Madlen's voices, but he wasn't paying attention to any of the words. He was sitting cross-legged on the bed, with his drawing things laid neatly out around him. But he wasn't drawing. Not yet.

Instead he was looking at his hand. He'd undone Serena's bandages and put them aside, and now he studied the wound, turning his wrist so that he could observe it from every angle.

Mrs. Mac looked in on him, but didn't stop.

Then Kate came. She'd wished Madlen good night, and left her to get to bed. She felt warmed and full of hope for the Future—whatever that turned out to be. But here, in the present, there was her son.

Bryn looked up and saw her hesitating in the doorway.

"Don't worry, Mum," he said. "It's going to be all right." And he held out his hand to her, and wrapped her up in his brilliant smile.

"What's wrong?" Mrs. Macmahonney filled the doorway of Cam's room.

"So, did it all happen? Or didn't it?"

Mrs. Mac closed the door and came to sit on the bed. It creaked under her weight.

"That's right," she said.

"No, I mean *which*? . . . Oh. I see. Both. Sort of?"

Mrs. Mac patted Cam on the head like a clever dog.

"But that's not what's worrying you," she said.

There was a long pause.

"Is it Ivory?"

Another pause, and then Cam muttered, "Is she—will she be okay?"

"Well, that depends . . . on how good you are at forgiving her for your mistake."

Cam looked up. "I thought she was mad."

"She was, a bit," said Mrs. Mac agreeably.

"Then I thought she was . . . evil."

"She is that too, a little."

"I used to think she was perfect."

"*That's* the one," said Mrs. Macmahonney.

Cam thought for a moment, then nodded.

"So what else is wrong?" asked Mrs. Mac.

Cam sighed. "It's . . . I don't know what's going to happen next. When we go back. Back home. I mean, I can see how it'll be for the others. On Kir they'll stop killing each other so much, won't they? But it'll still be cold and castle-y and . . ."

" . . . knee-deep in testosterone?"

Cam smiled palely. "Yeah. And Trentor won't be all sort of fascist, but it'll still be like itself. Just a better version, you know?"

Mrs. Mac nodded. "That's plausible," she said.

"But, don't you see—it can't be like that for us. My World's *over*!" Cam's eyes were huge. "The Holders are discredited because of what happened, and the dreaming's done because I threw the Corym away. Madlen and Bryn—their Worlds get to go on and—and develop. Their Worlds will get more like the good bits that already exist. But the dreaming *was* the good bit for us."

Cam looked down at its hands, twisted together till the knuckles showed white. It unclenched and held them out.

"Our hands really are empty, Mrs. Mac," Cam said, and it let them drop.

There was a moment of silence in the room, and then Mrs. Mac stood up. "Funny things, hands," she said cheerfully.

Cam shifted irritably. Hadn't she understood? Didn't she care? This was *important*!

Mrs. Mac started to potter about the tiny room, humming a little, and Cam could feel its anger grow.

If she wasn't going to be sympathetic, she could just leave!

Mrs. Macmahonney didn't appear to notice the change in temperature. "So you threw them out of the plane. The apple things, I mean."

"I said so," grated Cam.

"And there was quite a high wind."

"YES!"

Mrs. Mac nodded, and began to pace the narrow room, a few steps and turn, a few steps and turn. Then she started to swing her arm, back and forth in front of her. The action was vague at first, and then became more definite. It was as if she were throwing something away, again and again.

Cam stared at her, then looked away, refusing to ask what she was doing.

Mrs. Mac didn't seem to care.

"There's a painting," she murmured, almost as if to herself. "I'm not sure where I saw it, but I can definitely remember it. There was a stormy sky, and a field, and a man with great huge slabs of hands. He had a bag of seed on one hip and was striding along like a giant, flinging the seed out over the soil." She matched her actions to the words, and cocked her head to one side, watching Cam. "You had the feeling he could have kept it up forever. It was called *The Sower,* as I remember."

She stopped in front of Cam. "Imagine what kind of area somebody like that could cover, if they had a plane to sow from," she said thoughtfully.

Cam's eyes got bigger. "I don't . . . understand," it said.

Mrs. Mac patted it kindly on the head and turned to leave. At the door she paused and, without looking back, murmured, "Brilliant tactic, if you think about it. A totally unbiased way of distributing a limited resource. It takes real political genius to come up with a plan like that."

She left. Cam didn't notice. It was staring at the floor, thinking. When Kate came by to say good night, it nodded to her but didn't speak.

Mrs. Macmahonney had disappeared, probably back down to her kitchen, but Kate paused, and then settled herself on the top of the stairs to keep watch for a while over her family.

There were rustling noises, and then a sigh or two as the Questors made themselves comfortable in their beds.

For a while there was silence. Then, "Madlen?" called Bryn softly from his room.

"Hmm?"

"What do you think she was saying?"

Madlen turned over onto an elbow. "Who?" she asked sleepily.

"You know—Lady Beatitude—at the end there. She started to say something. Bull said, 'Why did you do it?' and she said, 'Because I c—'." Bryn sounded worried. "What do you think she was going to say?"

Madlen thought for a moment. "'Because I can't stand it anymore'?" she suggested. "Or 'Because I couldn't care less'?" She shrugged. "*I* don't know. She's gone now, Bryn, so leave it. It doesn't matter. Go to sleep."

Nobody spoke for a bit, and Madlen's brain began to drift pleasantly toward oblivion.

Then Cam's voice jerked her back.

"I think she was saying, 'I did it because I could.'"

Out in the hall, Kate could feel the change, feel the tension grow. The voices of the children began to rocket back and forth between the rooms, eating away at the peace.

"If she could, that means somebody else could too."

"It could all happen—all over again!"

"Yeah, but they'd know what to look out for, another time. The Prelates, I mean. They'd know how to keep us safe."

"Not if it happened differently the next time. I mean, it was one of *them* last time, for crying out loud, and they didn't notice a *thing*. How safe was *that*?"

"So it could all go wrong. It could not be over at all."

"But it *has* to be . . ."

"No it doesn't. It doesn't *have* to be *any*thing. There aren't any guarantees."

"I think we'll not be having this conversation just now." It was Mrs. Mac. Unnoticed, the older woman had joined Kate on the stairs. Kate looked round quickly, but not quickly enough to see what Mrs. Macmahonney did. There was a shimmer, a subtle shift, and suddenly the silence was one of sleep. Even Kate began to yawn.

"Oh . . . my. I can't keep my . . . eyes open. . . ."

Mrs. Macmahonney gave Kate a shove. "Off you go, then," she said. "Plenty more beds along the hall. Best thing for you all."

Kate did as she was told. "I've never . . . known . . . how you do that." Kate yawned as she went.

Mrs. Mac smiled smugly, and said nothing.

CHAPTER SIXTY-TWO

<u>Some Months Later</u>

Dear Bryn,
    Thanks for the invitation. It'll be great to see you! You say you've grown another inch? Unbelievable! Actually, *I'm* taller too.
    And I've got a surprise for you.

Counting the days—
Cam

Dear Madlen,
    Everything's ready for you two at this end. I've almost got full use of my hand back now, but I'm not being stupid! Drawing strictly rationed, and lots of exercises. In fact, it's driving me crazy.
    Cam says it's got a surprise for us. I hope it has something to do with planes! Imagine what you could draw from that kind of height. . . .
    So much to talk about! See you soon.

Bryn

Dear Cam,

Not long now! I'll meet you at the Kir port and we can go on to the Castle from there. Do you remember last time? Aagghh!

Can't wait!

Your sister,
Madlen

P.S. If the surprise has anything to do with planes, leave me out!

CHAPTER SIXTY-THREE

Now, That *Is* a Surprise!

A flurry of snow hurled itself in their faces, and the icy wind made them gasp.

"I keep forgetting how *cold* the cold is!" exclaimed Cam, stepping through the gateway.

Madlen followed—

—and there was Bryn, loping toward them with his arms full of furs. His face was one big indiscriminate welcome, until his eyes focused on Cam.

Bryn's mouth dropped open. His feet tangled up with each other and connected with a patch of ice, so that he landed on the ground in a scattered pile of fur, and slid gracelessly to their feet.

"Cam!" he spluttered. "You're not a . . . You're a . . ."

Madlen and Cam looked down at their brother, and laughed.